P9-DED-430

SANGRE DE CRISTO

A Novel of Science and Faith

by

Martin Hewlett

SR

Spirit Rider Press
Tucson, Arizona
1994

Copyright © 1994 by Martin Hewlett

All rights reserved under International and Pan-American Copyright Conventions. Published in the United States by Spirit Rider Press, Tucson, Arizona.

Library of Congress Catalogue Number: 93-87725

ISBN Number: 0-9639790-0-0

Printed in the United States of America

This is a work of fiction. Except for certain historical figures, all other characters, living or dead, are a product of the author's imagination. Locations described in the book, however, are real.

ACKNOWLEDGMENTS

I am indebted to many loving friends who stimulated, encouraged, and inspired me in the writing of this novel. To Douglas J. Donahue, Ph.D., whose dating of the Shroud of Turin stirred the idea for this story. To Martha Gore and Heather Winn, who critiqued my first stumbling efforts. To Fr. David Geib, O.P., whose call from the altar pushed the work to completion. To my diligent copyeditors and critics: Norreen R. Holmes, Thomas J. Lindell, Ph.D., Donna Mencinger, Fran Loubet, Donna Yeo Schwien, and the tireless MaryAnn Mead. To Peggy Hamilton Lockard, an editor and publisher in her own right, who mentored this enterprise. To George E. Holmes, Ph.D., colleague, friend, and brother in Christ, who captured the spirit of the book. And, of course, to my muse, editor, and publisher, Gail Hewlett.

Cover Illustration: Martin McCollum
Cover Design: Watson Design Group, Tucson, Arizona
Back Cover Photograph: Gail Hewlett

To Gail:

For long walks, for late night talks, and for your
unconditional love.

"Jesus Christ, the same yesterday, and today, and for ever."
Hebrews 13:8

"But evil men and seducers shall wax worse and worse, deceiving, and being deceived."
II Timothy 3:13

"Now faith is the substance of things hoped for, the evidence of things not seen."
Hebrews 11:1

PROLOGUE

GALLIPOLI, TURKEY
JANUARY, 1999

He walked along the rocky shore, the waters of the Dardanelles below and to his left. Strands of gray hair lashed across his forehead, driven by a wind whose breath stung of the mid-winter chill from the Steppes that could wring a shiver from any man. In response, he pulled his overcoat tighter around him, collar turned upward, and pushed his bare, reddened hands into the warmth of its pockets.

He faced the Straits, the ancient town of Gallipoli behind him, not yet stirring. It was just after sunrise, but the light of the January morning was further diluted by its passage through a leaden lens of clouds. The wind carried the musty smell of rain mingled with the acrid salt spray of the coast. He breathed deeply, filling himself with the sea, as was his habit on any shore.

Although the path was deserted, anyone who might have been watching would have assumed he was another affluent Westerner, perhaps on a brief holiday from his meetings in Istanbul. Costa Tarquin was indeed a very successful businessman, having built his small software company in San Rafael, California into an internationally competitive enterprise. His reasons for being in Gallipoli had nothing to do with being a CEO. Costa Tarquin was also the president of the Society of Arimathea, a secret order of men and women dating to the 1st century A.D.

The Society had been founded by the descendants of Joseph of Arimathea, the man who had asked Pontius Pilate for the body of Christ and had then wrapped the body in linen and laid it in a stone tomb which he had originally prepared for himself. After the Resurrection, the linen shroud had been recovered by Joseph. During the years following Christ's death, the shroud had passed first to the sons and then grandsons of Joseph. The Society had evolved within the family to ensure the guardianship of this holy shroud. Their secrecy was traditional since Joseph, a member of the Council of Elders in Jerusalem, had hidden the fact that he was a disciple of Christ.

The shroud had been given to the care of the Society and ultimately housed in a small church in Gallipoli. During the 14th century, battles had raged across Turkey between Christian forces from Europe and the Ottoman Turks, with Gallipoli as a strategic prize for both sides. The city had fallen to the Crusaders in 1366 and, in the ensuing occupation, the shroud had disappeared from the church. The Society knew nothing of its fate, save that it had been taken back to Europe with the conquerors. For hundreds of years, the members had passed on their traditions and had hoped for the rediscovery of their precious charge. The Society remained small but now its members represented many countries and cultures.

The leadership of the Society met each year in Gallipoli, largely for ceremonial reasons. Costa expected that at this meeting, like all others he had attended, the hope for the rediscovery of the shroud would be intoned, following the prescribed rituals. As before, they would leave the meeting and return to their public lives, believing that the search for the shroud would never be successful. Although these traditions had been deeply impressed on Costa by his uncle, who had preceded him as the leader of the Society, the younger man had never accepted the inevitability of the shroud's loss. Since his election to the presidency he had devoted himself to changing this situation. He awaited his opportunity.

CHAPTER ONE

L'ABBAYE D'HAUTECOMBE
LAC DU BOURGET, FRANCE

FEBRUARY 13, 1999

Even the sight of the lake could not get his attention on that morning. Usually, when Fr. Laurent Carriere walked into the garden courtyard outside of the cloistered residential wing of the abbey, he could not help pausing to gaze for a few moments at the waters of Lac du Bourget and the broad, rocky face of Mont de Corsuet. The narrow lake lay squeezed between two ranges in the western Savoy Alps, where Hautecombe commanded an inspiring view from its western shore. Although he had grown up on the other side of the Alps in the Rhône valley near the eastern end of Lac Léman, he never ceased to be captivated by the sight of blue-green glacial waters mirroring gray-brown peaks.

On that morning his steps were quick and purposeful and his mind was preoccupied with what he had to do that day. He crossed the walled courtyard, head down and hands grasped behind his back, his tall and angular frame contorted as though he carried a heavy weight. The winter sun had barely reached the western shore that lay covered in the snowfall of two days before.

Maurice LeFebvre was already at work in the courtyard garden, repairing a section of the watering system in anticipation of the coming spring plantings. He had cleared the few centimeters of snow from the ground and had started his excavation. As he worked, his labored breathing condensed into white plumes that swirled around his face in the chill air.

He was the caretaker of the grounds and buildings of the abbey. The monks had first met him several years earlier as he sat in front of the church gate, begging from tourists. During that same summer he had begun to do odd jobs for the priests and over the course of a few months had assumed the duties of caretaker as though this were the natural progression of things. Maurice spoke little of his past, revealing only that he was from southern France and that he had seen the debacle at Dien Bien Phu.

The bulky sweater he wore encased a body that told of years of hard labor, years that were counted by the shock of white hair trying to escape from beneath his old woolen cap. Quickly wiping away the rich, brown soil from his hands, he removed the battered cap and stood almost at attention, a broad grin on his face. Like many of the priests at the abbey, Laurent was young enough to be his son. Nevertheless, Maurice rose up from his work to greet him with the deference he had for all men of the cloth.

"Bonjour, mon père! Ça va, ce matin?"

"Ça va, ça va, ça va . . . "

Laurent said the words without recognition of the greeter, almost in irritation. He mumbled something unintelligible and hurried on toward the gate leading to the church complex. Maurice watched him as he left the garden, shook his head, replaced his cap, and returned to his work.

In a few minutes Laurent would meet with Fr. Gustav Holden, the Abbot of Hautecombe. The meeting would be the last before Laurent departed later that day. He could have gone straight from the cloister to the central office in the administration wing, but instead, had walked around the outside of the buildings, stopping in front of the monastery church. As his eyes wandered over the facade it was as though he were seeing it for the first time. Pulling open the massive door, he passed through the small vestibule chapel, entered, and faced the central altar, shivering as he looked up at the ornate vaulted ceiling. He had long ago come to believe that ancient stone buildings captured and stored the winter's cold and, as the ages passed, could no longer release it in the spring.

The church had been at the spiritual and physical heart of the monastery since its founding in the 12th century. A major restoration in the 19th century had brought it to its current state, a revival of its original Gothic architecture. It was both a place of worship for the monks and a local tourist attraction. During the summer months, steamers crossed the lake from Aix-les-Bains bringing visitors to view the tombs and monuments honoring the princes of the

House of Savoy. The Benedictines of the abbey were contemplative, preferring their private devotions to interactions with these visitors.

Laurent was not that kind of priest. He was a Jesuit scholar with baccalaureate and doctoral degrees in history and archaeology from the University of Geneva in his native Switzerland. After two years of training in the prestigious Vatican Museum, he had come to Hautecombe because of their historical collection, taking the position offered him as director of the tourist operation and as curator of medieval artifacts. The archives of the monastery library presented an untapped and uncataloged mine of information that he had just begun to explore. Nevertheless, to him the abbey was simply a milepost on his road to the directorship of a major museum, perhaps even a return to the Vatican, this time as a curator rather than as an apprentice.

He had not counted on Fr. Holden. The abbot had frustrated his attempts to increase the scope of the public presentations. They were constantly at odds about his activities and Holden had discouraged Laurent's efforts at scholarship, only reluctantly permitting him to travel. Laurent had come to see that in order to further his career he would have to make a name for himself in spite of Fr. Holden. The way had presented itself last October.

At the end of the last tourist season he had begun much needed repairs to many of the tombs and monuments within the church. One of these was the cenotaph erected in memory of Amadeus VI, the Green Count of Savoy. The monument, located just to the left of the main door, commemorated the burial of the Count in the monastery in 1383. With time, the stonework and statuary accumulated grime, covering the intricate carvings. In addition, settling of the floor had slightly tilted the entire memorial.

The work had to take place in the cramped space surrounding the monument, a section of the church constructed in the 16th century. At one point during the operation, a portion of the scaffolding slipped and fell against the wall behind the structure. The workers noticed that the stones at the base of the wall had been loosened and had fallen inward, exposing a dark cavity. Laurent was summoned immediately.

The crumbled stones were scooped out and the hole freed of debris. There was a hollow space between the walls of the church and the vestibule. Within the recess, Laurent had found a small cloth-covered bundle, obviously quite old.

The find had been removed and the wall repaired. Work on the monument had continued, although Laurent's attention had become focused entirely on this unexpected discovery. Ignoring the restoration work for the time, he had set out to investigate the object. He cleared a table in his office for this examination. He carefully peeled away the decayed wrappings from the bundle to expose a gold box. His curiosity was piqued, for here was another link to the past, the kind of mystery that a historian could not ignore.

The box was an ornately crafted chest, the still bright metal of its surface engraved with religious symbols. Laurent had known instantly that this artifact was a reliquary, a container for some sacred object, perhaps one associated with a saint. Reliquaries such as this were common in the Middle Ages and could hold anything from a piece of clothing to human bones.

The elegant chest had been locked, the cover secured with a clasp. Laurent was at a loss to solve this puzzle without damaging the metal until Maurice LeFebvre had volunteered his help. The old caretaker had stopped by the church to see the cause of so much excitement. He had quietly followed Laurent to his office and had watched and waited. Seeing the problem with the lock, he left and returned shortly with a small leather pouch. Using delicate wire tools and with obvious skill he opened the clasp, barely touching the precious chest. The amazed priest had questioned him about this talent, but Maurice had merely muttered something about locks and Marseille, and had quickly left the room.

Laurent's experience had prepared him for handling ancient artifacts with the necessary care. His training at the Vatican Museum had included all aspects of this discipline. His expertise had been further enhanced by the several consulting jobs he had performed throughout Europe. Still, he had been completely surprised by the contents of the chest. Within it he found a satin pouch; within the pouch was a folded, fragile linen cloth.

At this point he needed more space than was available in his small office. With stylized movements ingrained by years of practice, he carried the box to the abbey library and cleared the largest of the tables in the reading area. He then hurried to his room where he took two clean bed sheets from his closet. Back in the library, these sheets were spread out on the table to make as clean a surface as possible. Two monks who were engrossed in reading at small side desks found themselves suddenly at the edges of a swirl of activity.

With slow and deliberate movements, he lifted the pouch out of the open reliquary and placed it gently onto the surface of the sheet. Everything was studied and purposeful, with no sudden actions. As he began to draw the folded cloth out of the pouch, it became evident that the relic was indeed quite large and, once exposed, he could see several layers pleated back and forth. Gingerly opening the cloth from its approximate middle, he saw that the beige surface of the linen was discolored, stained in some way that created a pattern. He knew at once that the cloth was a shroud.

Laurent had seen such relics before. He had been a member of the team of religious and scientific experts who had been called to Turin some years earlier to participate in the first stages of dating the famous Shroud. Tradition had held for centuries that this relic was the actual burial cloth of Jesus. The project, using the powerful analytical techniques of modern science, had proven that the Shroud was of medieval origin.

The importance of religious artifacts to a church of the Middle Ages had been immense, since their presence could attract large numbers of worshipers and, with them, their money. The Shroud of Turin was most likely an elaborate construction created in the 12th century, possibly using a human victim. The years following the analysis of the Shroud of Turin resulted in the dating of other supposed "shrouds" to the same period. Laurent had no doubt that the cloth he had discovered would prove to be of the same ilk. Nevertheless, his excitement at the discovery and at the mystery of its existence in the monastery church was not diminished.

He could not open the shroud any further, given the facilities that existed at the abbey. There was the certain danger of breakage and the distinct possibility of contamination that might compromise any attempt to determine the age of the relic. He cautiously refolded the cloth, placed it back into its pouch and returned it to the gold chest, this time leaving the clasp unlocked.

Laurent began an intensive search for clues to the origin of what he now called the Shroud of Hautecombe. He spent long hours reading through the collection of documents held in the library and vaults of the monastery. In addition, he contacted his former colleagues at the Vatican Museum. By February, he was beginning to build the body of information that explained how the shroud had arrived in Hautecombe, although there was no clue to explain its presence within the wall. He was determined that this story be revealed by him in the scholarly setting he could only find outside of the abbey. He kept his research and his findings secret and, instead, began to formulate a plan that would take him and the shroud away from Hautecombe and the restrictive rule of Fr. Holden.

The flow of these plans through his mind was interrupted by the arrival of an agitated Fr. Phillipe Cand, the young assistant to the abbot, who entered the church through a side door. As was his habit in the midst of any crisis, his voice remained even and measured.

"Laurent. There you are. I've been looking all over for you." He gestured toward the door. "Father Holden is waiting."

* * * * * * * * * * * * * * *

"This is madness," the abbot said aloud, almost in desperate summation. He was at the window of his office, his hands behind his back and his eyes ostensibly taking in the view. He did not even see the lake and the surrounding peaks. His thoughts were not on the scene, but rather on the turn of events that could bring the abbey more prominently into the public eye. He had carefully guarded the cloistered lifestyle of the monastery for more than two decades. Now, this young Swiss Jesuit threatened the order and quiet of Hautecombe.

The elderly abbot was a recluse and his diminutive figure could often be seen wandering alone on the grounds of the monastery. He barely tolerated the annual intrusion of tourists who crossed the lake from Aix. For him, the winter months meant a return of solitude to the western shore of the lake. The discovery of the shroud had disturbed this tranquility.

Order had not always been present in Gustav Holden's life. As a young man, he had survived the turmoil of Nazi rule in Germany only to find his country divided, with his home in the eastern sector under the control of a new dictatorship. Gustav was deeply religious and intensely political. He became a priest out of love for God and in defiance of the ruling regime. In his fervor, he had become a militant, urging his congregation to resist the edicts of the Communist government. Ultimately, he found himself a part of a chain, a human conduit through Berlin to the West.

In 1964 he assisted in the escape plans of a young woman in his congregation in Dresden. More than just one of the faithful, she was his own sister. They had traveled together to East Berlin where she would attempt to cross the border, fleeing over the wall. Everything had gone according to plan. Gustav had watched from hiding one night as she made her way through a break in the barbed wire fence and entered the open space on the east side of the border. She was running, bent over low and arms pumping wildly, on her way to freedom, when the spotlight caught and held her in its glare. She was frozen for an eternity in that white blaze. Gustav remembered her almost as though she were posing for a picture, hands held at her sides like a schoolgirl in line. The staccato sound of machine gun fire interrupted the tableau and her body was thrown violently back by the impact of the bullets. In the silence that followed, his sister lay still on the ground, illuminated by the guard's light. The horror of that night had changed him forever.

His own escape from the East had left him with yet more scars, both physical and mental. He arrived in France where the Benedictines had granted him sanctuary and had allowed him to join their order. Gustav came to Hautecombe after a good deal of notoriety. The monastery, with its serene and remote location, was the perfect place for him. He worked first at the simple tasks of daily life but, over the years, became more and more interested in maintaining the lifestyle he had come to love. His appointment as abbot meant that he could secure his monastery as a place of refuge for himself and for his fellow priests.

He had meticulously organized the duties of each priest in his charge. Now one of his staff, Fr. Carriere, would be off on a journey that could only bring more attention to the abbey. Furthermore, the interest of the Vatican had been attracted to this shroud and the historian's expertise was required. The abbot was not happy.

A knock at the door brought him around. "Come in, come in."

The two younger priests entered and waited for his signal to sit or stand. They never knew whether a meeting with the abbot would be brief and to the point or would try the limits of their patience.

"Please, sit down." His assistant had begun to retreat toward the door, leaving the other two alone. "You too, Father Cand, if you please."

Laurent and Phillipe took chairs facing the large desk in the center of the room.

"Father Carriere, are your plans all set for this journey?"

Holden crossed to the desk and eased himself into his chair, his face a mask as he tried to keep his emotions in check.

Laurent sighed inwardly, realizing that he must go over the entire journey once again for his superior. He would remain calm. He had planned his escape and knew that the abbot could not stop him.

"Yes, Father. In about two hours I'll take the steamer for Aix. Later, there's a train that arrives in Geneva this evening. I can stay two nights at the rectory of St. Nicolas de Flüe with an old school friend. On Monday morning I have a flight from Cointrin to Frankfurt, then on to Dallas, and finally to Tucson, Arizona."

He concluded his recitation and sat back, his expression neutral.

"And where will you stay in Tucson?"

"I have made arrangements to stay with the Dominican community at the University's Catholic center."

"And how long do you expect to be gone?"

Laurent controlled himself, refusing to be baited by the repetitive questions he had answered so many times during the last two weeks.

"I'm told by the people at the University that the analysis may take as long as a month."

Holden considered this as if hearing it for the first time.

"Father, you know I object strenuously to this trip. I believe that it is quite unnecessary."

Laurent's absence from the abbey would coincide with the beginning of the tourist season. Although there were other members of the religious community who could handle most of the details, he knew that, without the curator, the involvement of the abbot himself would be unavoidable.

"I understand that, Father. However, the Vatican has asked that I personally accompany the shroud. Also, we are told that the University has no medievalist on staff. The dating team has requested that I stay throughout the project. As you know, the Vatican and the University are providing most of the funds for this trip." Laurent shrugged in mock helplessness.

"I know, I know. I just do not believe that this is consistent with our purpose here at Hautecombe. What about the shroud?"

Fr. Holden pointed to the wooden shipping case that sat on his conference table, occupying even his space.

"The cloth and its reliquary box are packed and ready for shipment. I will be taking the case along with me on the airplane. All of the transit papers are in order."

Holden rose suddenly and came around the desk, his composure broken by the smug, self-assurance of his curator. His anger was apparent in the bitterness with which he spoke.

"Father, you are obsessed with this shroud. You are letting it come between you and your priestly duties."

He now wanted both the curator and this relic out of his office and out of his thoughts.

Laurent rose slowly and walked to the conference table. He lifted the wooden case by its rope handles. Since it contained mostly packing material to protect its ancient cargo, it was a good deal lighter than it appeared. Holding the case in one hand, he extended the other to the abbot and smiled, "I cannot refuse a request from the Vatican, can I, Father?"

* * * * * * * * * * * * * * *

Laurent was much more nervous than he cared to admit. He sat in the passenger waiting lounge at Cointrin Airport in Geneva. The accidental discovery of the shroud had given him the opportunity for which he had waited. His attraction was to the artifacts of history that had been cloaked in mysteries woven by the passage of time. The Shroud of Hautecombe was a puzzle that he had found and that he alone would solve.

He knew that Fr. Holden would prefer to place the shroud back into its hole in the church wall and seal it away forever. For the abbot it was a threat, but for Laurent the ancient cloth kindled a thrill rarely available to a scholar of antiquity.

He had quietly engineered his "invitation" to the United States. The dating of the Shroud of Turin had taken place, in part, at the University of Arizona. As a result, the University had dedicated a center to the authentication and dating of such artifacts. Through his contacts at the Vatican Museum, he had arranged that the Shroud of Hautecombe be brought to Tucson for analysis and that he must accompany it.

After he left Fr. Holden's office his mood had been considerably lighter. He had again walked through the courtyard where Maurice was still at work. He greeted the caretaker as though he had not yet seen him that day.

"Hello, Maurice. How are you?"

The greeting caught the old man by surprise. "Fine, Father, fine. I hear you're leaving us for a while."

Maurice knew more of the business of the abbey than the abbot himself.

"I'm going to the United States. What can I get for you?"

Laurent had come to regard the old man as a dear and trusted uncle. He was one of the few people at the abbey in whom the young priest confided. He had made a practice during his travels of sending little gifts to the caretaker.

He could still picture Maurice standing, half-buried in the cloister garden, holding his cap in front of him, his face smudged with dirt.

"Oh, anything, Father . . . a postcard will do. Have a good trip, Father."

The airport public address system interrupted his thoughts. *"Mesdames et messieurs, American Airlines fait la première annonce d'embarquement du vol 435 . . . "*

In his excitement, he was on his way to the gate before the message was completed.

CHAPTER TWO

TUCSON, ARIZONA
FEBRUARY 15, 1999

Joshua Francis stood in front of the Life Sciences South Building at the west end of the Science Concourse. In one hand he held his briefcase, while, almost unconsciously, his other hand clutched at his stomach. The broad features of his face were knotted in a vain attempt to control the nausea welling up as he confronted the entry doors leading in off the plaza. The young assistant professor of molecular biology knew that his day would begin with a conference in the fourth-floor office of his department head. The agenda for the meeting would be his research, but in reality, the discussion would focus on his lack of progress. He would be warned again that his career at the University was in jeopardy.

Five years of graduate school at Stanford and an outstanding dissertation followed by three years of post-doctoral training in Paris had preceded his arrival in Tucson. He had been highly recruited at many universities because of the prestige of the laboratory in France and because of the elegant experiments in cancer biology he had conducted. Rather than take a position at one of the "big name" schools, he had accepted the professorial appointment at Arizona. The department was still relatively new and he saw this as an opportunity to make his way rapidly through the ranks of academia. He harbored the dream of someday returning to one of the Bay area schools as a full professor.

One year after he was hired, Josh had competed for, and been awarded, a five-year research grant from the National Cancer Institute, one of the National Institutes of Health. His area of research involved the rapid and fatal spread of cancer cells to other parts of the body, the property called metastasis. During his work in France, he had identified certain biological molecules that influenced the rate of growth and dispersion of these cells. His research proposal

23

to NIH had been to isolate and characterize these substances as possible targets for anticancer drugs. The senior faculty in his department had settled back, fully expecting him to develop as predicted, but things were not going as planned.

The problem was that everyone else thought this was a good idea at the same time. "Everyone else" in this case meant three large research groups at other universities and several biotechnology companies. The competition was fierce and Josh was constantly finding that experiments he tried to start had already been completed and reported by one of these other groups. During his four and one-half years as an assistant professor he had been able to publish only one short research note regarding a small technical achievement.

In one more year he would have to compete for a renewal of his NIH grant proposal. Even worse, in one more year he would have to face the tenure process. Both of these evaluations were brutal. And both required that he demonstrate "excellent research productivity" in order to succeed. This meant publications in prominent scientific journals. To date, he had none. Today's conference would address this issue, touching once more the raw nerve he wished to keep covered. Josh steeled himself, ran his free hand through the brown curls covering his head and, forcing an exterior calm he did not feel, entered the building and quickly got into the elevator.

The Life Sciences South Building was one of the newer structures near the southwest corner of the campus. The research laboratories were in the rectangular east block of the building, while the faculty and departmental offices occupied the west section. The office wing virtually took flight from the rest of the building, consisting as it did of a series of concrete vanes with interposed glass walls. The rooms along this side presented a spectacular view of the mountainous Tucson skyline. The administration of the Department of Molecular Biology occupied a suite of rooms on the fourth floor.

The receptionist at the outer desk greeted him with her accustomed cheeriness.

"Good morning, Doctor Francis. How are you?"

The secretarial staff secretly divided the faculty into "favorites" and "outcasts," depending upon the demeanor a particular professor displayed when in the office. Josh was included in the former category, because of his youth and the vulnerability he tried so hard to hide. She regarded him as he positioned himself in front of her desk, his solidly built body appearing to be at ease, his brown eyes steady. How could he remain so composed, she wondered, given the nature of the meeting he was about to attend?

"Just fine, Margaret. Is he in?"

Josh nodded toward the closed door.

"Yes. I think he's expecting you."

She walked over and knocked once on the door and opened it slightly.

"Doctor Stone? Doctor Francis is here."

Franklin Stone removed his glasses and rubbed at his eyes with his thumb and forefinger, a gesture which, to those who knew him, meant that he was trying to adjust not his vision but his mental state. He had been head of this department for almost seven years. After a long and distinguished academic career he had achieved the kind of renown for which most scientists hunger. In recognition of his contributions to molecular biology, he had been elected to the National Academy of Sciences. Now, in his late fifties, he was both a senior researcher and an administrator. It was the latter role that must predominate during this morning's meeting with his assistant professor. The next fifteen or twenty minutes would not be pleasant. He got up from his desk and moved to the door.

"Good morning, Josh. Come on in."

As the door closed behind Josh, Margaret lost the forced smile she had been wearing. The entire office staff knew of the problems that the young professor was facing. She had been around the University long enough to know the telltale signs. The tenure process could reward, or it could expel with frightening finality. She and the others guessed that Dr. Francis would ultimately suffer the second of these two fates.

* * * * * * * * * * * * * * *

After the meeting, Josh climbed the stairs to the fifth floor. His small laboratory suite was at the far end of the corridor. The newness of the building had worn off and, like most laboratory areas, the hallways were beginning to accumulate equipment and furniture. In university research environments, space was at a premium and the corridors eventually were converted into combination walkways and work areas, in spite of architects and fire marshals.

Josh made his way down the hall to his own laboratory. Narrow windows on the south wall provided light to the long, low table beneath them that served as desk space. Additional tables were along each side and, at a central island countertop, sat Christopher Warren, Josh's research assistant. Chris was five years younger than Josh and had completed a master's degree in molecular biology at the University of California at Santa Barbara. His face was framed by a mass of black curls and he wore thick-rimmed reading glasses, which he removed as he stood up and turned to Josh. The expression on his face telegraphed the depressing message he had for his boss.

"I'm afraid I've got some bad news this morning. Looks like all the cell lines are contaminated again. I think it's that yeast problem we've been having. What'll we do?"

Chris waited for some reaction. He had the uneasy feeling that Josh was losing touch with the laboratory and was more and more distant.

The cold, sinking sensation in his stomach tried to overcome him as Josh struggled for an answer. He had to accept another delayed set of experiments, still another failure. He feigned calm as he shrugged his shoulders.

"Oh, well . . . I guess we'll have to start fresh. Clean out all the incubators, check that everything is sterile and get some new vials of cells from the freezer. Look, I'll be in my office the rest of the morning. Have you seen Bill or Rita today?"

Bill Pierce and Rita Mitchell were his two graduate students, in their second and third years in the program, respectively.

"I think Bill's in class this morning. Rita's down in the library. Any messages when they come in?"

"No. I'll see them later."

Josh left the lab and hurried back down the hall to his office, which he entered, closing the door. The small room contained a curved desk with a writing surface and a computer, while one wall was covered floor to ceiling by bookshelves. Beyond his desk the large window overlooked the campus and mountains beyond. He sat heavily in his chair, clutching at his now reeling stomach. There was an audible croak as he asked of no one, "What next?"

The desk was piled with unread scientific journals and articles. He sensed that each new issue of *Science* or *Nature* or the *Proceedings of the National Academy* would bring further discouragement, more news that the others were continuing to pull farther ahead of him. He hoped that his two graduate students had not noticed his increasing difficulties in directing their research. He was almost certain that they had.

His eyes were playing randomly over the computer screen, while he idly toyed with the mouse, when the telephone brought him up with a start. He let the answering machine handle the caller. After a pause for his outgoing message and a click, a familiar voice sounded.

"Hi, Josh. It's Mac. Are you going to be able to meet Father Carriere later? Give me a call if . . . "

Josh grabbed the phone and quickly interrupted the message.

"Hi, Mac. Yeah, I can meet him. No problem."

He had promised to do this favor for his friend, Dennis McGovern, an assistant professor of chemistry. Mac was one of a group of scientists from a number of departments at the University who were part of a program to date historical or archaeological objects. The effort had grown out of the activity surrounding the dating of the Shroud of Turin. Mac had been drawn in as an analytical chemist.

"Listen, did I give you his flight information?"

"Yes . . . I have it here . . . just a minute . . . "

Somewhere on his desk, among the myriad of small, yellow adhesive-backed slips of paper he used for everything from messages to data calculations, was the note he had taken the week before.

"Here it is . . . American Airlines, Flight 1388 from Dallas, arrives at 4:21 this afternoon."

"Right. Thanks for doing this. After the Vatican arranged this visit, we realized that none of us speak French. I immediately thought of you."

"I hope he speaks some English. It's been a while since I carried on anything but a simple conversation."

"Well, he's actually Swiss. You know how compulsive they are about languages. He's staying at the Newman Center here on campus . . . on 2nd and Cherry. Can you get him there?"

"Sure. By the way, how do I recognize him?"

"I don't know. Why don't you hold up a sign or something?"

Josh recoiled at that idea. He suddenly saw himself standing at the airport, like a chauffeur, holding a crudely hand-lettered piece of paper. He would have to think of something else and he said nothing of this to Mac.

"Listen, I have an idea. Can you bring him to the conference room at the project offices tomorrow morning? We're going to have a short meeting and then get a look at this cloth he's bringing to us. You might find it interesting."

"Okay. I should be able to. I'll check my schedule."

There was really no need to do that, since he already knew that he would be there. This was exactly the kind of diversion he looked for to take him away from his office, his laboratory, and his troubles.

* * * * * * * * * * * * * * *

Josh was uncomfortable. He had agreed because Mac had prevailed on him. Here he was, stuck with the job of waiting for an incoming flight full of strangers. How would he recognize this Swiss priest? Would he be wearing a name tag?

The boarding area became, for a time, the limits of his world as he moved from one window to another during his wait. The pastel tones and ultra-southwest decor of the terminal could not disguise the fact that this was really a very tiny airport for a city the size of Tucson. Somehow the small town atmosphere had not yet been submerged in Tucson's rush to big city status.

"American Airlines announces the arrival of Flight 1388 from Dallas. Passengers will be deplaning at Gate 24."

Too late now. Josh decided to stand near the gate and try to look "professorial." How might a European cleric expect an American university faculty member to look? Surely not dressed as he was in his normal campus attire of jeans and a sports shirt. He knew that in this country, especially in the Southwest, his appearance could suggest practically any occupation.

The main bulk of passengers were starting to enter the terminal building, many caught up in the ritual airport greetings that somehow always managed to take place in front of the doorway itself. All he could hope for was that Fr. Carriere would be dressed appropriately. The remaining passengers were working their way through the mix of travelers and welcomers and, as yet, no priest had appeared, at least not by costume. Josh was deciding to have Fr. Carriere paged when he noticed a tall man in a black suit wearing the Roman collar of a Catholic cleric. No one would have necessarily said he was European. His straight black hair and sharp features could place his origin almost anywhere in the Western world, but his unshaven face and sunken eyes told of the length of his journey. In one hand he carried a wooden crate about the size of a small suitcase. He paused inside the terminal gate, looking somewhat dazed.

Josh approached the man. *"Père Carriere? Je m'appele Josh Francis de l'Université d'Arizona."*

"Hello. We can speak English, if you would like. Please call me Laurent."

They made their way toward the main section of the terminal and the baggage claim area, exchanging the awkward pleasantries that always accompanied the first meeting of two strangers. They passed under the small digital display sign, spelling out in red letters "Bienvenidos a Tucson! Home of the University of Arizona." Flights of stairs on either side of an escalator led down to the parking level where they joined the crowd of arriving passengers anxiously awaiting their luggage and the final stage of their journey.

Josh made an effort to aid his guest and reached for the wooden carrying case.

"May I take that for you?"

"No. It is fine, really."

Laurent was clutching the case with both arms as if it were a life raft and he were in danger of sinking into the floor.

His behavior took Josh by surprise. "Fine . . . okay. Let's get the rest of your bags."

The English word "bags" confused the priest until he realized that this referred to his luggage. Laurent identified his two suitcases as soon as they appeared on the conveyer belt. Josh quickly retrieved them, this time ignoring the wooden case that the other man still held so tightly.

The warmth of late February in the desert caught Laurent off guard. He had left his home in the Alps with tendrils of winter still clinging to the air. He paused at the door leading to the parking lot.

"Is there anything wrong? Did we forget something?"

"No. I am wondering . . . is it always this hot here or is this unusual weather?"

Josh smiled. "Well, it's a bit warmer than usual, but this is just typical 'Chamber of Commerce' weather."

" 'Chamber of Commerce' . . . what is that?"

"I only mean that this weather is good for the tourist business."

"Oh, yes. I see what you mean." Laurent pointed at several vans lined up along the curb, collecting guests who would be staying at one of the many resort hotels near the city.

"Come on. My car's over here. That Ford Bronco with the ski rack."

Josh led Laurent across the circular roadway on the lower level, past the gratuitous cactus garden, and out into the lot. Reaching his red 4X4, he opened the rear gate and lifted the luggage into the cargo bay. Once again he reached for the wooden shipping crate that Laurent carried.

"No. I would like to hold this, please." Again the priest clutched the case to his body.

"What's in that box, Father? Is it so fragile?"

"This contains the Shroud of Hautecombe, the relic that will be analyzed at the University. It is packed very carefully but I am reluctant to let go of it."

"Mac didn't give me any details about this relic. Where is it from? Is it like the one in Turin?"

"I will tell everything I know about it at the meeting tomorrow morning. Will you be there?"

"Yes. Mac, I mean, Doctor McGovern, has invited me. I'll be the one taking you to that meeting. I'll pick you up in the morning at the Newman Center on campus."

The two men climbed into the front seats and Josh maneuvered through the lot and past the pay booth out onto the airport access road. During the twenty minute trip back to the University, he entertained his guest with details about Tucson and the surrounding desert environment. By the time they had reached the campus, the brief exchange had struck a chord in each man, setting off the first strains of the melody of a burgeoning friendship.

* * * * * * * * * * * * * * * *

Leslie Alexander sat in the living room of her house that evening and followed Josh around with her eyes as he paced back and forth before the large picture window. The emotional connection between them, forged by their time together, caused her to sense his pain, to share in his frustration, and to taste his fear.

She was curled into the corner of the couch, shoeless, with her legs tucked under her skirt. Her face would have been considered plain were it not for her eyes, whose blue chambers captured and held whomever they wished. She wore her light brown hair short, framing her almost childlike features. The overall effect was much like a painting by Klee, except that in this case the innocent stare was often replaced by a frankly sexual presence. Leslie attracted attention in spite of herself.

She had arrived in Tucson five years earlier, intending to stop for a short while. As a free-lance photojournalist, her territory had covered all of Europe along with most of the Middle East and North Africa. Nonetheless, she had always been drawn to Tucson, a Mecca for all of the photographic arts. Once there, as she had made her pilgrimage through the smaller galleries, and at last to the artistic "Ka'bah" itself, the Center for Creative Photography, she had been transformed.

Her trip to Tucson had been by invitation, since some of her work was featured in a show at the Center. Somewhat to her surprise, she was offered a position as assistant curator at the gallery, handling mainly the journalistic acquisitions and exhibits. In recognition of her own work, the offer included appointment as an artist-in-residence. Unexpectedly, she enjoyed the feeling of constancy that the job gave her.

During her wanderings she had adopted France and its people, language, and customs. In order to soothe her "homesickness" for that country, she gravitated to anything with a Gallic flavor. One evening she had found herself at a foreign language film festival on the University campus, watching the very funny comedy, *Les Compères*. Although this version had English subtitles, the French was not always translated accurately or completely. She had noticed that the man seated next to her was also laughing at the same dialogue as she. During an intermission, she could not help but ask the question.

"Vous êtes française?"

"No, I'm American. Are you French?"

She smiled at him, laughed, and opened the doors of those eyes. He fell headlong into their centers.

She had watched him during the rest of the film. He appeared to her at once both serious and lighthearted. He had a strong face, brown-skinned and wide-featured. His eyes, also brown, were deep set. His hair, again a different shade of brown, curled crazily around his head. She knew instinctively why she had been drawn to him.

After the film they had gone for coffee together. They were as natural and easy as if they had known each other for years instead of hours. In the weeks that followed, their courtship dance spun itself over most of the campus between his office and hers.

They could often be seen, seated on benches beneath trees, or reclining on the grass alongside the wall fronting Park Avenue. The wonder of the dance brought them closer, both physically and emotionally. They shared lunches, dinners, and outings. As the steps of the dance became more intricate and more intimate, they found that they had become friends. Eventually, in the natural order of things, they became lovers.

It had been one year since they had met, and Leslie and Josh were together as often as possible. Yet, she kept her restored barrio home and studio, and he, his small house to the west of town. They now danced around the issue of living together, discussing it but doing nothing about it. That evening they were at her place after dinner.

Josh stood gazing out of the window, arms folded, holding himself tightly. He caught her looking at him and saw his own troubles mirrored for an instant in her face.

"I'm sorry, baby."

Josh crossed the room and sat next to her on the couch.

"Today was a bad day. Everything's messed up in the lab again. I guess I'm a little tense."

He reached out a hand to touch her hair. Leslie took his hand and held it against her face.

"It's all right, love. I understand."

There was much that she did know. He had told her of his desires, his accomplishments, and his failures. A career in science was all that he ever wanted, advancing by his intellect and talent rather than by any accident of genetics. And yet, throughout undergraduate and graduate school he had been both a victim and beneficiary of his racial background. He was an anomaly for most of his peers and his faculty mentors. He was Black, but not really. He was from New Mexico, but not Hispanic. He could never really make them understand what it was to be Creole. For a long time even he had not known what it meant. To many in academia it meant only that he was a minority, and therefore, someone to be carefully followed. As a result, each of his successes or failures was magnified and distorted through the white lens of equal opportunity.

She turned and leaned back against him as he cradled her in his arms. Perhaps another line of thought would move him away from this dark mood.

"How's Mac doing? I haven't seen him for several days."

"Oh yeah. Thanks for reminding me. I did that favor for Mac today. I picked up his visitor from France at the airport."

"Oh? And who is it?"

"A priest from Hautecombe Abbey in the Savoy Alps. His name's Laurent Carriere. He's brought along a relic that Mac and the others are going to date. It's a shroud."

"Like Turin?"

"Yeah. Mac's invited me to attend the initial examination of the piece tomorrow morning."

The sounds of the evening flowed in and out of consciousness.

They fell silent, vaguely listening to the rock station playing in the background . . . an old Jimi Hendrix tune . . . *Foxy Lady*. She could feel the tension in his body building as his mind continued to struggle with intractable problems.

Leslie sat up. "Let me give you a massage, Sonny. It'll make you feel much better."

Josh smiled as he always did when she used his family nickname. It had been the creation of his older sister. He left the couch, and stretched out face down on the floor. Leslie was wearing a blouse and wide skirt. She straddled his hips and began to knead the muscles in his back, working down from his neck to his waist. Josh could feel the pressure of her bare legs gripping him tightly. After a short while he turned over beneath her, pulling her down on top of him.

"Don't worry about me so much, baby."

"I have to, love . . . it's my job."

They both laughed and then, just as suddenly, they were kissing deeply. He stroked her back and arms, making her shudder.

Leslie pulled away slightly and whispered, "Let's go into the bedroom."

"What's wrong with right here . . . right now?"

CHAPTER THREE

TUCSON, ARIZONA
FEBRUARY 16, 1999

The lounge in the Newman Center was quiet at 8:00 a.m. Laurent sat in one of the soft chairs near the door, the wooden shipping crate at his side. He had attended morning prayers and breakfast with his Dominican hosts. At last, the effects of his journey were beginning to overtake him. He was drifting off to sleep when Josh arrived.

"Father Carriere, good morning."

Laurent jumped at the sound.

"*Oui, Oui! Je suis prêt* . . . oh, sorry."

Josh smiled, "A little jet lag, Father?"

"I guess so. But I am ready. I have the shroud right here."

"Is that too heavy to carry? We have about a fifteen minute walk."

Josh hesitated to offer his assistance, recalling how protective Laurent had been at the airport.

"No. It is actually quite light."

"Good. Then let's get started. You won't need that sweater. It's going to be in the mid-seventies today." Laurent's quizzical expression reminded Josh of yet another cultural difference. "Uh . . . that would be about . . . let's see . . . twenty-two or twenty-three Celsius."

The main campus of the University of Arizona covered more than one square mile, with the Medical School and its associated hospital and clinics in a separate section to the north. The University had gone through a tremendous growth surge during the decades of the seventies and eighties. Most of the buildings on the east side of campus were new. The architectural theme was red brick and variations were seen at every turn. The grounds were vast expanses of lawns with all varieties of trees and shrubs. In the middle of the campus, in front of the Administration tower, a small cactus garden was one of the University's few overt admissions that it sat in the heart of the Sonoran desert.

Josh led Laurent past the Main Library complex and along the mall to the center of campus. The area in front of the Student Union was alive with some of the 36,000 students, on their way to or from classes or sitting, in groups or alone, on the grassy areas. The mild Southwestern weather encouraged the wearing of shorts and T-shirts by most of the population.

The sciences and engineering predominated at Arizona. This fact meant that almost every part of the campus was infiltrated by a building devoted to some one of these disciplines, except for the fine arts enclave in the extreme northwestern corner. The mall itself was graced by one of the most recent additions, the seven year old Chemistry/Biological Sciences Teaching Building. The entrance to this five-story lecture and laboratory house was decorated with a metal arch, surmounted by cartoon-like human figures, each holding a larger than life representation of some field of research conducted at the University. One of the white-coated statues was even a paean to the physicist who had, a decade earlier, discovered the famous molecule Buckminsterfullerene. When it had been installed, the archway had been controversial, seen as great public art by some and as trashy pop art by others. Over the years it had assumed its own place in the lore of the campus.

Turning south at the Chemistry Building, the two men proceeded a few blocks further, arriving at the Gould-Simpson Building, a ten-story giant of brick and glass completed in the late eighties. The structure had a flamboyant character, distinguishing it from the neighboring buildings designed in the functional style of the fifties.

The dating of the Shroud of Turin had been directed by Dr. Richard Sutton, a professor of chemistry. This initial success had led to the establishment of offices and laboratories in Gould-Simpson, far removed from the rest of the chemistry faculty. Facilities for the dating project were on the seventh floor. The elevator spilled the two men out into a lobby area with a spectacular view of the campus and northeastern sections of Tucson.

Josh and Laurent reached a door with the imposing title "Laboratory of Atomic Chronometry, Dr. Richard Sutton, Director." Scientists loved to formulate lengthy names such as this and then, unceremoniously, to degrade them into acronyms. As a result, the laboratory was commonly known as "LAC." For Laurent, this shortened name instantly recalled images of glacial alpine waters rather than scientific instruments. They were met inside the door by a secretary.

"Good morning. May I help you?"

"Yes. This is Father Carriere and I'm Doctor Francis."

"Ah, yes, Doctor Francis. They're expecting you. Right this way."

The young man led them down a short hallway into a conference room. There they were greeted by Mac.

"Josh. How's it going? You must be Father Carriere. I'm Dennis McGovern from the Chemistry Department. I'm the analytical chemist on the dating project. Oh, I'm sorry. I don't speak French." Mac's personality was matched precisely by his nonchalant appearance, including the tousled blond hair that covered his ears and fell across his forehead.

"I am happy to meet you. And it is okay. I speak English reasonably well."

"That makes everything much easier, at least for us. Let me introduce you to some of the others. This is Dr. Sutton, the director."

"Yes, Professor Sutton. We met in Turin. Nice to see you again."

"Father Carriere, welcome to Tucson." The director adjusted his wire-rimmed glasses, pushed back several strands of gray hair at his temple, and extended his hand to shake that proffered by the priest. He was dressed less casually than the others, although in many East Coast circles his houndstooth check coat and school tie would have been considered quite informal.

Mac introduced Laurent around the room to other members of the LAC staff, scientists, and technicians who were involved in one or more projects.

Dr. Sutton moved to the long conference table and took his seat, again adjusting both his glasses and his hair before he spoke.

"Ladies and gentlemen, perhaps we can begin."

As everyone arranged themselves around the table, Dr. Sutton indicated that Laurent was to take a seat next to him. Josh remained at the edge of the conference, preferring to sit in one of the chairs away from the main group.

"I'd like to again welcome Father Carriere to the University. Perhaps the best place to start would be for Father Carriere to tell us as much as he can. Father, what is known of the history of the relic you have brought to us?"

Laurent drew in a breath and looked around the table. These were men of science, not of history. He had never before faced this kind of audience, but this was the opportunity for which he had waited. He began.

"The discovery of the shroud was quite accidental and its history is still relatively obscure. Nevertheless, I have pieced together the following information."

Laurent had discovered that Amadeus VI, known as the Green Count of Savoy, had led a Crusade against the Turks in 1366. He returned in 1367 and brought with him a cedar chest containing the shroud. The exact origins of the chest were not recorded, although references implied the Count had removed it from a small chapel of some kind in the Turkish city of Gallipoli. After the death of Amadeus, the shroud, sealed in a gold reliquary, had been enshrined on the great altar in the abbey church. The priests at Hautecombe had not taken advantage of the presence of the relic. There had never been any public exhibition such as that which had occurred in Turin.

All records of the chest seemed to end at the beginning of the seventeenth century. In December of 1602, Duke Charles Emmanuel of Savoy mounted an attack against the city of Geneva in order to destroy the Calvinist stronghold. The attack was repulsed and the armies of the Duke were driven away. The Abbey of Hautecombe reacted to the news of this defeat with panic. The priests feared that the whole of Savoy would be overrun by the Calvinist forces. The tide of reformation sweeping Europe often resulted in the destruction of religious artifacts deemed "idolatrous." Thus, the abbey was abandoned for several months until it was clear that the Genevese had no interest in wars of conquest. From this point on, however, no mention could be found of the golden reliquary.

The priest finished his presentation and sat back. He knew that this was the first time anyone had heard this part of the story. He realized that it had the desired effect on his listeners. The members of the team were quiet, their attention fixed on Laurent.

Sutton broke the silence.

"Father, what is known about the origins of the shroud before it was brought to Hautecombe? For instance, was it ever present in the village of Lirey?"

Laurent knew the history of the Shroud of Turin and its first appearance in that French town. "At this point, very little. My colleagues at the Vatican Museum are working to discover more. We suspect that Amadeus found the shroud in Gallipoli. We know that the reliquary box was constructed by a goldsmith in Chambery before the Count's death. We know little else; however, we do not think it originated in Lirey."

Sutton looked around the table.

"Are there any other questions before we begin? If not, why don't we have a preliminary look at this piece. Let's reconvene in the laboratory."

The group filed out of the conference room and crossed the hall. Josh trailed along behind, trying to remain in the background. They entered a room that resembled a surgical suite rather than a laboratory. An array of high intensity lights on the ceiling could be positioned at any required angle. In the center of the windowless room was a large table with a meticulously clean surface. Parked alongside the table were an assortment of utility carts, each containing monitoring devices. Video equipment was available to record, from different angles, all events occurring on the table. As the group moved into the room, various technicians went immediately to the assembly of instruments and began the setup and adjustment procedures.

"Father, if you would care to open the crate here, rather than on the clean table."

Sutton indicated a small workbench near the door that contained an assortment of tools.

Laurent placed the wooden crate on the bench and, using a pry bar, removed the lid. The crate was completely filled with foam cushioning. Nestled in the middle of the foam, in a fitted section, the reliquary sat wrapped in protective cloth. Laurent removed the bundle and took off the covering. By now, the attention of all within the room was focused on it. The metal case was about one foot square and five inches deep. The gold of the reliquary box reflected the light of the room with a blinding flash, causing Sutton and the others closest to Laurent to momentarily shield their eyes.

"Let's bring the box over to the clean table." Sutton motioned to the team of assistants. "You may begin recording any time."

The quiet hiss of video cameras began as Laurent set the reliquary onto the white surface. He recalled the scene at the Cathedral in Turin many years earlier. At that time, before the dating of the Turin shroud, the Church had informally admitted the possibility that the relic was truly the winding sheet of Christ. Because of this, the unfolding and examination of the shroud had been carried out with both the delicate treatment required for an ancient artifact, and the reverence dictated by the attending religious authorities.

Since then, it had been established that artifacts of this type originated during the Middle Ages, a time when a combination of religious fanaticism and potential financial gain made the construction of these "relics" quite common. Thus, the Shroud of Hautecombe was treated with the caution necessary for a centuries old object, but without the aura of sacredness present in Turin.

The reliquary box was not locked, remaining as it had been since Maurice LeFebvre had managed to open it. Laurent donned a pair of white linen "clean gloves," as did other members of the team who might have occasion to touch the shroud. He lifted the cover of the reliquary and gently removed the silk pouch inside.

"From the documents I have found at the abbey, I believe that this pouch was made about one hundred years after the arrival of the shroud at Hautecombe."

Sutton gestured to those taking notes as he spoke. "Excellent, Father. The fibers of the pouch will serve as a good control for the dating process. We have two others whose ages are known quite precisely."

With the pouch laying on the examination table, the gold reliquary box, itself of immense value, was laid to one side. Laurent opened the flap of the pouch and carefully removed the cloth. The ancient fabric, browned with the passage of time, looked as though it would disintegrate at the slightest touch. Working slowly, Laurent and the others began the process of unfolding the shroud.

The Shroud of Turin had been displayed in the Cathedral from time to time. Not so at the Abbey of Hautecombe. The reliquary had been on the altar before its disappearance, but was never opened. Beneath the glare of modern technology, the cloth was being exposed for the first time in centuries.

The material showed various stains and colorations, but no pattern emerged until Laurent, with help from one of the more experienced technicians, stretched the shroud to its full length. The cloth did, indeed, have on it the back and front images of a man in the repose of death. Just as with the other shrouds, the man appeared to have been cruelly treated before death. Dark brown stains were present at various places, including the head region, the hands, the feet, and the torso. The image conformed to what would be expected if the cloth had been used to wrap the body of a crucified man.

The sight of this image, finally displayed before him, caught Laurent off guard. He had known, of course, what to expect. However, the sheer visceral shock he received was not expected and his sharp intake of breath was heard by all near him.

"Father, are you all right?"

"Yes, yes. I am a little startled by this. I had not seen the cloth completely opened before."

Sutton outlined for Laurent and for the team exactly what would happen next.

"We'll leave the shroud unfolded for the time being. It will be protected by a special plastic cover that fits tightly over this table. Of course, this room and the entire LAC facility are under strict security at all times. What we'll do first is photograph the piece using a variety of cameras and filters. We'll also take measurements of the cloth itself and of the patterns on the fabric. After this, we'll need to decide on what samples we'll take for analysis. We'll need a small piece for the actual carbon-14 dating in the mass spectrometer. Another small piece will be necessary for fiber analysis, to establish the possible geographic origin of the cloth. And finally, we'll need to dissolve away some of the material in the stained regions to determine the nature of the discoloration, particularly to determine if it was produced by blood and if that blood was human."

Laurent remembered that very minute pieces of cloth were taken from the Shroud of Turin. He was concerned that without the pressure of religious significance, his shroud would not be treated in the same way.

"Doctor Sutton, how much cutting will be necessary? How much damage will you do to the shroud itself?"

"Father, please don't worry. Our techniques require no more than we were given in Turin. Doctor McGovern, would you care to comment about your analysis?"

Mac had remained off to one side, not really being trained to handle the relic itself.

"Yes. I only need a sample extracted from the cloth, not a piece of the fabric itself. We've developed a technique that's quite harmless. An area containing a stain is put in a small device and gently washed with a solution to remove anything that can dissolve in water. No damage is done to the shroud except that it is temporarily wet. The procedure will merely remove anything soluble that could have caused the stain, especially any components of blood, for instance hemoglobin or dried cellular contents."

Josh had been standing as far away as possible but close enough to see the events taking place around the table. He had become fascinated as the cloth was unwrapped and unfolded. Even at a distance, he could feel the thrill of the link to the past that surged through the members of the team. As Mac finished speaking, Josh became charged with intensity as a new sensation swept over him. He spoke up for the first time since the meeting had begun.

"Mac, what volume of solution do you get from this procedure?"

"Oh, about one milliliter, I guess."

"And how much of it do you use for analysis?"

"Just a few microliters, really. The rest will be dried and preserved. Why?"

"I don't want to interrupt further. I'll talk to you about it later."

Josh's mind had leaped at the possibilities. Mac had mentioned "dried cellular contents." What if within this mixture were contained fragments of DNA preserved through the centuries? What if Josh could recover some of this DNA from Mac's extract and capture it as a recombinant DNA molecule? Would he then have a clone containing a bit of DNA from some unfortunate whose death during the Middle Ages resulted in this shroud?

The work on the cloth continued. Josh had stepped back and away from the activity. He could feel the beating of his heart at the base of his neck and he noticed that his hands were beginning to tremble.

Sangre de Cristo

INTERLUDE ONE
Jerusalem
30 A.D.

The first light of day brings with it an overwhelming sense of renewal for anyone who rises to witness the gradual and unstoppable march of the sun's fire across the eastern sky. The dawn on that day, however, was unlike any other. He did not realize this at first but came to know it over the remaining years of his life as, in his mind's eye, he saw the series of events again and again.

On that day, however, he walked the pathways of a city that was waking from its Sabbath slumber. He looked neither right nor left, but rather, as if in a trance, moved in straight lines through the narrow lanes, making his way toward David's Gate and the southern exit of the walled citadel. The rays of morning were now tinging the rooftops. Early risers, looking out and shielding their eyes against the sudden brightness, would see a figure in rich robes, traveling alone. Those who caught a glimpse of his face might even recognize him, if they were at all aware of the religious and political life of Jerusalem.

He did not see them or their glances. He saw only the scene that had played before his eyes earlier. That and the bundle he clutched close to his chest beneath his cloak were all the reality he possessed.

The canvas of his life, up to that moment, had been painted with colors that denoted fame and success. Joseph, the rural unknown from Arimathea had become Joseph, the Pharisee and member of the Sanhedrin. How could he have, in a sweeping gesture of madness, overturned everything?

It was one thing to be a secret follower of the Master. It was quite another to declare this openly, especially when His enemies had won the day. Or so he had thought.

When his close friend and colleague Nicodemus had spoken out in the Council in defense of the Master a few weeks before, Joseph feared that all was lost for them. But they had survived, receiving only suspicious glances from the others, especially those who followed the Sadducean tenets.

The capture and trial of Jesus had been swift. Throughout the early hours on the day before the Sabbath, his hope was that there had been no time to assemble the evidence needed to convict Him and that He would be released. In spite of his political acumen, Joseph had not measured the strength of the opposition correctly.

Standing on the hill called Skull, off to one side, he had watched as they hammered the spikes through His flesh and raised Him up for all the world to see. He followed the anguish of His mother and the other women who were close to Him. Joseph stayed there the entire afternoon and watched Him die. At that instant, something in his own heart ripped.

Minutes later, he found himself in the palace of the Roman governor, petitioning this man for the body of Jesus. There was no way this could be kept from the members of the Sanhedrin. It was curious that he no longer cared.

The tomb had been closed in time for them to return home before the beginning of the Sabbath. Instead of going with the others who were openly disciples of Jesus, he went to his own house, seeking the solitude of his rooms. There he mourned alone, his wife and two children at a loss to know what was wrong or how to console him.

He had planned to be at the tomb at sunrise of the first day of the week. What little sleep he had managed had been fitful. His exhaustion, coupled with his grief, slowed his steps. Thus, he arrived in time to see the departure of a small group of the disciples. Even from a distance, he could hear their agitated voices. He did not call out to them.

As he approached the tomb he saw the massive rock that had covered the entrance moved off to one side. It had taken two of them to move that stone into place, and then with a huge effort. Inside, he found the slab on which, less than two days before, they had laid the body of the Master. All that remained was the linen cloth with which they had wound Him in death. Joseph picked it up and saw the image of Jesus' body imprinted by the marks of His wounds. Without thinking, he folded the cloth and placed it inside his shirt, next to his heart.

He had re-entered the city, passing the Pool of Hezekiah and walking through the Gennath Gate. Unconsciously, he was fleeing the centers of power represented by the temple and the royal palace, intending to leave, perhaps to travel to his home city by a circuitous southern route. As he approached the Roman guards stationed at David's Gate, his footsteps slowed and he halted. Why was he running? He had not seen the other disciples flee. Had Jesus tried to avoid capture? Was this the lesson He taught?

He wanted to be a part of whatever had occurred at the tomb that morning, of the events that had been placed in motion. In the next days or weeks or months there would certainly be trouble for the followers of the Gallilean. Perhaps even more would die. None of that mattered. The Man who had been buried in the folded cloth which he held tightly under his shirt had burned a path into his soul.

Sangre de Cristo

CHAPTER FOUR

TUCSON, ARIZONA
FEBRUARY 22, 1999

"I think you're crazy. But, if you want to try it, go ahead."

Mac McGovern leaned back in his chair with his legs stretched out in front of him, his hands folded behind his head. Mac's casual air was in no way affected. He truly was what he appeared to be: a mellow and totally unpretentious man. His blond hair told of long hours in the sun. His youthful face barely hinted at the intelligence that lay behind it. His clothing was always a mixed metaphor of style: today it was a Hawaiian print shirt, sweat pants, and sneakers. His office in the Marvel Chemistry Building reflected his eclectic personality with a mixture of scientific texts, rock concert posters, and mountaineering souvenirs. Strangely, his desk was in perfect order, with neat stacks of papers and journals carefully arranged in what were obviously specific locations.

"I really think it could work," Josh argued. "I know it's a long shot, but I think it could work."

"Look, Josh. What are the chances that any DNA at all has survived on that cloth for hundreds of years? I mean, be reasonable."

"DNA has been cloned from several ancient sources, some older than this shroud. For instance, bits of genome were extracted from mummified remains. Even more amazing, a small amount of nucleic acid was cloned from a leaf found preserved in a Paleolithic deposit. With polymerase chain reaction we can recover even single molecules. Look at the work that was done on the Lincoln samples. It is possible."

Josh was striding back and forth before Mac's desk as he delivered his little lecture. He had read reports, published some years previously, demonstrating that DNA had been recovered from dried blood on clothes worn by the assassinated president. Mac held up his hands to stop the onslaught.

"Okay, okay! Take some of the extract. Give it a try. Who am I to stand in the way of progress?"

Mac got up and walked from the small office into the hall.

"I've got the extracts stored over here in the lab refrigerator."

He entered his laboratory, similar in layout to Josh's, yet different in many ways. The working spaces were the same, but the instrumentation was devoted to another discipline entirely. Mac's lab looked more like an electronics shop than a chemistry laboratory. Much of his analytical equipment was computer controlled and, as a result, the lab countertops were populated with a variety of keyboards and monitors, most with instructional menus displayed, ready for use. Mac crossed to a small refrigerator against the far wall. He removed a rack with four sealed glass tubes, each containing a small amount of clear reddish liquid.

Mac turned to Josh, who had followed him into the laboratory.

"Here are the extracts. You can have, oh, 200 microliters, okay?"

"That should do it, Mac. Thanks. Look, this won't be a problem with Sutton, will it?"

"You worry too much, Josh."

Mac fitted a disposable tip to an adjustable pipeting device designed to handle micro-scale samples. He transferred the 200 microliters of the red-tinted extract from the first glass tube into a plastic vial, numbered it "99-216-A" and placed it into an empty rack. He repeated the same procedure with tubes marked with the same set of numbers, this time lettered from "B" through "D." As he carried out the procedure with a casualness that spoke of years at the lab bench, he narrated the history of the extracts for Josh's benefit.

"Sample 'A' was extracted from the area of the shroud that covered the head. Sample 'B' is from the hands, 'C' from the torso and 'D' from the feet. The buffer solution is essentially isotonic, neutral pH and has a mild detergent. Here you go."

Without further ceremony, Mac handed the small rack containing the vials to Josh and turned to close up the original rack and return it to the refrigerator. "You'll find some small containers over there on top of the ice machine. You'd better keep those chilled on your way across campus."

Josh regarded the tiny amounts of liquid in the vials. He felt the familiar tingle of potential discovery, of experiments waiting to be performed. This time the excitement had the added flavor of something almost forbidden. He fought the excitement, trying to make his voice portray a composure inside him that did not exist. He forced a shrug as he spoke.

"Thanks, Mac. You're probably right. This is really a long shot. I'll try it anyway. Do me a favor. Don't tell Sutton and the others about this just yet. Let's see what happens first."

An expression of curiosity flickered across Mac's face.

"Sure. I don't see why, but if that's what you want, no problem. Good luck."

* * * * * * * * * * * * * * * *

Chris Warren was at his desk and Rita Mitchell was standing before her section of the laboratory bench when Josh entered the lab, holding a styrofoam container in which the small rack of vials was buried in crushed ice.

"Hi, boss. What've you got?"

His research assistant stood up and walked toward the door to greet Josh.

"These are some samples I'm going to work on as a favor to Doctor McGovern. I'll do what needs to be done myself. Is this space free?"

Josh indicated an apparently unoccupied section of lab countertop.

Chris and Rita exchanged glances as Josh turned to arrange his work area. The number of times that Josh worked in the lab had become fewer during the last two years. Chris had assumed Josh was becoming one of those scientists who directed and administrated, but no longer got his hands "wet."

In truth, Josh had become a scientist because of his love for the experimental work. In the past, he would spend hours in the lab, losing track of time as he traced all the myriad of tiny and intricate steps necessary to coax a new bit of information to emerge.

Now, he was a faculty member and found that getting grant support for his research led to hiring other people to do the experiments. In the end, he, like many scientists, wound up cut off by their advancement from the activity they most enjoyed.

Josh had his back to the others as he spoke.

"Look, Chris, I'm going to need some solutions, PCR primers, a cloning kit with a vector for picking up rare sequences, maybe pUC19. Also, I'll need some competent, high efficiency cells and some nutrient agar plates with ampicillin. Do we have any hot ATP in the freezer?"

In his element now, Josh flung the jargon of molecular biology out at a rapid-fire pace. His assistant was totally fluent and missed none of the meanings.

"Sure, boss. You can use my solutions on the shelf above my desk. The primers, cloning kits and enzymes are in the minus twenty freezer on the left. The cells are in the ultra-low freezer and there are some fresh plates in the cold room. We got in a new vial of ^{32}P-ATP yesterday. It's in the ultra-low also. Anything else?"

"No, no . . . that'll be fine . . . just fine."

Josh was making notes on a pad and was no longer paying attention to his assistant. Chris turned back to his desk, commenting sarcastically under his breath, "Now, this should be interesting."

The excitement was building and poured out through his pen as Josh worked quickly, drawing out his plans as a flow chart on the pad. He would start by concentrating any DNA that might be present in the extracts, keeping the samples separate and using the numbers Mac had given him. He would then begin the construction of the recombinant DNA molecules. His first job would be the amplification of DNA fragments in the shroud samples using a high-temperature procedure that drove the synthesis of many copies of any molecules present in the sample. After purifying the products of this reaction by gel electrophoresis, he would use one of the many combinations of cutting and splicing enzymes available in the modern arsenal of molecular biology to link any DNA that might have come from the shroud with a vector DNA molecule. Once these chimeras had been formed, he would literally force them into bacterial cells. Those fortunate cells that got either the vector DNA by itself or the recombinant molecule could grow happily in the presence of a penicillin-like antibiotic. The growth of all other cells would be inhibited.

Josh would take advantage of this. He would put the collection of cells onto an agar plate containing the antibiotic. He would also make use of another property of the DNA vector used for these experiments. Bacterial cells that received the vector alone would be tinted blue because of a reaction with a chemical in the agar plate. The cells containing the recombinant molecules he sought would grow to form small, whitish colonies on the surface of the plate.

There would be further steps needed to prove that the colonies harbored a bit of the DNA he was after. To do this he would use a number of small probes, pieces of artificial DNA that would identify human genetic material among the clutter of bacterial DNA found inside the cells. This would be the final test of whether or not he had cloned a piece of DNA from the shroud.

Over the next few hours, Josh executed the first stages of his experimental plan. He concentrated the molecules from the shroud extracts, using ethanol and extreme cold to bring them out of solution and into a solid form. He began a series of enzymatic reactions to amplify and convert any DNA present in the samples into a form that could be coupled with the recombinant DNA vector. The vector was a circular molecule of DNA made so that it could invade a bacterial cell and be reproduced within that cell. In return, it conferred the resistance to the antibiotic that Josh would use in the selection.

There were several times during the day when waiting was necessary: enzyme reactions and electrophoretic separations took time. Josh spent these minutes nervously pacing the hall between his lab and his office. He tried to clear some of the paperwork from his desk, but got nowhere. It was not until early evening that he was ready to mix the DNA and bacterial cells in the final stages of the day's work. It would take overnight for the bacteria to grow on the agar plates.

Josh was alone in the lab. His efforts had yielded four small plastic tubes containing the potential recombinant DNA molecules and another set of tubes with various positive and negative control reactions. He went across the lab to the ultra-low freezer and recovered three small vials of frozen bacterial cells.

These were the famous *Eschericia coli* bacterium, the workhorse of modern molecular biology. The microbe had lived within the human intestinal tract unnoticed until the end of the nineteenth century when it was "discovered" by bacteriologists. Much of the history of molecular biology in the twentieth century was the tale of explorations into the life and loves of this tiny organism. With the advent of biotechnology, the bacterium had assumed a new niche in the pantheon of the laboratory.

The procedure Josh used called for mixing the DNA molecules with small amounts of the cells, subjecting the mixture to a series of incubations at various temperatures, and then spreading the mixture out onto the surface of an agar plate containing the proper amount of the antibiotic ampicillin. It took nearly two hours to complete the necessary steps. In the end, Josh inserted the stack of petri plates into the bacterial incubator set up in one corner of the lab. He would know nothing further until the next day.

* * * * * * * * * * * * * * *

Josh arrived early at his lab the next morning with more excitement than he'd felt in months. At dinner the previous night with Leslie at El Charro, a Mexican restaurant near her house, he had told her about his experiment. The restaurant, in a converted home north of the downtown complex, was decorated with memorabilia from its many years as one of the city's premier Sonoran-style kitchens. Unlike other occasions, Josh barely noticed the food or the atmosphere.

Leslie felt conflicting emotions. True, Josh seemed to have broken out of his somber frame of mind. On the other hand, he was almost manic in his attitude about the project.

"Aren't you doing this as a favor for Mac?"

"No, Les. This experiment is totally my idea . . . mine. If this works, it'll really be something. Think of it. I will have cloned DNA from someone who died maybe 900 years ago. This could be a whole new direction for my research."

He had continued, rambling on about the examination of other ancient artifacts using molecular biology. Leslie had said no more. They had finally returned to her house in silence. His sleep was restless and he arose in the early hours. He had taken only coffee for breakfast and rushed off to campus before Leslie had even been fully awake.

Josh was anxious to look at the agar plates from the night before. The open incubator exuded the smell of fresh growing *E. coli*, a faintly seminal odor that some found slightly offensive. He examined the control plates first. All seemed as expected. The plates had small round bacterial growths called colonies, all of which were bluish in color against the light brown of the agar surface. He next picked up the set of plates containing the colonies made from the shroud samples. Three of them had only blue colonies, meaning no recombinant molecules had been formed. Josh looked at the fourth and his heart began to pound. The last plate, coming from sample 99-216-C, had, among all the blue colonies, three small white circles of bacterial growth. The cells within these colonies contained recombinant DNA molecules.

He brought the plates to the lab bench, forcing himself to breathe slowly. Chris Warren was at his own desk, lost in the reading of a journal. The two graduate students had not come into the lab as yet that morning. Josh opened his lab book and methodically recorded the results, noting the number and color of the colonies on each plate. He tried to push down his mounting elation. He realized that he must prove that at least one of these colonies contained human DNA. To do this, he would transfer a small amount of bacterial cells from the colonies to the surface of a membrane on top of another agar plate. He would once more allow them to grow overnight, and then process the membrane to release the DNA from the cells. He would also make an exact copy of the membrane to keep as a source of more cells.

This procedure took about an hour and Josh soon had the new agar plates in the incubator.

"How's it going, boss?"

Chris had come up behind him at the incubator.

"Huh? Oh, fine, Chris, fine."

In spite of his growing confidence, he was still reluctant to reveal exactly what he was doing.

"What's going on? What's this big experiment?"

Josh was evasive again.

"Nothing, really. As I said, it's simply a little favor for Doctor McGovern. I'm not even sure if it worked yet."

"McGovern? Doesn't he have something to do with the Laboratory of Atomic Chronometry that's trying to date some newly found shroud?"

Josh was more than a bit surprised.

"How do you know that?"

"Oh, there's a small blurb right here in *Lo Que Pasa*."

Chris handed Josh a copy of the weekly faculty/staff newspaper. In the lower right hand corner on the second page was a brief story: "LAC to Analyze Ancient French Shroud." Josh scanned it quickly and realized that it was verbatim from a short news release put out by the LAC office. The article named Sutton and Mac and referred to Laurent as the scholar who had brought the shroud to the University. Josh decided to admit some of his involvement.

"Actually, Chris, I'm trying to see if there could be any DNA preserved in the cloth. If it's there, I'm trying to make a recombinant DNA from it. I don't know yet if it worked."

"That sounds like a real tough experiment."

Chris was trained well enough to recognize the unlikely chance of success that Josh faced.

"I know. I thought I'd try it anyway. Mac provided the samples and . . . well, we'll see in a couple of days."

"What will you do if it works?"

Josh grinned, "Call a press conference, I guess."

* * * * * * * * * * * * * * * *

Midnight, and Josh was agitated. He nervously toured the bounds of his living room, stopping now and then to touch or adjust something on a shelf or table. His small house in the western hills overlooking the city had been built in a Southwestern style, reflecting for him, when he first saw it, his childhood years in Albuquerque.

The interior of the house had been designed to have a look and feel that matched the adobe and beam exterior. However, Josh had other ideas. True, much of the furniture was contemporary, with the square lines and pastel shadings of Santa Fe. But, here and there were touches of his New Orleans heritage.

A heavy wooden wall unit served as an entertainment center and bookcase, including on its shelves an assortment of objects culled from his past: woven baskets he had found in Tucson, a piece of pottery from Acoma that reminded him of his first trip to that mesa, and a replica of a polychrome Mimbres vase.

An incongruous Mardi Gras mask his grandmother had bought for him many years before attracted his attention. Mélanie Francis embodied his earliest memories of his ties to the Crescent City. There was never a time when the soft contours of her face, nut-brown with piercing black eyes, did not hover over him.

It was to her that he ran in terror one day when, at age ten, he and his younger brother, Walter, had disturbed what turned out to be a very large and equally frightened king snake in the vacant lot across from their home. Mélanie had armed herself with a broom and marched, with the two boys in reluctant tow, straight into the tall grass.

The snake, more than likely assuming that danger had passed, now found himself confronted by the imposing sight of an outraged grandmother. The two eyed each other suspiciously. Her judge-ment made, she turned to the boys and laughed. "Listen, chers, he's harmless, you see. He has a right to his life, too. Just because he's a snake don't mean he's bad. There's lots of folks who look at you kindly and are more poisonous than he'll ever be." There were times when he wished for her wisdom, and her instinctive ability to tell the good from the evil. He put the mask down and resumed his nervous rounds.

Leslie had been at work most of the evening, unpacking and cataloging a recent shipment that the Center had received. He had not seen her that day, having spent most of the time in his labora-tory and only picking her up at 8 p.m. for a late dinner. This time they had returned to his house. She was asleep now, having given up on his anxious watch an hour earlier.

His experiment was in its final stages. The samples had been processed through the necessary steps to allow the small pieces of human probe DNA, made radioactive, to bind to any human DNA that might be released from the bacterial cells growing on the nylon membrane. The last step in the procedure was to lay the nylon membrane against a piece of sensitive film. Wherever radioactivity was present on the membrane, a dark spot would appear on the film. Sufficient time had to pass for this exposure to occur. It would take until about 1 a.m. And so he paced.

12:30 a.m. and he was ready. Josh was out of the door and into his car. The city streets were all but empty on the west side of town as he drove downhill on Speedway Boulevard toward the campus. A right on Park Avenue and several blocks to the south brought him to the deserted lot next to his building. He was through the doors and in the elevator by 12:50 a.m.

The halls were illuminated by the low-level lighting necessary for patrolling the buildings. He made his way to his lab door and entered the darkened room. The sounds of the research laboratory at night would be mysterious to the uninitiated: clicks of electrical relays in regulating panels for a variety of incubators, gurgles of water circulating through small heating baths, the whine of centrifuge motors turning at high speed during an overnight experiment. But for Josh these sounds were like the steady beating of his heart. He flipped on the light switch, bringing up the full fluorescent glare of the overheads.

The membrane and film were contained in a sealed metal case inside his ultra-cold freezer. He opened this unit and, wearing thick gloves, retrieved the film container. The interior of the freezer was kept at minus ninety degrees Celsius. At this temperature, contact between his skin and the metal of the film holder would be painful. As he withdrew it from the cold, the container was instantly covered with frost and enveloped in clouds of moisture condensing from the air. He left his laboratory and crossed the hall to one of the common darkrooms used by everyone in the building.

The door into the darkroom consisted of a rotating cylinder arrangement. He entered the open side of the cylinder that faced the hall and turned the entire tube around until the opening allowed access to the inside of the room. His eyes took several moments to adjust to the red glow of the safe lights. He placed the container on a small counter and reached over to press the "on" switch of the automatic film processing machine. Working in the red light, he opened the film container. The nylon membrane was wrapped in thin plastic and pressed tightly against a sheet of X-ray film. Josh separated the two and fed the film into the receiving tray of the processor. A small bell sounded, indicating that the end of the sheet had engaged the rollers and had begun its slow entry into the machine.

The entire processing would take no more than two minutes, minutes that always seemed to be occurring in some alternate time frame. Josh could remember other times, especially as a graduate student, when he had spent what must have been long hours in the darkroom only to exit and find that less than twenty minutes had passed. His mind was drifting along all the possible outcomes of this experiment when he heard the film drop into the output tray of the processor.

Josh grabbed the developed film and quickly turned on the normal room lighting. He held the sheet up against the white glare for his first view. The vague outline of the membrane that had been pressed against it could be seen. Along the lower edge was a series of dark spots indicating that the positive controls were as expected. And in the right center of the film, corresponding to the position of one of the bacterial colonies, Josh saw the dark spot revealing the presence of radioactivity at that site on the membrane. The experiment had worked. He had a DNA clone from the shroud.

CHAPTER FIVE

SAN RAFAEL, CALIFORNIA
MARCH 1, 1999

Costa Tarquin let his copy of the *San Francisco Chronicle* fall onto the table in his office. He turned to the window that framed a view of San Pablo Bay, the northernmost extension of the great landlocked arms of the Pacific, spread out behind the Golden Gate.

The office was uniquely suited to the man who was founder and CEO of Delos Systems, Incorporated. The dominant feature of the room was not, as one might expect, a desk. Instead, two computer terminals, linked to mainframes, along with Macintosh and DOS machines, occupied space at four work stations. The middle of the room contained a conference table arrayed with publications and software manuals for the product lines of DSI. It was onto this table that Costa had dropped the morning paper, folded open to the fourth page, revealing the story headlined "University Team Finds New Twist to Dating Ancient Shroud."

The company had been built from the ground up and Costa had overseen every aspect of its development. He had started alone, operating out of his garage in South San Francisco, and now presided over an operation that included managers who coordinated both domestic and foreign offices. But DSI was not his only driving passion.

His memories of early childhood were riddled with scenes of his father and uncle at their home in the Southern California port city of San Pedro. The Tarquin brothers had left their Aegean birthplace to fish for tuna in the warm currents of the eastern Pacific. They spoke of the sea, of the lines and nets, and of the boats that were dearer to them than women.

While he remembered the stories of fishing, he had been captivated by the other tales of the ancient and holy shroud and the Society sworn to its safekeeping. At first, there had been vague

61

references. As he grew older and as the men drew him more closely into their circle, the stories took form and substance. He learned the real purpose for the yearly trips the brothers took, ostensibly to Greece, but in reality to Gallipoli. The story of how the shroud had been lost was told and retold. By the time he was initiated into the Society he had inherited their longing for the return of its sacred charge.

Costa had not inherited their love for the sea, at least not as a way of life. Instead, he found another talent he could utilize: mathematics. Complex formulas and abstract symbols were merely second nature to him. His talents brought him at last to the University of California's Berkeley campus. The revolutionary times of the sixties had pulled him, not into the counterculture of the Bay area, but into the dawning of a new age in the region that would become known as Silicon Valley. He was a founding father.

Family traditions were central to his philosophy and he had not turned his back on his past. Thus he had built a company named for the island home of his ancestors and had an office window from which he could watch the ships come and go.

The intercom on his small desk buzzed, followed immediately by the voice of his administrative assistant, "Costa . . . Nikos is here." Cheryl had been on a first name basis with him almost since her arrival twelve years earlier. But, just now, the familiarity rankled him. His son was the last person he wanted to see. He left the window for his desk and jabbed at the switch.

"Tell him to come in."

Nikos Tarquin walked into his father's office and, as always, stood nervously to one side of the door. Beyond the family resemblance, Nikos was but a shadow of the older man. Where Costa was broad, Nikos was slight. The roughly carved features of the Old World had been smoothed out in this next generation. Costa emitted a tangible energy while his son sought to hide from the light.

After four years at the University of Pennsylvania he had returned with a degree in business, although he had barely made it through the program. Now, he was a vice president in charge of sales at DSI, and it was clear that the position was his only through nepotism. Within the company network he was considered dangerous. While totally deferential in the presence of his father, he was ruthless in his absence. In short, everyone knew that he would never be another Costa.

"Come in, Nikky, and close the door." One hand motioned his son toward him while the other reached over to touch the intercom. "Cheryl, no interruptions for fifteen minutes." She knew that as code, meaning if Nikos wasn't out within fifteen minutes, find some pretense to break in. He looked up at the younger man who had remained across the room.

"Sit down, Nikky, sit down. What do you want?"

Before the rest of the world, Nikos at least appeared decisive; before his father he was reduced to whimpering. He always felt that he was being tested, even now, though he knew his father had merely asked a simple question. His voice was lurching around for an answer. He hated this feeling.

"Papa . . . uh . . . was wondering . . . have you seen . . . that is, did you read . . . have you looked at the *Chronicle* today?"

Costa was afraid of this. The news article that had attracted his attention, and that of his son, was still clear in his memory.

> TUCSON (AP). A research team at the University of Arizona has announced a novel development in their attempt at dating an ancient linen cloth believed to be a shroud similar to that kept in Turin, Italy. Dr. Richard Sutton, Director of the Laboratory for Atomic Chronology, revealed that a molecular biologist has been able to extract fragments of DNA preserved in the linen cloth and produce from them a recombinant clone. The experiment, carried out by Dr. Joshua Francis, is one of only a few successful attempts to recover biological material from such artifacts.
>
> The relic, believed to date from the Middle Ages, was brought to the University from the Abbey of Hautecombe in France by its discoverer, Fr. Laurent Carriere. Fr. Carriere believes that the shroud may have originated in Gallipoli, Turkey and might have been captured there during the Crusades.

For Costa, the words in this report had been electric, sending currents deep into the circuitry of his past. He had immediately begun to construct the broad outlines of a strategy that would realize his dream of returning the shroud to the Society. His son's entry had disturbed his train of thought.

"What are you talking about, Nikky?"

"The article about dating this shroud from France." Nikos glanced toward the conference table and the open newspaper. Costa followed his son's gaze.

"Yes, I've seen it."

"Well, isn't this the one? What are we going to do?"

"We? I didn't think this meant that much to you. What do you have in mind?"

Nikos had been inducted into the Society as a matter of course. He did not, however, share Costa's commitment. For him, the traditions and ceremonies were remnants of the Old World. But he knew enough of the history to realize the significance of the news story. His father's challenge had put him on the defensive once again.

"Papa . . . let me try to get it back."

"You? How?"

"Let me go negotiate with this priest. Perhaps he would be willing to sell the artifact to a collector. Especially if he doesn't know its true nature. Monks always need money. Maybe he would part with it."

For most of his life Nikos had tried to please his father with his accomplishments. He had never seemed to succeed. He was not charismatic; he was not brilliant; he was not Costa. He saw a way to win favor permanently.

Costa rose from his chair and stood before the window, silhouetted against the waters of the bay. His right hand drifted to the narrow scar that ran along his jaw line, a souvenir from one of the summers he had spent on the docks. The mannerism indicated that he was reviewing the logic and sorting out the possibilities of what he would do next. He did not have the slightest confidence that Nikos could accomplish anything, let alone the purchase of the shroud. On the other hand, he saw that he now needed his son out of the way during the implementation of his plans. Sending him to Tucson might serve a purpose after all. Nikos might even create a much needed diversion.

"What makes you think the cloth would be for sale?"

"They don't know what it is, Papa. They think it's like the others, some artifact made during the Middle Ages. I'll say I represent a wealthy collector. It could work."

Costa was silent for a while. He reached into the open collar of his shirt and retrieved the gold medallion he wore, fitting it into the palm of his hand. He could feel the contours on its face, tracing the raised image of three crossed nails. Along the lower edge, in Greek lettering, was the word "ARIMATHEA." He had worn this since his induction into the Society as a youth. Nikos, too, wore the medal, but without the same reverence.

The habit of fingering the medallion, either openly or through his shirt, whenever Costa was lost in thought, was almost superstitious. However, Nikos knew that it meant a decision was imminent.

"All right, Nikky. You try to negotiate the purchase. Go to Tucson. Meet this priest. See if he accepts an offer. Take as much time as you need."

"Trust me, Papa. I won't fail."

He watched as his son left the office, then turned back to the view of the bay. Their conversation was all but forgotten as he mentally checked off the series of phone calls that must be made.

* * * * * * * * * * * * * * * *

"Cheryl. Get me reservations for Tucson, Arizona. I want to be there next Monday. I'll need a hotel near the University and a rental car. And don't mess anything up. This is top priority."

She watched as the younger Tarquin swaggered off toward his office. She recognized the signs. He had obviously been given what he considered an important job by Costa. She knew that he would spend the rest of the week terrorizing the secretarial staff. As he closed his door, she made a grimace at his disappearing back.

Nikos shut out the rest of the company and tried to contain his emotions by marching back and forth in front of his desk. This time perhaps he could rout his demons forever.

He was the second child born to Costa and Alexis Tarquin. His older sister had already co-opted the aggressive, compulsive personality of the firstborn, leaving Nikos to play another roll within the family. For his father, however, there was no other possibility for a male offspring. Costa expected that the boy would fit into the mold from which the older generations had been formed.

The incident that had formed, in one stroke, the Nikos who struggled for Costa's acceptance had occurred during his junior year in high school. His father had insisted that Nikos run for class president. In spite of the boy's reluctance, he had no way of refusing. He placed his name in contention and began to campaign in what was, at best, a halfhearted effort. He made speeches, lacking in any kind of fervor. He appeared at school rallies, feeling foolish and uncomfortable. His only consolation had been that, after the election, he could return to his normal mode of behavior.

To his utter amazement, he won. When the votes were counted, he had been swept into office by a decisive majority. For a brief time he began to believe in himself, to see in the mirror something of what his father wanted him to be. He appeared before his classmates draped in confidence.

Little by little he began to sense that something was not right. He caught sidelong glances or snickering remarks that ended as he walked into a room. It took a good bit of investigation. By asking the right questions of the right people he found out the truth. Costa had secretly organized a group of his classmates as an underground campaign committee in his son's favor. Money was put at their disposal to essentially buy the votes needed to elect him. The students actually took it as a lark, some voting for him more as a joke, others as a protest against the system or even as a vote for Nikos as some kind of mascot. No one took him seriously.

In anger, he confronted Costa with his discovery, only to be told "I knew you couldn't do it on your own." His father's words would echo through him for the rest of his life. He was outraged and humiliated and had barely endured the balance of his term of office. To avoid further political activity, he threw himself into his sport. He had been a swimmer for many years and now spent extra hours at practice, letting the long, slow laps dull the pain he felt.

During this time he changed. He modeled himself after one part of his father. He became ruthless and manipulative, but lacked the compassion that made Costa a leader. The aftermath of the election had followed him to college and from there into the company. When he walked through the hall on his way to his office, he imagined that he could still hear the gibes and see the half-hidden glances. But this time, he was in a position of power and could make their lives miserable.

He stopped the pacing that had become more and more frenetic and yanked the telephone from its cradle. He pushed one of the interoffice buttons.

"Cheryl. Have you got those reservations yet?"

"It's okay, Nikos. I have someone working on it."

He slammed the receiver down in anger. When he ran this company, it would be "Mr. Tarquin."

CHAPTER SIX

TUCSON, ARIZONA
MARCH 4, 1999

Richard Sutton, Ph.D., Professor of Chemistry and Director of the Laboratory of Atomic Chronometry entered his office in the Gould-Simpson Building at 7:30 that morning. He looked forward to at least one uninterrupted hour before the rest of his staff began their day. He would use those precious minutes to scan the latest issues of the scientific journals he had received that week. By the time his administrative assistant was at his desk in the outer office, Sutton's schedule would commence, filled with project reports, budget details, and other managerial chores. All of these duties were added to his regular responsibilities as a professor, including his afternoon lecture section of Introductory Chemistry. Prominent during the morning would be a meeting he had called with Drs. Francis and McGovern and Fr. Carriere.

The Southwestern desert had been his adopted home for more than twenty years. Those who had known him as a child would be hard pressed to find traces of little Dicky Sutton from Leeds. His Midlands accent had been erased long ago by his British public school education. He carried the bearing of a Cambridge don with a practiced dignity he had cultivated during his undergraduate years. In his case, it was not simply an air. Sutton was, in fact, a consummate scholar. His role as director of LAC was often at odds with his academic yearnings.

The 10 a.m. conference he had scheduled would require a mixture of his academic and administrative roles. The unexpected experiment conducted by the young professor of molecular biology had provided a much-needed publicity boost for the LAC team. Interest in dating archaeological finds had been high following the initial success with the Shroud of Turin. In the succeeding years, as each artifact was meticulously characterized, the news value had waned. The University Information Office continued to issue press notices, but these met with little response. The latest release, with its mention of recombinant DNA, had caught the attention of the media.

As a scientist, Sutton was, of course, interested in the scholarly potential of this new direction. However, he was also keenly aware of the effect that the publicity might have on the laboratory and its funding. The meeting had been called as a planning session.

* * * * * * * * * * * * * * * *

Mac McGovern arrived at the University at 9 a.m. in his customary style. This meant biking in from his home a few miles north of campus. He rode up to the door of the Marvel Chemistry Building and dismounted. His long, blond hair created a manic fringe around the edge of the fluorescent green cycling helmet he wore. The well-used backpack, slung over his shoulders, contained journals, papers, and his lunch. His "uniform of the day" consisted of a red-checked shirt and jeans coupled with a pair of old running shoes. No one was certain if the image of eccentricity that he portrayed was studied or actual.

Here was a man whose heart and soul were permanently camped on the beaches of his beloved Southern California. He had grown up in Torrance, had worked toward his bachelor's degree in chemistry at U.C.L.A., and had then moved 100 miles south for graduate work at U.C. San Diego. However, when the department at Arizona was seeking to make an appointment in analytical chemistry, they found Dr. Dennis McGovern at the Massachusetts Institute of Technology, where he was considered one of the more brilliant postdoctoral fellows. Mac was not an Easterner and the three years in the Boston area had produced withdrawal symptoms, but no permanent damage.

The atmosphere at M.I.T. appeared to Mac, at first glance, quite casual. Most students and faculty dressed in a fashion that seemed familiar to the transplanted Californian. In spite of this, he soon found out that the mood was definitely cerebral and intense. Postdoctoral fellows were expected to be in the lab seven days each week. Their lives centered around the Institute. Mac's breezy Western style was different from that of his colleagues. It was only after they realized that he was a literal master of both theory and practice in the laboratory that they began to accept, more likely to ignore, his quirks. The sound of heavy metal rock became a normal replacement for the classical music that existed in the lab before his arrival.

Neither the Institute nor his own successes there impressed Mac. At the end of his post-doctoral term, he had been actively pursued by several universities. He had chosen Arizona because of the research facilities and the location. The University's reputation and status had not been important.

The scientist in Mac thrived on solving mysteries. The mystery of the shroud had deepened and that fact added an extra thrill to his day. He walked into the Marvel Building, wheeling his bicycle alongside, and boarded the elevator. On the way up to his third floor office, he wondered again about the implications of Josh's experiment. He had not expected it to be successful. It apparently was. And now, Sutton had called a meeting to decide how they should proceed, given this new direction. He leaned his bike against the wall outside his lab, opened the door, and reached up to the radio on his bookshelf. The room filled with the thump-thump of a classic rock back beat. Mac hummed along.

* * * * * * * * * * * * * * * *

At 9:30 a.m. Laurent left the Newman Center for the walk to the Gould-Simpson Building and the offices of LAC. After two weeks, the routes through the campus had become relatively familiar. Even so, he had been uprooted and cast into an alien environment with little time for adaptation. Laurent experienced that dizzying, almost surreal, view of the immediate world that often slams unpredictably into a traveler's awareness.

One month earlier he had taken a short vacation and had returned to his family's home in the vineyards of Le Châble, a small Swiss village at the base of the Alps. He had grown up there, in the canton of Valais, near the great lake that everyone, except the people of Geneva, called Lac Léman. As a boy he had been more attracted by the ancient Roman ruins in the nearby town of Martigny than by the life of a vintner. His love of scholarship had led to ridicule at the hands of his older brother. The university at Geneva had been a welcome refuge for him.

The train ride from Geneva along the shores of the lake and up the Rhône valley to Martigny had been both welcome and frightening; frightening because he had felt once more the unwanted emotional tug of the snow-covered terraced slopes perched above the glacial river basin.

At Martigny he had to change to a narrow-gauge train for the final stage of the trip to Le Châble. The little farming community sat demurely in a notch below the Grand Saint Bernard Pass. Above was the fabled ski resort of Verbier with its network of gondolas, chairlifts, and cable cars leading up to Mont Fort.

The day after his homecoming he had skied from the very top all the way back down to Le Châble, a run he and his brothers loved. It took them through the flashy resort town and dropped them along virtually unmarked trails down to the level of the valley below. The last part of the run was through the vineyards themselves and required skiing off the edges of the terraced slopes. They had ended the day in the family home, with the entire clan gathered in the great room in front of the fireplace.

Laurent had tried to tell everyone of the excitement he had experienced with the discovery of the shroud at the abbey. The looks on the faces of his brothers and even his father told him they were not impressed. The familiar mix of anger and hurt that had so often driven him from the fields as a child welled up within him. His mother's smile kept him from fleeing once more. He let his description drift to an end with "So, next week I'm on my way to the United States." After a polite pause, the conversation turned to local gossip and the prospects for the next growing season. Laurent watched the flames consume the edges of the log and imagined what the coming trip would be like, mentally leaving the fields again.

Here, in this foreign land, he was in the milieu of a scholar. His opinion was sought after by faculty of the Religious Studies Committee. They included experts on the period of the Reformation, but none whose specialty was the Church during the Middle Ages. Laurent was in his own element, if not in his own climate.

The meeting in Sutton's office that morning would be different. Laurent did not fully comprehend the scientific principles involved in the dating process or in this new aspect of recombinant DNA. Nonetheless, he was being called in as an important contributor. He was a long way from the vineyards of Le Châble or the gardens of Hautecombe.

* * * * * * * * * * * * * * *

Josh and Leslie drove in that morning from his foothills home. Leslie had spent the last few days keeping close watch on him. She sensed a subtle change in him but could not clearly identify it. His excitement over this new discovery could barely be contained. Yet, she knew that this was not at the core of the difference.

The night before, they had made love. As always, their bodies responded so well, so intensely to each other. This time Josh had been more tender than before, somehow gentler. She was awake long after he had drifted off, trying to touch in her mind the elusive source of this change.

They left the car in the parking structure north of the Fine Arts complex and crossed through the pedestrian underpass beneath Speedway Boulevard onto the campus. The brick walkway was full of students and faculty arriving for morning classes, some on foot, others on bicycles. The clatter of loose stones echoed in the tunnel as the wheels rattled over them.

The Center for Creative Photography was the second building on the left as they exited the tunnel. Josh climbed the first set of steps to the entrance with Leslie. A small espresso cart and a set of outdoor tables occupied the space in front of the entrance to the Center. They would often linger there for coffee before parting; today, there was no time, especially for Josh.

"I'll see you for lunch, Les." He held her for a moment and kissed her slowly before moving off.

Leslie remained for a time on the Center steps, startled into immobility. Josh had never been comfortable with public displays of affection. Now he was kissing her openly, as though it had been happening all their lives. She watched him until he disappeared among the crowd of people heading south into the heart of the campus.

Any change in his own behavior had not registered with Josh. His mind was eagerly following the expected path of the days events. The meeting at 10 a.m. in Sutton's office was the focal point for these thoughts. He made his way toward the Life Sciences South Building and his office, following a route dictated by the buildings in the oldest part of campus.

The western side of the University had been built first, designed during the early part of the century. A prominent feature was the large number of olive trees lining the streets and foot paths. Walking between their gnarled trunks, lost for a moment amidst lawns and shrubbery, took away any link to the desert ecosystem that enclosed the campus.

Josh had spent his undergraduate days on home ground at the University of New Mexico in Albuquerque. He was a native of that city by birth, but his cultural roots extended far to the east, touching down at last in New Orleans. His parents had quite unexpectedly settled at the base of the Sandias. They had left the Mississippi bank as part of a general westward migration. On an overnight stop, they had fallen instantly in love with Albuquerque. Eventually, they were followed by other family members, including their own parents. Josh had been raised in a Creole family transplanted into a community rich in Hispanic and Pueblo Indian influences.

The New Orleans culture of his heritage was very distinct and all but unknown to most of the white world, especially outside of Louisiana. The most common reaction was to confuse "Creole" with "Cajun," a mistake that would infuriate Josh's grandmother, Mélanie. It was she who had given him the distinctly un-Creole, but Biblical, first name of Joshua. She would tell him, holding him upon her lap as she sipped her café au lait, "You know, cher, a child born on Friday the 13th, he's going to need all the help he can get, yeah." She could not restrain herself, however, from imposing on him at least one French name. Joshua René Francis honored both the Old Testament and his great uncle.

Josh had never seen himself as a minority, at least not until he had left his home town. He had grown up in an extended family, a virtual tribe, full of the language and traditions that gave a child a center. Then too, the emphasis in New Mexico on Hispanic and Native American values made any feeling of second-class status remote. This continued through his years at the University in Albuquerque.

As he moved beyond these familiar confines, however, Josh was called Black and then African-American, definitions imposed, in effect, by the majority. Josh had tried to embrace these classifications, even though his ethnic experience was in many ways distinctly different from that of the average Black American.

His problems began when he rose higher into the rarefied atmosphere of academia. He found, to his dismay, that, too often, people assumed he was given a position because of his race, not his ability. In a perverse way, this produced in him a kind of quiet rage, akin to, but different from, that felt by previous generations who were denied entry to the upper echelons of society. The result was that Josh set out to prove himself at every turn. He was determined to be the best, regardless of the content of pigment in his skin. He could never admit to himself that he could not succeed on his own merits. This attitude only heightened the tension brought on by his flagging research efforts. The shroud offered a way out.

The time he had spent outside of New Mexico, in Northern California and in France, had been culturally disorienting. Here, on another Southwestern campus, he felt at least as at home as he had ever been, or as lost.

* * * * * * * * * * * * * * *

The office of the director of LAC had few of the trappings expected for an administrator. There was no large desk, no conference area with tables and chairs set aside to facilitate interactions. Instead, his office looked much like the others he had occupied during all the years of his professorship. The walls were lined with bookshelves, overflowing with texts, journals, and reference books. His desk was organized but stacked with papers. There were extra chairs in the room, but these too had either magazines or monographs covering the seats. A window that looked out onto the street north of the building gave light, but the view was obscured by charts and tables taped in various places.

Professor Sutton sat at his desk reading one of a series of reports dealing with the progress of his research team. His thinning gray hair was splayed haphazardly across his scalp and was constantly being rearranged by an unconscious habit of running his hand over his head while he thought. He had the slightly pudgy and pale appearance of the bookish. His wire-framed glasses were perched precariously on the bridge of his nose. In spite of living in Arizona for so long, he had never lost the habit of wearing a coat and tie each day.

A soft knock at the door preceded the entry of the LAC administrative assistant, Harold Flynn.

"Doctor Sutton. Everyone's here for the meeting."

"Fine, fine. Show them in, please, Harry."

The three men filed in and began clearing the chairs.

"Good morning, Richard." Mac eased himself into a seat near the window.

The director visibly recoiled at the informality of the younger professor. "Good morning."

Josh and Laurent arranged themselves in the remaining chairs and greeted Dr. Sutton.

"I'm glad you could all be here. Coffee, anyone?"

Sutton prided himself on his attention to details for such meetings. He already knew that a fresh pot of coffee was available. Harry waited at the door to collect the orders. Once everyone had been served, Sutton opened the business of the morning.

"I'm sure you all realize that the dating of the Hautecombe shroud has attracted considerable attention because of the experiment Doctor Francis has performed. The question to be asked is what we wish to do next. How shall we proceed?"

Josh had been waiting for this moment. He spoke before anyone else, gripping the arms of his chair in his eagerness.

"I know this may sound a little sudden, but I think we're moving in a new direction for us. The field of study is called "molecular archaeology": the examination of human or animal molecules isolated from artifacts such as the shroud. I assume you have materials that have been extracted from other items you've dated. I could use the same procedures with those samples."

76

Mac was the first to respond, raising an obvious note of caution.

"Hold it, Josh. How likely is it that the other samples might contain something that you could clone? Wasn't your success more fortuitous than anything else?"

Josh did not hear the objectivity with which Mac spoke. Instead, he was stung, being challenged from an unexpected source, and he became defensive.

"DNA has been isolated from mummified remains, even from fossilized organic matter thousands of years old. I don't think this is unlikely at all. On the contrary, I think it's not only possible but probable. The importance must not be overlooked. Isolation of these molecules would give us a direct analysis of changes in human DNA that have occurred over time."

The others remained silent during this short lecture. Sutton studied the young scientist with interest. He cleared his throat to signal his intention to speak.

"Well, Doctor Francis, this is all quite interesting. I'm sure that this could be the topic of much further discussion. But, my real question this morning has to do with the item currently being investigated: the Shroud of Hautecombe. We have caught the interest of the media and I wish to follow up as soon as possible."

Josh sat back in his chair, somewhat deflated, feeling his enthusiasm trampled by the LAC director and by Mac. Laurent had remained impassive up to this point, drifting in and out of the discussion. With the mention of the shroud, his attention returned to the meeting.

"What do you propose, Professor Sutton?"

"The carbon-14 analysis should be completed tomorrow. I'm calling a press conference to announce the results. The conference will take place on Monday at 2 p.m."

Mac spoke up again.

"Richard, don't you think we need time to analyze the data before making this kind of announcement?"

Sutton was a full professor of chemistry. More importantly, he was a product of the English university system. He held a mental image of himself strolling aloofly along the Cam, undergraduates, graduate students, and junior faculty politely parting before him.

This vision persisted in his mind, almost ghostlike, whenever he crossed the Arizona campus. To have Mac repeatedly refer to him as "Richard" caused unwanted distortions of this scenario. Sutton glared at Mac with icy detachment.

"Doctor McGovern. I presume that your results are completed?"

"Why, yes, they are."

"Very good. And would you be so kind as to tell us your conclusions?"

"The stains on the cloth were made by blood of human origin."

"Thank you. The accelerator mass spectrometry results will be completed by tomorrow afternoon. We will 'analyze the data,' as you call it, on Saturday and Sunday. The press conference will be on Monday as I have arranged. I presume there are no further questions. Thank you all for coming."

During this final statement, the director had risen stiffly and, striding across the room, had opened the door for his visitors.

* * * * * * * * * * * * * *

"Well, that was kind of sudden."

The three men stood in the lobby area of the LAC offices as Mac made this observation. Indeed, he appeared to have no clear idea about what had led to Sutton's abrupt dismissal. The formality of rank was as foreign to the young chemist as the glitter of L.A. streets must have been to the director.

Laurent's thoughts were elsewhere. He dreaded an end to this experience and a return to the confines of Hautecombe.

"Do you think the results will really be ready by Monday?"

Mac had been idly toying with a magazine at the reception desk. He remained unchanged in his opinion.

"Yeah, probably. I don't think I like taking that kind of chance . . . announcing a press conference before we can go over the data."

Josh had been quiet, still stinging from the rebukes, both real and imagined, delivered during the meeting. As he was about to speak, the LAC administrative assistant appeared at the door of his office.

"Father Carriere, I have a message for you."

"Oh yes, Mister Flynn, thank you."

"A phone call came to our office for you this morning." He referred to a slip of paper in his hand. "A man named 'Nikos Tarquin' wishes to speak to you. He says he represents a wealthy collector who might like to purchase the shroud. He says the amount is up to you."

"To buy the shroud? But why? I do not understand."

"I guess the collector is interested in medieval artifacts and has the money to indulge his taste. Mr. Tarquin implied that the purchase could provide a nice sum for the abbey."

"I have no authority or intent to sell the shroud, but I suppose I should speak with him. How can I telephone him?"

"Oh, you don't have to. He'll be coming to Tucson next week."

CHAPTER SEVEN

TUCSON, ARIZONA
MARCH 6, 1999

Leslie could not stop herself from watching him across the room, following his moves as he and Laurent walked from picture to picture. They were at the Etherton/Stern Gallery for the opening of a photographic exhibit. The gallery, on the second floor of a large building in the downtown arts district, was perfect for such shows. The room was large and open, the off-white walls illuminated strategically, and the hardwood floor punctuated with low benches for sitting and viewing, at leisure, the works on display. This was one of the premier houses in Tucson's artistic community and represented a variety of artists working in several media.

Although he loved her work, Josh would usually object to attending these events, feeling ill-suited in a nonscientific setting. Tonight had been different. She had asked if he would go with her and he had said yes without hesitation. He had even suggested bringing Laurent along. Leslie's intuition had again told her that something in him had changed.

She had always believed that intuition was a much maligned sense. For most people, especially men, it had the connotation of guesswork, of action accompanied by no thought. For her, intuition was a highly tuned instrument, used as the framework for logic and decision making. The information she received in this manner had guided her through a number of difficult situations.

Leslie was a child of the Peninsula cities south of San Francisco. Most of her early years were spent in Redwood City where her father, a civil engineer, worked, and her family lived. Her mother anchored their home, caring for Leslie and her two older brothers. Their very conventional family life was nurturing and, at the same time, stifling for her.

81

She excelled in high school and was lured by and accepted to Stanford. Her intuition signaled a warning at this point. The honor she was given and the pride her family felt was weighed against what she sensed might happen to her during four years at this esteemed center of learning. She would work diligently, submerge herself in courses, devote herself to studies and, in the end, perhaps lose her independent core that was just beginning to harden into form. She decided, instead, to attend Menlo College, a small yet highly respected liberal arts school in Palo Alto.

During her freshman year she discovered photography. Capturing an image on film became more than recording a scene or event. She used her camera as a means to suspend the flight of time, freezing both the action and the emotion before her.

She had majored in art and history, combining her interests in interpreting human actions and events. She had also developed a reputation as an exciting photojournalist. Her work was used by many of the Peninsula papers. She had even had a photo published in the *Chronicle*, a dramatic picture of antinuclear activists chained together in front of the entrance to the Stanford Administration Building. It was no surprise that, following graduation, she was offered an assignment with Reuters news service at their London office.

After three years and photographic work over most of Europe, North Africa, and the Middle East, she had enough contacts and credibility to work free-lance. Following her heart, she based herself in Paris, a city that would become a second home for her. Her pictures began appearing in newspapers and magazines almost immediately. Being independent, she could choose her subjects, choose her settings and follow her intuition to produce a collection of images on a theme.

Leslie could be seen or not seen. She could appear at one time seductive and feminine and, at another, almost asexual. If she chose to wear a tight-fitting dress, black stockings on long legs accentuated by high-heels, she could enter a room and have the instant attention of every male over five years old. Just as easily she could dress in baggy slacks, a nondescript shirt and sweater, tuck her hair into an old baseball cap, leave off the makeup, and all but disappear into the scenery, leaving only the unquenchable force of her eyes peering out from behind the disguise. In this way, with camera bags over her shoulders, she had prowled the cities of Europe and the Middle East, capturing scene after scene on film.

In the wake of the appearance of some of her work in an anthology entitled *Les Visages de Paris,* she had begun to receive calls from galleries instead of newspapers. The photographs that had attracted the most attention were of prostitutes and other inhabitants of the streets and alleyways near Place Pigalle. The story of these images told something of Leslie herself.

Before taking even one picture she had frequented the small bars and cafes near Pigalle, becoming a part of the nighttime scene. After several weeks, she arrived with her camera bag. She asked and received permission to shoot in and around a brasserie on Rue Frochot. Her photographs, processed during the days in her darkroom/kitchen, revealed a sensitivity and depth of emotion that went far beyond the grains of silver on the paper.

This was the body of work that had attracted the attention of the Center for Creative Photography in Tucson. The show and the resulting job offer had unexpectedly altered her course, and her intuitive sense was once again required. One phase of her life came to a close and a new one opened.

Josh and Laurent had been slowly working their way around the gallery, pausing at various photographs. At last they had found an unoccupied space, apart from the exhibit, where they were lost, deep in conversation. The two men had become quite close during the last few days. She could see a growing friendship that went beyond the professional relationship that brought them together. Leslie drifted toward them, stopping at various exhibits in order to give the two more time and, finally, joined them, hearing Laurent in mid-sentence.

" . . . although I suppose it could be done. Nothing like that has been suggested before. I am not certain that Father Holden would approve."

"Approve of what? Who is Father Holden?"

"Ah, Leslie, I am enjoying this exhibit. Thank you for the invitation."

As Laurent spoke, Josh slipped his arm around her waist, an uncharacteristic, yet apparently unconscious, gesture.

"Laurent has received an offer to buy the shroud."

"Oh? From whom? For what purpose?"

"We think it's from some wealthy collector who read a news report about the dating project. The person's agent will be here next week. Laurent is not certain how to handle this."

"That is true. I really do not know who owns the shroud. It might be the abbey. On the other hand, France has some interesting laws regarding historical artifacts, especially after what happened during the Second World War. It may also be that the Church claims ownership. I am not certain that I can actually negotiate with anyone who wants to buy it."

Leslie considered for a moment. "Would you want to sell it?"

"No, not if I could decide. The Abbot of Hautecombe, Father Holden, would probably choose differently, especially if the sale included me as well."

"I don't understand."

"Well, Father Holden and I have not seen, I think the phrase is, 'eye to eye' on this matter. For him, the discovery of the shroud has been a great distraction. He is something of a recluse."

"Perhaps you should ask him about the sale."

"Perhaps. I will wait and see what this Mister Tarquin has to say next week."

* * * * * * * * * * * * * * *

They lay on the couch in each others arms, two figures caught in the soft glow from a candle. Throughout the room were her photographs, in various stages of completion. Even though the renovated barrio home had an adjoining studio, the space never seemed able to contain her creative process. The work spilled out to fill all corners.

Hours earlier they had returned Laurent to his temporary quarters at the campus Newman Center. The short drive to her house had been in silence. Once inside, Leslie had gone straight to the kitchen.

"Want some coffee?"

"Sure."

"I bought some flavored beans . . . amaretto . . . the other day. How would that be?" She had already started pouring the aromatic coffee into the electric grinder.

"That'll be fine, love."

He had stood in the doorway, watching her busy with preparation. She was wearing a beige skirt that clung to the lines of her legs and a tight-fitting sleeveless shirt. She had discarded the light sweater she had worn during the evening. She had kicked off her shoes as soon as she got home, as was her habit. Idle conversation had continued during the ritual of coffee preparation, the smell of the brew filling the kitchen.

They had moved back into the living room, mugs in hand. Josh had closed the curtain over the picture window, locking out the world, and lit the large candle in the holder on the table opposite the couch. They had sat, mostly in silence, finishing their coffee. Josh had taken the empty cup from her and placed it on the floor along with his.

"Turn out the lights, baby."

Leslie had gotten up and moved to the wall switch to darken the kitchen. She recrossed the living room to where Josh now stood. He touched her hair, letting his hands move slowly along the sides of her face, onto her shoulders and across her breasts. She gasped and pressed closer to him.

They had undressed each other slowly. He had lowered her onto the couch, lying down next to her. They had made love, gently at first, and then more forcefully, ending in a cascade of sensations for both of them.

Later, she lay on top of him, watching the flickering yellow light play against his brown skin. The slow subsidence of their passion took the form of playful kisses and cuddling as their bodies continued to meld together. After a while, she propped herself up on one elbow and changed to a more serious tone.

"What's going to happen at this press conference, Sonny?"

"Oh, I guess Sutton will announce that the Shroud dates to sometime around the 11th century, Mac will add that the stains were caused by human blood, and I'll comment on the cloning. I don't think the press will make much of it."

She sensed that he was more excited than this casual description implied.

"Come on, Sonny. There's more to it than that."

He looked up at her for a moment before answering, absorbing the intimacy in her voice. He let the fervor of his new-found hope infuse his voice.

"If Sutton agrees, I'm going to make this my main area of research. I'll be one of only a few molecular archaeologists in the country. I could be isolating biological substances from artifacts that are hundreds, maybe thousands, of years old. Sutton's lab has samples stored from projects they've already completed. I can start with those."

"Can you really do that? I mean, can you repeat this experiment that easily?"

"I think so, Les, I think so. They've got samples of all kinds: mummified remains of humans, along with animal and plant material collected from a number of archaeological sites. If I can do this, it would mean a whole new direction."

She lay back down on his chest, listening to his heartbeat. The sound and rhythm were evidence of his excitement. She held him closer.

"Les. Why don't we move in together?"

"What?"

"Why don't we move in together? I have the house and enough room. We could convert that back bedroom and bath into a studio and darkroom. It's not that far away. Why not? What do you think?"

She remained very still.

They had never discussed this, mainly because he had been the reluctant one. The last time she had even hinted at it, he had gone on a lecture tirade about their need for "personal space." He had not really said "no." He had made it clear that "yes" was not an option.

Now, he was asking the question. She didn't answer.

"What's wrong, Les?"

"I . . . I thought you didn't want that. You said that you . . . we . . . need space. What's changed, Sonny?"

"Nothing's different."

Even as he said the words, the first inkling of some transition was creeping into his awareness. He was no longer the same.

CHAPTER EIGHT

TUCSON, ARIZONA
MARCH 8, 1999

The hallway outside of the LAC offices might as well have been a cage for Richard Sutton. He walked back and forth, hands behind his back and head down, pausing occasionally to look at his watch or to run his hand through his already disarranged hair. Each time he passed the lobby waiting area, his nervousness mounted as he watched the minutes tick off on the wall clock. It was nearly 1 p.m. The press conference was scheduled for 2 p.m. and he did not have the results of the dating of the shroud.

The bravado with which he had scheduled the conference flew in the face of every one of Murphy's Laws. Shortly after the meeting with Josh, Mac, and Laurent last Thursday, he had learned that the linear accelerator was inoperative. Repairs, he was told, would take about five to ten hours.

Those hours had extended well into the weekend as first one component and then another of the intricate instrument was tested. By Saturday noon the accelerator was pronounced ready. Fortunately, the cloth samples from the shroud and the control fabrics had already been prepared for analysis.

The minute bits of cloth had been cleaned to remove any twentieth-century contaminants, and then carefully burned to produce carbon dioxide. The gas had been sequentially converted first into carbon monoxide and then graphite. The almost microscopic amounts of carbon powder would then be used as targets in the linear accelerator. Bombardment of these targets and computerized analysis of the resulting emissions would yield the amount of carbon-14 present in the sample. This, in turn, would reveal the age of the fabric.

A series of replicate determinations would be necessary to confirm the age. The analysis had begun Saturday evening, but the data would not be available until Monday morning or early after-noon, prior to the press conference. And so, Sutton stalked the hall, lost for a time in his own recriminations.

He had returned to his office and closed its door when he heard voices in the lobby. He rushed out in time to see Josh, Laurent, and Mac standing with Harry Flynn in the reception area. They all looked up as he opened the door.

The administrative assistant shook his head. "No word yet, Doctor Sutton."

Laurent spoke first. "Is there a problem?"

"Actually, no. We're waiting for the accelerator data from this weekend's analysis."

"The results for the shroud?"

In spite of himself, Laurent could not keep the tone of distress out of his voice. Sutton pretended to ignore this.

"Well, yes . . . the final calculations, actually."

Displaying obvious disapproval, Mac leaned against the recep-tion counter.

"Richard, I thought that was done last Friday."

Sutton became the outraged don, firing back his retort.

"There were some technical complications over the weekend. Everything's come 'round now. I do hope that your results are ready for presentation."

"I have my data right here." Mac touched the pocket of his shirt. Sutton noticed for the first time that Mac was tieless.

Laurent was in his formal black suit and Roman collar. Josh had on a sports coat and knitted tie. Sutton wore his customary bow tie and blue suit. Mac was dressed in tan slacks and a floral print shirt.

"Doctor McGovern, we have some time if you'd like to go back to your office and change."

"No, I think I'm fine like this, thanks."

Josh had always assumed that Mac was oblivious to the con-ventions and dictates of academia. Watching this exchange, and the effect it had on Sutton, he suspected that Mac was more pur-poseful in his actions.

A young man hurried into the lobby, breathless and holding out a sheaf of computer printouts.

"Doctor Sutton. Here are the results. I think you should know that . . . "

He cut him off, taking the data.

"Yes, yes, thank you, John."

"But, Doctor Sutton, I think . . . "

"Thank you, John, that will be all. Gentlemen, shall we move into my office? Harry? No interruptions."

The young technician was left at rigid attention, empty hand still extended as Sutton led the others into the director's office.

They seated themselves as they had days earlier. Sutton stacked the data sheets on his desk and adjusted his glasses.

"Right. Let's see. Controls all seem to have worked fine. Here's the medieval linen sample from the British Museum and the Egyptian sample from the Cairo Department of Antiquities. Yes, those are as expected."

He was really speaking to no one in particular, although the other three sat attentively, as if in class.

Sutton stopped his narration suddenly and concentrated on the page in front of him. He leafed quickly through the pile once more.

"There must be some error here. I don't understand."

Again, he shuffled the papers, looking at first one set of numbers and then at a second. The other three exchanged questioning glances.

Sutton picked up the phone receiver on his desk and rapidly punched in seven numbers. He kept his head down as he waited for an answer.

"Yes, Herman? Sutton here. I'm looking at the final data analysis and . . . " He paused to listen.

"No, John didn't say anything to me when . . . " Again he paused.

"Are you sure . . . is this certain?"

The answer must have been an emphatic "yes."

"Herman, you must do a repeat analysis as soon as possible . . . I know you're sure it will be the same . . . do it anyway." He placed the receiver down slowly.

Sutton looked around the room at his three colleagues and ended their suspense. He rested one hand on top of the report.

"It seems that the Shroud of Hautecombe dates to about the year 30 A.D. The results are conclusive."

* * * * * * * * * * * * * * *

The large conference room in the LAC facilities that had been used for the meeting when Laurent had first brought the shroud for analysis had now been rearranged for the press. Rather than having a single central table, a smaller one was placed at one end against a combination marker board and projection screen. An overhead projector had been set up at about the middle of the room. Four chairs had been positioned behind the table. Other seats were arranged in classroom fashion for those in attendance. Since the room also served as a small library for the LAC staff, two walls were lined with bookshelves containing journals and texts.

As the group that had been meeting in Sutton's office entered, technicians from the local network affiliates were setting up their equipment. A phalanx of microphones decorated the table, with cables trailing across the floor to various camera tripods. The subdued lighting of the library atmosphere had been replaced by the harsh electronic glare necessary for video recording.

The jolt of Sutton's announcement had left Josh and Laurent in astonished silence. Mac had been the first to speak up. He had argued that the conference should be called off until they could analyze the data and consider the implications. Sutton was adamant that the conference go on as scheduled. He would take the lead, describing the methods of analysis used and making the announcement of the shroud's age and then refer specific questions to one of the others as necessary.

The three scientists and the priest/historian sat behind the table, Sutton taking the chair facing the central bank of microphones. Josh and Laurent were to his right while Mac occupied a chair to the left, removed a slight distance away. Harry Flynn, the LAC administrator, was busy ushering in members of the print and broadcast media. A small cart near the door held coffee urns and a tray of cookies. Most of the press were gathered there, manipulating cups and napkins along with their note pads.

At 2 p.m. Sutton caught Harry's notice and nodded to him. Harry stood at the front and spoke up to be heard over the conversational noise.

"If I could have your attention, please. We're ready to begin. If you would please take your seats."

Reporters moved to the chairs, camera operators stood by their equipment, and the room began to focus on the figures seated behind the table.

At the back of the room a man stood unobtrusively against the wall next to the door. He had arrived in Tucson on a late morning flight from San Francisco. A phone call to the LAC office had informed him of the open press conference that afternoon. Nikos Tarquin had quickly signed out his rental car and found his way to the campus in time for the start of the meeting.

Harry Flynn was speaking again.

"Ladies and gentlemen, Doctor Sutton will present the results of the analysis carried out by the LAC staff and will introduce the other experts available to you today. His presentation will be short, followed by an opportunity for you to ask questions. Doctor Sutton . . . "

Harry gestured toward the table and stepped aside.

"Thank you, Harry. And thank you for coming today. I am joined here by Father Laurent Carriere, a specialist in medieval history from the Abbey of Hautecombe in France, Doctor Joshua Francis of the Department of Molecular Biology, and Doctor Dennis McGovern of the Department of Chemistry."

He had pointed, in turn, to each man sitting with him. The assembled reporters took few notes, since the printed press kits had most of this information. The releases, prepared over the weekend, did not have the final results that were to be announced.

"As you know, we have radiocarbon dated a variety of objects, using accelerator mass spectrometry as our main analytical tool. Our most recent study has involved a linen cloth, discovered by Father Carriere at the Abbey of Hautecombe. The cloth has on it markings that could be interpreted as the image of a man, much like that of the famous Shroud of Turin."

Sutton described very briefly Laurent's history of the Hautecombe Shroud and the preliminary examination by the LAC team, including Mac's chemical analysis. He did not mention Josh's experiment.

"We have completed the radiocarbon dating analysis and we now have the results to present to you. Would you turn down the TV lights for a moment so that we can use the projector?"

He motioned to Harry who went to the overhead projector and flipped on the switch. A hastily prepared transparency containing the data that Sutton had received less than one hour before appeared on the screen.

"Here you see our analysis. Samples 1 and 2 are controls. Sample 1 is a piece of cloth obtained from the British Museum and historically dated 1380 A.D. Sample 2 is taken from the cloth of the funereal wrappings of Pharaoh Amenhotep III who died in 1375 B.C. Sample 3 is a fragment of the silk pouch that was found with and contained the shroud. We have evidence that this pouch was manufactured in about 1460 A.D. Finally, sample 4 is a piece of the shroud itself."

The data on the screen was displayed in the following way:

SAMPLE	AGE (YRS. B.P.)
1	570 ± 23
2	3330 ± 56
3	476 ± 37
4	1922 ± 33

Sutton explained that this table contained the actual data, including the range of experimental error. Radiocarbon dating was calculated and reported as "years before present," in reference to the number of years before an agreed upon date, that being the year 1950. The numbers in the table were close to the actual ages for the known samples. He interpreted the data for the press.

"Therefore, we conclude that the pouch that contained the shroud was manufactured in about 1440 A.D. The material of the shroud itself, however, dates from about 30 A.D. We would be happy to answer any questions."

Jeffrey Hoffman was the science reporter for the *Arizona Daily Star* and had an extensive technical background. He raised his hand almost immediately.

"Doctor Sutton, can you tell us where the shroud was made? What part of the world was the origin of the cloth?"

"Yes. Fiber experts have concluded that the linen fabric was produced somewhere in the eastern Mediterranean. This is based on the properties of the fibers and the weave used for the cloth."

Another hand went up, this time one of the TV field reporters.

"Doctor Sutton, what is the nature of the image? What caused the coloration on the cloth?"

"Perhaps Doctor McGovern would answer that question."

Mac sat forward in his chair.

"Chemical analysis of material extracted from the shroud indicates that the stains forming the image were produced, in part, by human blood. Tests for dyes or other pigments were negative."

Jeff Hoffman of the *Star* spoke up again.

"Doctor Sutton, this is the shroud from which the sample was isolated to produce the recombinant DNA clone, isn't it?"

"Yes, it is."

"Could you comment on that experiment, please?"

"Doctor Francis is here and will say more about that."

Josh had been wondering if this topic would come up, since Sutton had pointedly avoided mention of the cloning experiment in his summary. Given these new developments, he was unsure of his answer.

"The matter dissolved away from the shroud by Doctor McGovern was used as a source of DNA for the construction of a plasmid. I was able to isolate one such plasmid and I have confirmed that it does contain sequences of human DNA."

Another hand was waving for attention.

"Professor, do you mean that you could reconstruct the person who was buried in this shroud?"

Josh had expected this misunderstanding of the word "clone."

"No, of course not. The DNA I've isolated is only a tiny fragment, less than one-millionth of the total genetic information that made up the person."

Hoffman had been waiting and spoke before anyone else could be recognized.

"So, you have a linen cloth, potentially used as a burial sheet, that dates to the time and geographical location of Christ and that contains coloration produced by human blood. In addition, you have produced recombinant DNA molecules that include the DNA of the person whose blood is on the cloth. Is that correct?"

Sutton saw clearly where this line of questioning was going. He made a vain attempt to head it off.

"There is no evidence, historical or otherwise, that links this cloth to any particular person. The data we have presented speaks to the age of the cloth and the nature of the coloration on it. The DNA experiment was a side project, not a part of the original plan."

"But, Doctor Sutton, there is the possibility that the cloth is, in fact, the one used as the burial sheet of Christ, isn't that so?"

"I can't comment on that from our data. Perhaps Father Carriere would address that issue."

Laurent had not yet fully recovered from the effect of learning the true age of the shroud. His mind had been racing along the new avenues that had opened and he had barely followed the presentation of the data by Sutton. He heard his name as if in a dream and looked up to find all eyes, both human and electronic, focused on him.

"I have information about the history of the shroud that places it at Hautecombe at the end of the Crusade led by Count Amadeus IV. He apparently claimed to have recovered the cloth from a chapel in the Turkish city of Gallipoli. Beyond that, I have no information. I have asked my colleagues at the Vatican Museum to search for other records. This has not been completed. What you say is certainly conceivable, but we have no way of proving or disproving the statement at this time."

Laurent's answer was intended to defuse the question. Instead, it had the opposite effect. Admitting to the likelihood, however remote, that this was the shroud that had been used for the body of Christ gave the media the kind of story they wanted.

The effect on the gathered reporters was evident as they wrote furiously. A multitude of hands were in the air as more questions were asked, more speculation demanded from the experts at the table.

At the edge of this sea of information turmoil there was one island of icy calm. Nikos heard the revelations about the shroud and realized that his plan to simply purchase it for the Society had evaporated in the heat of the press conference. The priest would never sell the cloth. In addition, the Society must face more than the fact that the shroud had been rediscovered after more than six centuries. Unknown to the scientists, they had in their hands the DNA of Christ.

INTERLUDE TWO

The Port of Joppa
320 A.D.

The sounds that filtered below deck were no more than those expected for a harbor of that size. Yet, every voice that shouted an order or a response, every thump of cargo against the ship's side, and every pitch of the vessel as men moved up and down the narrow gangway, caused him to jump uncontrollably. He was huddled against the bulkhead, keeping as far away from the other passengers as possible. As he sat on the rough wooden floor, he clutched tightly in his arms the canvas bag that held his few items of clothing and, most importantly, the wooden box containing the shroud. In his eyes could be seen all of the fear and uncertainty that tumbled around inside of him. Fortunately, for the sake of his mission, anyone looking at him would only see a twelve-year old boy who was traveling on his own for the first time.

The night before—had it only been then?—his father had taken him aside and told him of this journey.

"Benjamin, listen to me carefully. I'm going to ask you to do something very difficult. You're going to take a long trip, by yourself. You're going to visit your cousin and his family in Byzantium."

His father certainly knew that the name of that city had been officially changed to Constantinople. He refused to acknowledge the reality of world politics. In fact, the ebb and flow of rulers and their conquering armies was not really his most immediate concern. For him, and for the other members of the Society of Arimathea, there was only the safety and secrecy of the shroud.

Their world was rapidly becoming Christian under the influence of the emperor. Ironically, for the Society this presented the greatest threat to their charge, in the person of the devout Augusta, otherwise known as Helen, mother of Constantine.

She had taken it as her personal quest to restore to the Church all of the physical materials associated with the life, death, and resurrection of Christ. Descending upon Jerusalem with her own army of scholars and religious authorities, she had literally turned over the city in her search. At her side, a constant and mysterious presence, was Judas, now known as Cyriacus.

Helen had already found the Cross. Somehow, Judas had the information necessary to lead her to its location. Cynics in the city claimed that she had been duped. No one, however, doubted the miracle that had taken place when the wood of the Cross had been touched to the dead body of a young girl and she had been restored to life.

Benjamin BarSimon was just a child, but he could see the effect these events had on the men in his family. He knew of the shroud and was at the beginnings of his initiation as a full member of the Society. Until the previous night, however, his main occupation, outside of his studies and his work in his father's shop, had been that of any boy: having as much fun as possible each day.

Along with his younger sister, Tamar, and his friend and co-conspirator, Samuel, he would sneak into the rear of the shop for one of their favorite activities. In that place were stored the huge bundles of canvas to be cut and sewn in the production of tents and awnings. The mounds of fabric became gigantic cushions for their frenzied leaps and airborne gymnastics, until they were inevitably caught by one of the workers or, even worse, by his father.

It was while they were hidden among the rolls of material, waiting their chance, that they overheard a conversation that presaged the journey he was about to take.

"Mark my words, Simon, this man Judas knows about us. It's only a matter of time before he tells her about the cloth."

His father had paused some moments before answering while the other man continued to look back toward the shop, watching for someone who might be listening.

"I believe you, Matthias. And, because of that, I have made the following arrangement. We'll send the shroud away from Jerusalem."

The other man shook his head violently as he opened his mouth to protest. Benjamin's father raised his hand to stop him.

"Hear me out. We'll send it to the care of my cousin, whom you know, in Byzantium."

"Constantinople? Why not just present it directly to the emperor with our compliments?"

"Don't you see, Matthias? She'll be turning over Jerusalem for the shroud and everything else associated with our Lord's death. Why would she think of looking in her own house?"

"But, how will we get it out of the city? She has her agents and I'll wager we're all known."

"I have another idea that should work quite well, as much as it grieves me to do it."

The sounds of the port once again intruded into his awareness, causing him to press his travel bag closer to him. Insistent voices of command indicated that the time had come for departure. He heard the sound of the gangway being drawn aboard. The running feet of sailors pounded overhead as they made their way along the side to cast off the lines that held the ship to the dock. The hull shook around him as the men pushed hard to move the vessel out into the sea.

The shroud, in the charge of one small and frightened boy named Benjamin, was on its way.

CHAPTER NINE

MARCH 11, 1999

HAUTECOMBE ABBEY, FRANCE

The sun had fallen behind the mountains, plunging the western shore of Lac du Bourget into shadow. Gustav Holden stood at the edge of the abbey garden, hands clasped behind his back, his features shadowed by more than the setting sun. The news of the dating of the shroud had reached the abbey minutes before telephone calls from the press began. Reporters and tourists would soon be swarming across the lake, clamoring to see the spot where the famous cloth had been discovered. His greatest fear, the threat to his sanctuary, had been realized.

Even worse, he had received a message from Rome. The head of the Vatican Museum was asking for custody of the shroud. The abbot's inclination was to agree right away, except that the relic was in the United States with Laurent. He would dictate a letter the next day, instructing Laurent to return as soon as possible. He knew that such a letter would be viewed by the young priest merely as a request, not a command.

Maurice had been at work in the garden, finishing the last of the spring plantings that would line the pathways in color during the summer season. The old man jammed the shovel into the moist earth and wiped his hands along the back of his overalls. He was a few feet behind the slouched form of the old priest and waited for a moment before speaking.

"Father? Excuse me for intruding."

"What? Oh, yes, Maurice, what is it?"

"Father, I have heard that Father Carriere has learned that the cloth he found here is truly the burial cloth of Jesus. Can this be?"

"All that has been learned is that the cloth is much older than suspected, perhaps old enough to have come from the time of Christ. No one knows anything more than that."

"Father, forgive me for asking, but how did this cloth come to the abbey?"

"It seems that it was brought here from the Middle East after a Crusade lead by one of the Savoy counts. I really don't know the details, Maurice. I must go now."

Fr. Holden was moving away, trying to retreat to the safe haven of his office. Maurice watched the abbot until he entered the cloistered section of the monastery. He returned to the shovel, pausing thoughtfully before resuming his careful tilling of the soil.

* * * * * * * * * * * * * * * *

BAKERSFIELD, CALIFORNIA

The telephone at the edge of his oak desk would ring at any moment. Reverend Edwin Slaughter knew that his call to Washington would be returned as soon as possible. He busied himself with some minor paperwork while he waited for his secretary's alert.

The offices of the Christian Revivalist Movement occupied the top three floors of the newly constructed Corporate Trust Building in downtown Bakersfield. Rev. Slaughter's office was much less ostentatious than might have been expected for the leader of a religious network as immense as CRM. Edwin Slaughter did not fit the stereotypical image of a television evangelist.

Growing up in the small town of Earlimart, amidst the vast farmlands of central California, had given him a set of values in common with the majority of his flock. His early religious training had been Southern Baptist with strict biblical interpretation. Edwin was an ordained minister who also held a degree in business management from the University of California at Berkeley. After serving in two brief pastoral appointments he had decided to strike off on his own.

The simple Christian principles and values of his message had touched the hearts and consciences of the people in the surrounding farm communities when he first began his evangelical ministry

some 20 years earlier. At age 58 he found himself at the head of a religious organization that included publishing and broadcasting, both in the U.S. and Latin America. He had avoided the disasters that had befallen others, especially the more prominent televangelists. Scandal had not found him because he was, at the core, the simple preacher he seemed to be, and nothing more.

He counted among his closest friends Sam Johnson, now U.S. Senator Samuel Johnson, the senior congressman from California. The two of them had roamed the San Joaquin Valley together as children and as young men. They had fought together in Vietnam and had returned to the communities of their youth to follow their separate careers. Sam had been among the first to join his movement. Edwin, in turn, had been a loyal supporter of his friend's political campaigns. By the time Sam Johnson made his move on Washington, Rev. Edwin could muster the considerable force of his flock in support.

Slaughter finished reviewing the financial report for the last month. On his desk, next to the telephone, lay a copy of the *Los Angeles Times* opened to the third page of the first section. A news item, headlined "University Team May Have Identified the Shroud of Christ," was circled in red. He had read the article more than once, and with each reading, his anger grew as the words grated together in his mind.

> " . . . Dr. Joshua Francis, a professor of molecular biology, was able to extract a fragment of DNA from the cloth and has used this to construct a DNA clone. Although no conclusive evidence exists, it is possible that, if this cloth is the true shroud of Christ, then Dr. Francis has isolated material of great religious and historical significance . . . "

Slaughter had been on many campuses and considered himself a well-educated man. He did not accept the image of "godless scientists" as one that could be universally applied. Nonetheless, he had seen the effects of the objective application of science, coupled with the attitudes of those he called secular humanists. Within his own belief system, these two accounted for most of the ills of modern society. His movement had been intended as a fight against these values, or, as he taught, lack of values.

The news report was the latest and perhaps most blasphemous example of the evils that could come from the amoral world of academia. His initial reaction had been that someone must stop this. He was convinced that he was that person.

The DNA of Christ. There was no way that such precious material should be in the hands of scientists. The only proper place for this substance was with the believers, the people of Christ. With the coming of the new century, the appearance of the shroud and the creation of this DNA was certainly a sign. Rev. Slaughter would make it his personal task to take this DNA from science and give it to those who would revere it. His call to Sam Johnson was the first step toward this goal.

* * * * * * * * * * * * * * *

THE VATICAN

André Bernay almost ran through the corridors connecting the storage and research areas to the offices of the Vatican Museum. The public was restricted from these sections and so the halls were empty, save for the occasional scholar or technician. He was holding one of the many specialized containers used for the preservation of ancient documents. His destination was the office of the Director, Monsignor Giancarlo Corsini.

The priest who was in charge of the vast activities of the museum and libraries had risen to his post after recognition of his considerable talents. He had, of course, received the appropriate doctoral training in his discipline. In addition, he had directed an impressive number of studies and excavations. His home in the port city of Maratea on the southern Italian coast of the Tyrrhenian Sea had benefited from one of his earliest archaeological projects: the restoration of the ancient church of St. Biagio on a promontory overlooking the harbor. As a part of his design he had proposed the installation of an imposing statue of the Risen Christ that now looked down on the city. His posting at the Vatican had followed several equally successful ventures.

Msgr. Corsini had been appointed director after his supervision of the marvelously intricate restoration of the Sistine Chapel, a challenge that both the Church and the art world viewed as dangerous, if not foolhardy. With the unveiling of the brightly renewed frescoes his reputation was secured.

André Bernay was a senior staff member of the Museum and a longtime assistant to Corsini. As such, he did not stand on ceremony and entered the director's office unannounced.

"Monsignor. You must see what I've found."

"Yes, André, what is it?"

"I've been tracing records related to Hautecombe Abbey, looking for any reference to the shroud. I've managed to reconstruct Father Carriere's account, including the arrival of the shroud at the abbey with Count Amadeus IV. Also, I've found this."

He opened the case and carefully removed a plastic sheath containing a crumbled parchment with words barely discernible on its surface. He arranged the ancient document on the desk in front of the director.

"This letter was written in 1375 and addressed to Pope Gregory XI. It's difficult to make out most of the words. What I've translated thus far indicates that it was a follow-up request, urging the Pope to continue his assistance in the recovery of a sacred relic. The letter is signed by someone who claimed to be the head of some society. The name of the society is barely legible. See . . . just here. The name begins 'Arim' . . . the rest has been destroyed."

Msgr. Corsini bent over the parchment, following his assistant's gestures.

"I don't see what this has to do with the abbey or the shroud."

"This parchment was in a case containing papal documents related to the Abbey of Hautecombe."

"André, you know as well as I that the time of Gregory XI was one of great turmoil. The Holy See was in exile in Avignon. I'm not surprised that documents of this type have been misplaced throughout our archives, simply due to the confusion. Does it mention Hautecombe or the shroud anywhere?"

"No, Monsignor."

"Then I really don't see that this applies. It's most likely a case of medieval misfiling. But, leave it here for me. I'd like to inspect it in more detail."

The assistant withdrew, leaving the plastic-encased document with his superior. Corsini considered the situation. He had already contacted the abbot of Hautecombe. From him he had confirmed that the priest who had discovered the shroud was not a French Benedictine but the Swiss Jesuit, Laurent Carriere. The young historian had spent more than a year at the museum and, although Corsini had not worked directly with him, reports had come back to the director. He knew that this headstrong young priest would not be easy to handle. It was clear that even Fr. Holden was reluctant to issue an order bringing him back to France.

The next course of action would be direct. He would contact the office of the Papal Nuncio in Washington, D.C. Perhaps a visit from an official representative of the pope would get this Jesuit historian's attention.

The director's eyes drifted again across the parchment before him. That had been close, too close, really. The last thing they needed was for the name of Arimathea to surface at this time. He touched the medallion he wore beneath his cassock. The parchment would be refiled, this time out of the way. The shroud would be returned to Rome and, through him, to the care of the Society.

* * * * * * * * * * * * * * * *

SAN RAFAEL, CALIFORNIA

It was frustrating to simply sit and wait, especially for a man used to acting. Costa Tarquin was certainly not used to waiting. He had set several wheels in motion and now he must impatiently watch their progress.

When Nikos proposed buying the shroud from the abbey, he had not discouraged his son. Of course, he had realized immediately that this naive approach would never work. How could Nikky expect to just walk in and announce, "I'd like to buy that medieval relic; how much is it?" Costa was, as always, disappointed in his son and realistic about his abilities. He had sent him to Tucson in the hope that he might be of some use, even as a distraction, and to keep him away from the real center of activity.

Immediately after Nikos had left his office, Costa had telephoned a certain firm of private investigators. He had used them in the past in matters related to his business competition. The two men he had requested were each former members of the intelligence community. He trusted their work and didn't question their methods. At present, they were in Tucson with instructions to investigate everyone connected with the shroud, making sure that Nikos remained on the outside.

The next call had waited until late that night, at a time when, in Italy, offices were opening for the day. There had been the expected delay as his name was reported through the Vatican switchboard to the man he wanted. Eventually, Msgr. Corsini had been informed that the shroud had been rediscovered.

Now that the dating had revealed the age of the cloth, the recovery would be more complicated, but not impossible. The existence of the DNA clone presented an additional problem apart from what the Society might accept as its charge. If he could bring both the shroud and the clone under the protection of Arimathea, it could go a long way toward healing six centuries of loss.

* * * * * * * * * * * * * * * *

TUCSON, ARIZONA

Nikos stared into the darkness of his hotel room. This was madness. How could he have believed that it would be as easy as writing a check? Because the world suspected what the Society knew, it would be next to impossible to get the shroud openly. Another way must be found. That other way would have to involve subterfuge.

After the high school election incident, Nikos had developed a style that payed little attention to the rules. Whenever necessary, and especially when he thought he would not be caught, he cut corners. He cheated on examinations, ostensibly because "everyone did it," but, in reality, because he believed the end justified the means. He found that money could always be used to ease his passage; he had learned this from his father. During his senior year, he decided that his primary objective was a university degree to give him credibility. His purpose would be to return to his father's company and win his rightful place. He was still a long way from achieving this.

He was faced with an opportunity that could not be lost. He had not forgotten the look on his father's face when he last left his office. He had tried for years to earn respect in Costa's eyes. This was his chance and he would have to use all of the skills he had. He would recover the shroud by some means. He knew he would do it by any means.

CHAPTER TEN

TUCSON, ARIZONA
MARCH 15, 1999

The plastic rack sat in the middle of his desk in a space he had cleared. It held four glass ampules sealed under vacuum, each in appearance much like a miniature bottle and containing a brownish powder. The four vials held the dried and preserved bacterial cells harboring the recombinant DNA molecule he had constructed. He had cultures of the cells growing in the laboratory, in preparation for further experiments. He also had samples of the cells carefully stored in his ultracold freezer. These ampules were his final hedge against any possible loss.

Josh watched the vials as if hoping for some revelation, some clue as to which direction he should go. The events of the week that had followed the press conference had not been what he expected. The press had focused on the possibility, however slight, that the shroud was the actual burial cloth of Jesus and arguments to the contrary went unheard.

The news stories had appeared the next day. By Wednesday, Josh was receiving a steady stream of calls from reporters around the country. His message tape on his answering machine had filled each day before noon.

He was not the only one besieged. The LAC offices had similar requests; for interviews, for more information, or for confirmation of this or that rumor. Harry Flynn had been fielding most of these, although some managed to get through to Sutton's office. The LAC director was not happy.

The University was also receiving calls. Opinions were beginning to come from the public and, more importantly, from state legislators and the Board of Regents. It was not surprising that the University president had called a meeting at 10 a.m., to include

Sutton and the other members of the research team who had held the press conference.

Josh had hoped that the isolation of the clone would initiate a new line of research for him. He had foreseen analysis of this DNA, derived, he originally thought, from someone who lived during the Middle Ages. He had imagined becoming a scientist who identified changes that had arisen in the human genome with the passage of time. In his mind's eye he became one of the consummate experts in this new discipline.

Some years earlier, molecular biologists had undertaken the monumental and controversial project of determining the exact structure of the entire human genome. The task was well under-way, in spite of early opposition from several prominent scientists. Josh could even see a role for himself in this enterprise, and had begun to sketch out a way to tap into this large source of funding.

Now, with the dating of the shroud to around 30 A.D., his visions were in turmoil. On the one hand, the data merely indicated that his DNA sample was simply older than he had first assumed. On the other hand, the popular perception that the shroud was real, and the religious implications this raised, made the future of his research uncertain. He would go to the president's meeting today prepared to defend his experiments.

* * * * * * * * * * * * * * * *

The office of the University president was on the very top floor of the administration tower that dominated the center of the campus. The building only missed being made of ivory and covered with vines. It was the epitome of isolation.

Elizabeth Varner enjoyed the view from her office. During the past year, as she had settled into the presidency, she had come to relish the sanctuary of this building. She had taken over the reigns of a major state university, with all of its prestige and problems. In that short time she had weathered several crises, many of them the result of long years of conflict that had remained unresolved.

Telescopes had been built on a nearby mountain peak by a consortium of university research groups, including Arizona. The project had been bitterly, and at times violently, opposed by environmentalists, using as an unwitting pawn a threatened squirrel species. The administration had doggedly pursued the issue, flexing its research arm and beating back opponents with money and lobbying. The mountain top had been closed, the telescopes had been constructed, and the astronomers had gone about their quiet pursuit of the secrets of the universe. The squirrel population actually doubled during the years following the construction, resulting in a mixed blessing for the environmentalists and a Pyrrhic victory for the administration. The controversy had left open wounds in many parts of the academic body and had caused the administration to become much more sensitive to outside criticism.

Dr. Varner had requested the meeting with the LAC group as a consequence of the initial reaction to their press conference. Her office had received a number of calls from private citizens outraged that the University was engaged in research dealing with such sacred objects. These comments had been referred to the Office of Public Information. But when two members of the Board of Regents had called, each demanding an explanation, Dr. Varner had decided that she must take direct action.

Her office was spacious enough to accommodate a small-sized group meeting. The large central desk at one end of the room was set against a backdrop of bookshelves containing the various volumes that recorded her academic life: her years as a scholar of the classical period of Greece and her move through a variety of administrative positions, most recently as provost of a major Midwestern university.

The opposite end of the room was outfitted as a conference area. The table had been prepared for the meeting with enough chairs for those invited. In addition to the four involved in the press conference, she had requested the presence of the Vice-President for Research and the Dean of the Faculty of Sciences.

By 10 a.m. most of those expected had arrived and were waiting in the outer office. Dr. Varner's secretary ushered the group in at the correct time and indicated the prepared seats. Introductions were made for those who did not know each other. Josh, Laurent, and Mac took seats together as Sutton moved to the other side of the table. Dr. Varner seated herself at one end along with Dr. Gerald

White, the Vice-President for Research. To Sutton's left was Dean William Rossman. Dr. Varner called for their attention.

"Thank you all for coming this morning. I'd like to begin by having Doctor Sutton summarize for us what has occurred up to now. Doctor Sutton?"

Sutton arranged his notes before him, cleared his throat, and began.

"Yes. Well, as you know, this has been the latest in a series of mass spectrometry dating projects we have conducted. This particular object was brought to our attention by the Vatican and Father Carriere some three months ago."

He proceeded to chronicle the events surrounding the analysis of the shroud.

"We had every reason to assume that this object, like the others, would have originated at some time during the Middle Ages."

Dr. White interrupted the narrative.

"Doctor Sutton, if I may ask, what led to the experiment involving the DNA?"

"That was very much a side project. Doctor McGovern can tell you how that came about."

Mac had leaned back in his chair, his legs stretched out underneath the table. He sat up as he spoke.

"Sure, Richard. Josh came to see me shortly after our first examination of the shroud. He was interested in my analysis of the coloration on the cloth. I had extracted samples from several locations on the fabric that were identified during the initial workup. Josh proposed that these extracts might contain fragments of DNA from the person who had been wrapped in the cloth at burial. I gave him a few hundred microliters of the extract."

"Did you authorize this experiment, Doctor Sutton?" The vice-president was clearly on a specific tack.

"No. I didn't learn of it until after the fact."

"Doctor Francis. What was the purpose of your experiment? Did it relate to some other ongoing work?"

Josh was becoming increasingly uncomfortable. It was apparent that the reason for this meeting was more than simply gathering information.

"The idea came to me as I watched the shroud being examined at LAC. DNA has been isolated from similar sources; mummified or fossilized remains, for instance. It was obviously a chancy experiment but I convinced Mac to let me try it." Josh continued, warming to the subject as he prepared to describe his move into this new area of research. President Varner lifted one hand and gestured to interrupt him.

"Yes, Doctor Francis, but how does this relate to your current research program dealing with cellular growth factors?"

"It really doesn't. At this point, it's merely a side project."

The vice-president exchanged glances with the president. Dr. Varner decided to end what she felt was becoming an interrogation.

"I'm sure you all realize how much the University supports interdisciplinary work of this kind. Past efforts have brought considerable prestige to our campus. I have no doubt that this current project is of similar high quality. On the other hand, the public perception is that we are overstepping our bounds. There exists the sentiment that the University ought not to be dealing with an object that may be related in some way to Jesus Christ."

Dr. Sutton was prepared for this point and his answer was tinged with the indignation of the injured scholar.

"Doctor Varner, there is no evidence that this cloth is the one used for the burial of the historical figure Christ. All we can conclude is that it originated in the Middle East, was constructed around 30 A.D., and contains stains produced by human blood. Many hundreds of people must have died in that geographical area and been buried in the same manner. This cloth could have come from any one of them."

The president smiled and shrugged in sympathy.

"I appreciate that, Doctor Sutton. That is certainly the most logical and reasonable view to take at this time. Unfortunately, that is not the popular view. It is certainly not the view expressed to me by members of the Board of Regents."

Dean Rossman motioned for recognition.

"Perhaps Father Carriere would tell us if any more is known regarding the history of the shroud."

The historian, called upon for an opinion, puffed his cheeks slightly and blew outward in that familiar Gallic gesture of uncertainty.

"It is possible that the researchers at the Vatican Museum will uncover additional information. I have no way of telling at this time."

Dr. Varner assumed the role of mediator and peacemaker.

"Given that, I suggest the following. Let's hold off on any further work on the shroud until more historical data is available. Doctor Sutton, is the cloth secure?"

"Quite. We have examined museum pieces that are literally priceless. To satisfy our collaborators, we had to install a special climate-controlled safe. The shroud is presently locked inside it. The combination is computer-activated, with only myself and my administrative assistant, Mister Flynn, knowing the password."

"Excellent. And Doctor Francis, what about the clone?"

"Oh, I have it stored in several ways, both frozen and dried. That is, I've got desiccated samples of the bacterial cells sealed away in glass."

"If you're planning any new experiments, I think it might be a good idea to wait on those, also. Perhaps the preserved cells should be kept in Doctor Sutton's safe."

Sutton held up one hand, waving it back and forth quickly.

"I'd really rather not, Doctor Varner. We're not equipped to handle such things."

Josh sat in silence during this exchange, unsure of how to respond to the request that he not continue this new line of research he was convinced could rescue his flagging career.

"Fine. For now, Doctor Francis, please refrain from any more experiments on these samples. Let's wait until some of this furor dies down a bit. Then we can all go back to work."

* * * * * * * * * * * * * * *

As the meeting broke up, Sutton stayed behind, pulling Dr. White over to one side for a private conversation. Josh, Laurent, and Mac left together, descending by elevator and exiting the building. They crossed the expanse of lawn, heading for the mall at the center of campus.

The area in front of the Student Union was filling up with students breaking for lunch. A crowd had gathered at the southeast quadrant of this section. A sign proclaimed this "Speaker's Corner." During the sixties and early seventies, the University had set aside a space where anyone could stand and speak on any subject. At that time, the "corner" was a location directly in front of the Student Union. With expansion of the building, the "corner" had been moved onto the grassy area of the mall.

While the original use of Speaker's Corner had been by political activists, in the current times of relative student apathy it had come to be used, almost exclusively, by the mall preachers. The preachers, mainly Christian, stood on the grass delivering their messages to whomever would listen. Some garnered no attention whatsoever. The more flamboyant ones attracted a crowd. One of these was a tall man with a mane of flaming hair outlining a face anchored by eyes of glacial blue. Brother Redemption was enveloped in a crowd of students, many of whom had come to taunt and jeer.

As Josh and the others stepped onto the mall, Brother Redemption was speaking, quoting from the book of Revelation.

" 'And I saw three unclean spirits like frogs come out of the mouth of the dragon, and out of the mouth of the beast, and out of the mouth of the false prophet. For they are the spirits of devils, working miracles, which go forth unto the kings of the earth.'

"The scientists of this University have committed sacrilege. They have profaned the things of God and of His Christ. Those who ally themselves with them shall also perish. And look . . . the ones I have named are here!"

He pointed at the three men who had slowed to watch. The students and others who were listening turned to see who he meant. As the crowd parted, Brother Redemption, his arm outstretched and his finger held rigid and at eye level, was face-to-face with Josh.

"You are the one! You are the man who has taken of the Lord and made of Him a vile experiment. You shall be cursed! And all those who stand with you."

Josh was trapped. He had been walking along without really hearing or seeing those around him. The president's request at the meeting had already left him cold. Now, he was frozen, caught in the icy glare of Brother Redemption's eyes. He was awash in the venom that spewed forth; confused, embarrassed, and frightened, all at the same time.

Mac saw what was happening and stepped between Josh and the preacher. He dragged his friend away, forcing him to walk.

"Come on, Josh. Don't get involved in that. Let's keep going."

As they continued toward the Chemistry Building, Josh could still hear the accusations ringing in the air.

"He has blasphemed! He will be punished!"

CHAPTER ELEVEN

TUCSON, ARIZONA
MARCH 15, 1999

Nikos watched from his vantage point at the edge of the crowd as the preacher railed against the three men. After the confrontation ended and the men moved away, Brother Redemption returned to his theme with even greater vigor. His audience had been quieted by the incident, since this was the first time any of them had seen the preacher attack someone directly. The jeering and argumentative comments had stopped. Nikos had seen enough and drifted away from the mall in the direction of his hotel.

His first instinct after the press conference had been to abandon any idea of recovering the shroud. Costa had insisted he remain in Tucson and continue his efforts. In reality, he knew that he couldn't return to his father empty-handed.

In the week since the age of the shroud had been revealed, Nikos had drawn more and more into himself. In the evenings he would take his meal in his room. During the day he would make his rounds on the campus.

Each morning he left the hotel and crossed the street onto the northernmost section of the University grounds. Each time his path was purposeful, leading him first to one corner and then another of the sprawling campus. And each day his pilgrimage would bring him to the same set of shrines.

He would stand across the street from the north entrance to the Gould-Simpson Building, watching the seventh floor windows of the LAC facilities. He would lean against the corner of the student dormitory, keeping himself away from the sidewalk. The traffic of students and faculty rushing back and forth between classes flowed past him unnoticed and unnoticing.

After long minutes at this station, he would walk around the building in ritual fashion. After some time, he would continue on to the Life Sciences South Building. In his mind, the clone had become an extension of the shroud and must, therefore, be included in the charge of the Society. He would end by sitting on the round stone bench in the plaza, alternately counting the windows of the laboratory wing and tracing the pattern of the bricks at his feet.

Nikos was not conscious of his outward behavior. During those walks his mind turned over scheme after scheme designed to recover the shroud and the clone for his father, and the Society that he led.

Throughout his life Nikos had found it difficult to face Costa without feelings of insecurity and inadequacy. When it came time for college, he leapt at the chance to leave home, if only for four years.

All of the aptitude tests he had taken predicted he would be a good but not outstanding student. Consequently, he was not admitted to any of the two or three most competitive schools that Costa would have preferred. However, he was accepted at several excellent universities. He chose the one farthest from the Bay area: he picked the University of Pennsylvania.

His years in Philadelphia were some of the calmest he could remember, if only because he was away from the constant judgmental gaze of his father. In spite of this, he knew that he would eventually become a part of the company. He majored in business and competed in swimming. The long hours required by both of these endeavors gave him no time for any social life. This was just as well since he had little warmth to offer. The women he met eventually saw this and his relationships were few and short.

Once back in San Rafael he had moved immediately into Delos Systems, both drawn to and repelled by the need for Costa's approval. He managed the sales efforts of DSI with efficiency, implementing with skill the strategies laid out by his father. Nikos could not, or, more likely, would not be innovative. And the disappointment again was registered in his father's eyes.

Nikos walked a fine line, keeping a low profile in front of Costa, but always seizing every opportunity to twist a situation to his own advantage. Within the company he was obeyed, but not out of respect. The competitors of DSI simply bided their time, waiting for the day when the old man would no longer be in charge. When that time came, they were certain the talent and customers at Delos Systems would be theirs for the taking.

As Nikos left the mall area of the campus, the beginnings of a new stratagem formed in his mind. He saw a possibility in the exchange between the preacher and the scientist. Fear had registered on the face of the man who had cloned the DNA. Perhaps he could exploit this reaction. Perhaps through intimidating him, he could force the scientists to turn over the shroud and the clone to the Society. He walked quickly toward his hotel, his steps and his thoughts accelerating along his next course of action.

* * * * * * * * * * * * * * *

Two other men had observed the events on the mall that day. They were dressed to blend in but, on close inspection, did not look like students. They wore jeans and sweatshirts and had the requisite backpacks. The taller man had sandy-brown hair and an unremarkable face. The other man, although shorter and darker, was equally nondescript. Both men had the ability, cultivated by years of practice, to be seen and subsequently forgotten.

The two were stationed to one side of the group circling the preacher. They, too, had watched the exchange with Josh and the others. They also saw Nikos. As the scientists and the priest retreated in one direction, and the son of their client left in the other, the two men exchanged glances, nodded, and separated, each following one of the objects of their surveillance.

* * * * * * * * * * * * * * *

Mac was concerned about his friend's demeanor in the face of the onslaught from the preacher. He and Laurent were reluctant to leave him alone. Standing outside of the Marvel Laboratories, the two of them had tried to judge his mental state.

"I'm fine . . . really, I'm fine. I just need a little time to settle down."

Mac did not completely believe him and took his arm, pulling him toward the door of the building. "Would you two come up to my office for a minute? This won't take long." The elevator closed before they saw the man who had followed them to the entrance.

Once in his office, Mac directed them to each take chairs. He sat behind his desk and pushed some stacks of papers around absently before speaking.

"I've decided to get rid of everything in my lab that's left over from the shroud extractions. I'm going to incinerate the balance of the samples in my lab furnace this afternoon."

"Why?" Josh understood the implications of this, for it would mean that no additional DNA clones could be made from the shroud samples.

"Well, if it should turn out that this really is the burial cloth of Christ, then we're dealing with something quite sacred here."

"But Mac, we don't know that. Anyway, what's that got to do with our work? I don't see how faith and science are at all related."

"You don't? Maybe that's part of the problem. It's true that we don't use faith as a tool in our work on a daily basis. But there's something more subtle to consider. Don't you see that, in order to even conceive of a hypothesis or design an experiment, we, as scientists, must have an inherent faith in the order of the cosmos? We believe that the physical world can be understood, without any *a priori* evidence to support that belief.

"I've always operated on the proposition that my chemistry is only a way to observe the fine details of God's creation, the works made by the hand of God. I don't see that anything I would ever find by my methods could be in conflict with faith.

"In fact, I believe that theology is just another way of looking at creation. Sacred writings are expressions of the mind of God in language that we can understand. They can't really be at odds with science.

"That preacher out there may believe that everything in the Bible must be taken literally. From his words today he doesn't seem to have much regard for science. In my view, the wonders of God's handiwork are revealed by the Bible as well as by *Fundamentals of Chemistry*." Mac pointed to the shelf above his desk where, in fact, both books could be seen.

"You're a scientist, Mac. How can you acknowledge within the framework of your chemistry anything that can't be measured?"

Josh spoke, but with little conviction in his voice. This unexpected and, before now, unknown side of his friend and colleague challenged his basic assumptions.

"Josh, I'm a scientist; but before that, I'm a human. My motivation for doing science, which is an entirely human activity, has always been an attraction for the mysteries of this universe God has made." He sat upright in his chair, leaning forward for emphasis. "What is your motivation? Why do you do this, Josh?"

The question remained unanswered and, for a time, was a palpable presence in the air of the office. Josh rose and took the handle of the door, opening it into the hall.

"Look, I can't really deal with this now. There's too much going on. I need some time to think. I'll be in my office."

His departure left his two friends in silence, each with his own fears for him.

* * * * * * * * * * * * * * *

Josh sat in the darkness of his fifth-floor office. The lights were off and he had closed the slats of the vertical blinds that screened out the view. He needed to be isolated for a while. He was still shaken from the events in the Administration Building and on the mall, and he was challenged by the question Mac had posed.

In the days that followed his construction and isolation of the DNA clone, he had developed a scenario that saw him becoming an expert in a new field of investigation. He believed that there would be little competition, that the LAC group on campus would be a ready source of samples for him, and that everyone would support his efforts, including the granting agencies.

This rosy picture of his future had begun to fade. Sutton had been less than receptive to his plans, focusing his attention on the analysis of the Shroud of Hautecombe. The announcement of the age of the shroud had taken everyone by surprise. Still, his project was not really altered. His DNA isolate was older than he first suspected, nothing more.

The public perception of his work had not filtered through the cloud of his own reasoning. The meeting in Dr. Varner's office changed this dramatically. The upper administration was always more attuned and sensitive to opinions from outside the halls of academia. The call for a halt to work on the shroud was evidence of this.

As he left the meeting, he was already rationalizing, deciding that this was a temporary setback. He was convincing himself that everything could proceed as he wished, as soon as the initial reaction had died down. These were the thoughts occupying him when the mall preacher confronted him.

The trauma of that encounter was still fresh. The violence of the verbal assault was unexpected. Josh had been raised in a devoutly Roman Catholic family, which meant that he viewed evangelical street preachers, such as Brother Redemption, with skepticism. But, charges of blasphemy and sacrilege touched a chord in him.

Many academicians of Josh's generation had rejected the spiritual in favor of the scientific, seduced by the intellectual comfort of the testable hypothesis as opposed to the subjective challenge presented by the metaphysical. Josh had rejected God, but had done so deliberately.

During his junior year at the University of New Mexico, his younger brother, Walter, had come down with what seemed like a cold that would not go away. After an interminable series of tests it was determined that he had leukemia. The initial diagnosis was frightening but not hopeless, since treatment of this form of cancer had met with great success. Tragically, in this case, the statistics were meaningless.

At Walter's birth, Josh, then four-years old, had formed an immediate and powerful attachment to his sibling. Throughout their childhood they had been more like twins than like older and younger brothers. There had been little rivalry between them.

The news of Walter's condition tore at Josh. During the months they waited for improvement, he visited his parish church often, reciting the prayers he had learned as a child and asking that Walter be spared. But as time went by, his brother's cancer did not remit. In the end, Josh had been at the bedside, holding his hand and watching the last labored breath Walter had drawn.

Josh had left the hospital and walked alone for hours. At first he had cried. Finally, however, he had come to the conclusion that if God could be so cruel as to take Walter from him, then God was not needed in his life. He did not become an atheist. Rather, he chose to take matters into his own hands. It was this that drove him as he pursued his graduate training and his career.

Mac presented him with a question of faith. The words Mac had used recalled for him the conversation he and Walter had shared two days before his death. In spite of his weakness, his brother had wanted to speak to him. His voice was faint, but clear.

"It's a mystery, Josh. We don't need to know how long life will last. We only need to accept the gift from God and know that all of it is important." He tried to squeeze the hand that held his own. "Don't be sad. And don't forget me . . . okay, Josh?"

In the years that followed, those words of his brother had become lost in the whirlwind of his flight from God. Mac had brought them back.

The rational arguments that he and the others involved with the shroud had been using were in juxtaposition to the faith that his brother and he once held so dear. Of course, there was no proof that the shroud was the same one used for Christ's burial. The DNA he had isolated could have come from anyone dying 2000 years ago. Never mind that the image on the shroud showed all the features of someone who had been crucified. That was just coincidental; there was no proof.

As he struggled with these arguments, he noticed a figure waiting in front of his office, the form visible through the opaque glass panel that ran the length of the door. The figure stepped away and, a few moments later, returned, stopped in front of the door briefly, and then moved off again.

Josh had the distinct feeling that this person was still present outside his office. Often, timid students would come by, find the door closed, and be too afraid to knock, yet too anxious to leave. He got up from his desk and went out into the hall.

Next to his office was a bulletin board containing seminar announcements, class notices, and departmental information. Standing in front of this board was an older student. He was casually reading a memorandum regarding disposal of radioactive material from laboratories.

"Can I help you with something? Were you looking for me?"

"Oh, no. I'm looking for the main office."

"It's on the fourth floor, down one from here. There's a stair-case by the elevators."

"Thanks."

Josh watched as the sandy-haired man walked down the hall. Something bothered him, something that didn't seem quite right. Perhaps it was the man's age, or the backpack he carried that seemed unusually empty, or even the newness of the sweatshirt he wore. Or perhaps he was simply on edge from his encounter on the mall. He dismissed the thoughts, returned to his office, and closed himself inside once more.

* * * * * * * * * * * * * *

"We almost had a problem."

"Why? What kind of problem?"

"One of the subjects, the biologist, almost made me."

The two men sat in their car, parked some distance south of the campus.

"I tailed him to the Chemistry Building and then on to his building. I saw him go in, waited, and followed a few minutes later. When I got to his office, it was dark. I thought he wasn't there. He opened the door on me and I had to fake it real quick."

"Look, you've got to be more careful than that. We're not being paid to have our cover blown the first few days."

"Okay, okay! No problem. I'll handle the tail. He'll never know he's being followed."

"He'd better not. Let's call Mr. Tarquin and make our report."

Interlude Three

Jerusalem
1172 A.D.

Every footfall on the gravel path produced a sound that seemed loud enough to awaken the entire city. The light of dawn was hours away and, in the pallid shadows of the full moon, she imagined she could see, lurking at each turn, an attacker wielding a death stroke. Sweating more from terror and from the tension of her mission than from exertion, she continued on, climbing the Mount of Olives, clutching the cedar chest beneath her arm.

The European conquerors of Jerusalem were about to be deposed as this land, now sacred to three religions, once again played host to bloody strife. With their downfall would come an end to Christian control over the holiest of sites, including all those associated with the final days of Jesus' life. For the Society of Arimathea, this was of no immediate consequence. Instead a new threat had arisen, in the form of the militant order that ruled the Christian world: the Knights Templar.

As the final days of their tenure in the kingdom they called "Outremer" came near, the knights were seeking to strengthen their position in preparation for a retrenchment to their European strongholds. This would include gaining possession of as many of the relics of Christendom as could be found. It was during this effort that their searchings uncovered evidence of the Society. All too soon their investigations would lead them to Gallipoli.

Miriam d'Anjou was well aware of the danger this represented for all that she held dear. The medallion she wore beneath her garments was only one sign of her dedication to the ancient charge she had inherited. Thus, she had volunteered as part of the desperate plan to fend off the Knights.

In the years that followed the transfer of the shroud from Jerusalem, the Society had become adept at creating diversions to keep itself and its precious relic a secret. They had perfected the art of constructing false shrouds, imitations of the original, treated to appear hundreds of years old.

Now, their plan was clear: induce the Knights Templar to accept one of these fakes as authentic. There were two things the leadership realized immediately: they needed a believable contact with the knights and they needed the best forgery they could manage. The first requirement would be met by Miriam, the child of a French nobleman who, after his conquest, was himself conquered by the arms of a daughter of Zion. The second had plunged the Society into a moral crisis. The only believable shroud would be one that had been used to bury a man who had died the same death as Christ. Someone had to be crucified.

Miriam had spent months convincing one of the knights that she was disaffected with the Society and that she feared the shroud would fall into the hands of the Saracens when the inevitable conquest happened. Slowly, she had led him to believe that she considered the Knights Templar the only safe haven for the relic, and that, because of her French ancestry, the shroud should be enshrined in that country.

That night was the final step in the plot. She would turn over the manufactured relic to the Templars, meeting the one whom she had deceived. She carried with her the ultimate sacrifice of a man whose name she did not even know.

The path climbed past the garden of Christ's final agony and wound among the olive trees that covered the mount's western slope. As she struggled with the incline, her breath forced and rapid, she prayed in whispered gasps, "Please, Lord, I cannot fail. Not after all we've done." From her left a cloaked figure appeared to materialize from the gnarled trunk before which he stood.

* * * * * * * * * * * * * * * *

Guillaume de Lirey watched her climb the path toward his position. The woman was dressed for the cold night air with a hood pulled tightly around her head. He knew that it could only be Miriam, given the time of night and the burden she carried.

Eight hundred years before, St. Helen had scoured the Holy Land for any and all relics of Christ. The shroud was one of the things that had escaped her search. And now he, a humble knight in service to the Church, was called to bear it in triumph to the Christian world.

He knew exactly what he would do, once he managed to secret the relic out of Jerusalem. He would not trust to the superiors of his order the task only he could complete. He must bring the shroud to France and ultimately to his home in the village of Lirey. There, in the local church, the holy cloth could be displayed for all to see and venerate.

As Miriam approached closer he stepped out from hiding. He was pleased with the effect his appearance had on her, having exchanged his accustomed white tunic for black. The woman had been completely surprised and now he was in control of the meeting.

"Did you bring it?"

"Of course." She held the chest close to her, reluctant to part with it so soon. "Will you do as we agreed? Will you take it to France?"

He reached out to take the cedar case from her. "That is exactly what I will do. You have nothing to fear."

"Oh yes I do. I have broken my vow to the Society. I fear both their retribution and God's."

"You have done the best thing, Miriam. Believe me, the shroud will be safer in France than here in Jerusalem. Your Society will come to see that in time."

"I pray that you are right." She pulled her cloak tighter, the cold air chilling the wetness that had accumulated along her skin. "I must go, before what I have done is discovered."

The knight covered the chest with his cloak. "Yes, yes. I will leave by another route."

She retraced her steps, following the winding path down toward the city. Guillaume watched her until she had turned through the trees. He shook his head and said aloud, "God have mercy on her and on me for what I must do."

He motioned to his right. From deep within the trees emerged another dark figure. This one was an old acquaintance, a member of the Hashishim, the Islamic counterpart to the Templars. He was an assassin.

Miriam had betrayed her vow and had delivered the shroud as agreed. However, the Society must never learn what had become of the relic until it was too late. For this reason, Miriam could not survive.

The silence of the moonlight was broken by the strangled cry of a woman, cut short, he knew, by the single stroke of a knife. He turned away and, with deliberate steps, began his retreat from Jerusalem and his march to his destiny in France.

CHAPTER TWELVE

TUCSON, ARIZONA
MARCH 18, 1999

The Committee on Religious Studies
Presents

"The Medieval Church and Religious Artifacts"

Laurent Carriere, S.J., Ph.D.
Curator and Historian
L'Abbaye d'Hautecombe
France

Thursday, March 18, 1999
Room 232 Modern Languages
3:30 p.m.

The seminar announcement had been circulated two weeks earlier. The faculty of the Religious Studies Committee had persuaded Laurent, with little resistance on his part, to give this presentation. The arrangements had, of course, been made before the press conference and the ensuing public reaction. Laurent decided that he would focus on the known cases where artifacts, supposedly originating during the time of Christ, had been proven to be elaborate fakes. He planned to avoid any lengthy discussion of his discovery.

This was exactly the kind of opportunity for which he had hoped. It would not be a talk given in the vineyards of the Valais, or even in the cloisters of Hautecombe. Instead, this would be a scholarly discourse delivered to a group of his peers who looked to him as an expert on the subject.

Like most seminars at the University, this one would also be open to the public. Because of the recent notoriety, the faculty expected a larger than normal attendance. Laurent had been asked to arrive early so that preparations could be made for slide projection and lighting before the audience began filling the room.

Modern Languages 232 was normally used for classes. There were about 100 desks, affixed to the floor on metal pedestals, and arrayed in rows, sloping up toward the back of the lecture hall. The rise was gentle, unlike the steep, almost amphitheater-like setting found in medical schools. In front, there were three panels of green chalkboard, the central one covered by a lowered white screen. To one side was a small lectern with controls for light and sound. The walls were a combination of red brick and white acoustical tiles, giving the room a stark and relatively sterile feel.

Laurent entered about 20 minutes before the start to find more than one-third of the seats already occupied. Halfway up the center isle was a small cart holding a slide projector. He introduced himself to the young woman who was busily involved with setting up the equipment. She gave him a circular magazine and instructed him in the correct way of inserting his slides.

When Josh came into the hall, he found Laurent seated in the front row, ordering the illustrations he intended to use for his talk and loading the slide tray. Josh sat at the adjoining desk.

"Are you about ready?"

"What? Oh, yes. I have a few more slides to arrange."

Josh could sense the nervousness that was always a part of the minutes before a seminar. He said nothing else to disturb his friend and, instead, surveyed the room as more and more people filed in. Although it was still some ten minutes before the announced time, the available seats were rapidly being taken. Sutton was present and had already positioned himself in one of the middle rows when Mac slid casually into the chair to director's right.

As the last of the crowd jockeyed for the remaining empty spots, Josh scanned around the hall. Most of the other people in attendance were unfamiliar to him, being made up of faculty and students from the humanities side of campus. He did recognize two reporters who had been at their press conference. His gaze came to rest on a sandy-haired man whom he thought he might know. He had caught the man looking at him and, as their eyes met, the man turned suddenly away. Josh remembered. This was the student he had seen outside his office three days earlier. Why would a science major be at a humanities seminar? Perhaps it was the cloning angle that had attracted him. He recalled that something seemed odd about this particular student. His train of thought was interrupted as the faculty member in charge of seminars for the Religious Studies Committee rose to introduce Laurent to the waiting audience.

Laurent's host tapped on the small lapel microphone, producing a series of muffled "thuds" over the PA system in the room. The sounds served notice that the afternoon's program was about to begin.

"I am pleased to introduce today's speaker. Father Laurent Carriere comes to us from the Abbey of Hautecombe in the French Savoy Alps. He holds a Ph.D. in history from the University of Geneva and is an ordained priest in the Society of Jesus. Father Carriere is an expert on both the historical and archaeological data relating to the medieval Church in Europe. His topic today is 'The Medieval Church and Religious Artifacts.' Father Carriere . . . "

Laurent stood behind the small podium as the microphone was attached to his lapel. He arranged his notes in front of him and began.

"Thank you for this invitation. I hope that my English and my accent will not be a problem for you."

He had given many seminars of this type at universities throughout Europe, using English when French would not serve. He always found that it relaxed him as well as his audience, however, if he used this disclaimer at the start.

"During the Middle Ages the Church was the literal and figurative center for all activities in the community: religious, social, legal, and otherwise. Individual churches, fighting to survive in this climate, often found it beneficial to have an attraction that would draw the faithful and their support. This resulted in an intense competition for the possession of relics. Therefore, the setting was ideal for the 'manufacture' of artifacts, especially those that could be claimed to be traced to Christ himself."

Laurent proceeded to describe, in detail, the attitude of believers and clerics that might have led to widespread public acceptance of a supposed relic. He used slides taken from his own work with medieval materials or taken from collections he had seen. He spent a large amount of time dealing with the work concerning the famous Shroud of Turin, touching on the major contribution of the group at Arizona. In all of this, he judiciously avoided any mention of Hautecombe or the shroud he had discovered.

At the end of his forty-minute presentation there was applause. The moderator rose and faced the audience.

"I'm certain that Father Carriere would be glad to answer any questions. Yes. Professor Halser."

A senior member of the History Department had raised his hand.

"Father Carriere. Do you believe that these fakes were produced with the full knowledge of the Church?"

"If by the 'Church' you mean the higher religious authorities, for instance, the bishops, then my answer is 'no.' If, on the other hand, you mean the local church in a town or village, then I would have to say that sometimes they may have been completely aware of the true origin of these supposed relics."

Professor Halser pressed his point further.

"Why, then, did the authorities in Rome never suppress the veneration of these objects, such as the Shroud of Turin?"

Laurent detected the decidedly anti-Catholic bias of his questioner. He did not want his seminar to devolve into a sectarian clash.

"You have an excellent point. Indeed, Rome should have taken a firm stand and done more to stop the misuse of such objects. In many cases, however, the Vatican was not aware of the existence of a supposed artifact until long after the people had built a great legend around it. In these cases, suppression may have been out of the question or too late."

Halser had not expected agreement with his statement and found himself suddenly without an adversary. He sat back in his chair and satisfied himself with a studied stroking of his beard.

Two or three questions from students were related to specific objects that Laurent had described. His answers were instantly converted into notes. At last, a graduate student from the Religious

Studies Committee raised his hand and his mentor, the moderator of the seminar, recognized him at once.

"Yes, John. You have a question?"

"Yes. Father Carriere, how does the Shroud of Hautecombe fit into this picture? I mean, if it dates from the time of Christ, how could it be an artifact created during the Middle Ages?"

This was the question that most in attendance had waited to hear asked, and that Laurent had tried to avoid. The other members of the dating team waited for his answer, each sharing in the tension that this question provoked. Josh watched Laurent, anxious to see how he would respond. The LAC director twisted in his chair to glare at the questioner who sat two rows behind him. The young man tried in vain to look away. Mac slouched further down in his seat in an effort to withdraw from view.

Laurent assumed a scholarly stance next to the podium and began the response he had mentally prepared.

"Little is known of the history of this shroud. Its presence at Hautecombe began near the end of the 14th century and it had disappeared by the beginning of the 17th century. During this period of more than 200 years, practically no information can be found about the shroud. It was not used to enrich the abbey church and was rarely, if ever, displayed. The monks of Hautecombe profited by their association with the royal house of Savoy rather than by the presence of the shroud. Therefore, it is difficult to compare this relic with the others I have mentioned."

To Laurent's dismay this answer did not serve to end the topic. Several hands shot up as soon as he finished.

"Professor Halser, you have a comment?"

"Doesn't the fiber analysis of the fabric confirm the stories of the shroud's origin somewhere in the Middle East?"

Sutton could no longer remain silent. He raised his hand and motioned to Laurent for attention.

"I believe that Doctor Sutton from the dating project will be able to answer this question better than I."

"Yes, quite. Thank you, Father. Our analysis of the weave of the cloth and the composition of the fiber does point to a geographic origin somewhere in the eastern Mediterranean. I must emphasize, however, that the data we have acquired speaks only to the chronological age and physical nature of the shroud. There is nothing in these data that suggests a link to any particular person. The fact that the cloth was discovered at Hautecombe is purely circumstantial."

Halser had at last found a worthy opponent.

"Clearly, Doctor Sutton, someone was buried in that cloth. You merely quote the data and would have us believe you are not even the least bit curious about who the unfortunate victim was."

"Curiosity is one thing, professor, while fact is another. Indeed, I am curious. But, I am also a scientist. I restrict my curiosity to those things that I can hope to examine by an application of the scientific method. Everything else is speculation, which I leave to other areas of endeavor."

Sutton had forgotten for a moment where he was. His well placed jab at the nonscience side of campus may as well have been a stick shoved into the heart of a hornet's nest. While Halser's face reddened with his rising anger at the delivered insult, several other faculty members murmured their discontent.

Laurent found his seminar getting rapidly out of control. He tried once more to put the subject of Hautecombe to one side.

"In any case, we have neither scientific nor historical evidence to say very much more about this particular relic. Our investigations are continuing and we hope that soon this mystery will be solved."

Throughout the seminar and the question period Nikos had been leaning against the wall on the left side of the room. He had seen the announcement for Laurent's talk three days before in the campus newspaper but had arrived too late to find a seat. He spoke up without raising his hand, his voice drowning out the sound of protest within the hall.

"I have a question. What if the Shroud of Hautecombe is authentic? What if it truly is the winding sheet of Christ?"

Along with Laurent, all heads turned to regard the man who spoke. From his dress he was neither a student nor a professor. His gray suit and understated tie represented the business world rather than the university. His appearance would have been entirely unremarkable except for his face. Sleepless nights, and days of wandering lost in thought, had given a haunted and slightly manic cast to Nikos' features. Buried within this setting were two eyes that burned with a zealous fire.

"We have no evidence to suggest this cloth is in any way related to Christ."

"Yes, but 'what if,' Father? 'Speculate,' please. You are not a scientist. What if this cloth is real?"

"Then, I suppose, it would be the most significant historical and religious find in the annals of Western civilization. But there is no . . . "

Nikos cut him off before he could complete his answer.

"In that case, Father, who should be the custodian of this shroud? Who should be its caretaker?"

Laurent had no answer. The silence that followed was broken by the seminar moderator.

"I'm sure there's much room for discussion in cases like this and we are all looking forward to more information as it becomes available. I would like to thank Father Carriere again and invite any of you who have additional questions to stay for a few moments afterward."

Applause was accompanied this time by a general movement of the audience toward the doors. A number of students and faculty came forward to continue the discussion with Laurent. He did not see them. His attention was focused on one person. Nikos remained for a few moments at the side of the room, isolated as those heading for the exits flowed around him. Their eyes met and locked. After an eternity, Nikos walked to the back of the room and left the hall. Laurent watched the door long after Nikos has disappeared.

CHAPTER THIRTEEN

TUCSON, ARIZONA
MARCH 20, 1999

The mail room that served the Department of Molecular Biology was a small, windowless alcove adjacent to the main offices. Along two walls were compartments for each member; large slots for the faculty, small slots for the graduate students and staff. Once each day incoming letters and packages would be distributed by a student assistant. Once each day everyone gathered up their correspondence and retreated to their offices.

Josh saw that his slot was stuffed to overflowing. His mail normally contained University memos and notices, advertising brochures from scientific supply houses, scientific journals, and the occasional message from some colleague. For the last few days, this had been augmented by an increasing number of letters, most addressed by hand and all coming from outside the University. Josh was almost reluctant to touch the stack of mail and only collected it with great effort.

As he left the mail room he met Franklin Stone.

"Say, Josh, do you have a few minutes?"

"Sure, Frank."

"Fine. Come on into my office."

The air of casualness between the department head and his faculty might have seemed unusual at first. Even senior graduate students eventually learned to call him "Frank." Stone had cultivated this informality throughout his career, preferring this manner to the staid academic atmosphere common in many European and some American institutions. Nevertheless, the imposing figure and reputation of the senior scientist held sway in every interaction. No one ever doubted his leadership.

The two men made their way through the reception area and the outer office toward the open door of Stone's chambers. As they

139

passed, staff members acknowledged them with a smile and turned quickly and inconspicuously back to their work.

Stone closed the door after them and gestured to the conference table near the tall vertical windows. Josh dropped the large bundle of mail he was still holding onto the table and lowered himself into one of the chairs. Stone sat across from him, staring alternately at the pile of letters and at his own hands.

"How are you doing, Josh?"

"Okay, Frank. I'm doing okay."

There was little conviction in his voice. Stone glanced once more at Josh's mail.

"I mean, how are you handling this pressure? I've heard from both the dean and the president that public reaction to your experiments has been quite strong."

Josh nervously rearranged the letters in front of him, as though trying to hide the many obvious pieces of outside mail by covering them with innocuous circulars and seminar announcements.

"It's really not that bad. I've gotten some comments, but nothing I can't handle."

"Tell me how you see these experiments fitting into the overall research goals for your laboratory."

Josh leapt at the answer to this question, excited that he could discuss the results of his experiments with Stone.

"Actually, I see this as a completely new line of endeavor for me. In fact, I can see how the analysis of DNA sequences from ancient sources could tie in nicely with aspects of the Human Genome Project. I believe I can get funding for this as soon as I publish these early observations."

Franklin Stone sat back in his chair. He had personally recruited Josh from the laboratory in Paris headed by an old and close friend. Like many department heads, he had a professional and sometimes paternal interest in the success of his junior faculty. In the case of Joshua Francis, these feelings were intensified by the "family" ties that crisscrossed the substructure of the international scientific community. Josh had become more of a protégé than he had intended. His anxiety about the young scientist's tenure chances clouded his mind.

"What about your work on cellular growth factors? Are you planning to give up your grant funding for that project? What about your graduate students? How can you continue this new work in the face of the public outcry?"

Josh was not prepared for this barrage of questions. He became defensive and flustered. He tried to ignore the part about his failed efforts to establish himself and, instead, pressed his point about the experiments with the shroud.

"As soon as the reaction dies down, I'll be able to finish the work with the clone. After all, what I've isolated is merely some DNA from a cloth proven to be nearly two thousand years old. There is no historical or other evidence linking this cloth to any person. The furor will soon be over." Josh spoke the words but could not ignore the hollow sound with which they echoed in his mind.

"Josh, don't misunderstand me. I'm not against your work. I'm simply trying to alert you that it's dangerous to change directions this close to the time for your review. The committee will have little hard evidence that they can use to judge this new research. I'm only suggesting that you might be better off directing your energies at your original project."

"Frank, I know you're trying to help. I need a few more weeks to follow this through. If it's not going anywhere, I'll drop it."

He could see that Stone did not agree with this plan. In any case, he knew that no more would be said now. The department head rose and walked to the door leading directly from his office to the hall rather than back through the reception area. Josh gathered up his mail and followed.

"Thanks for the concern, Frank. Whatever happens, I know you've been on my side."

"Be careful, Josh. The tenure system can be brutal, but it's nothing compared to what they'll do to you outside the University."

* * * * * * * * * * * * * * * *

"Francis lab . . . "

Chris Warren cradled the receiver of the wall telephone against his ear as he maneuvered himself around to face the laboratory. Sitting at desks against the far wall, Rita Mitchell and Bill Pierce watched, somewhat nervously, as the tenth incoming call of the day disturbed their work.

"No . . . I'm sorry . . . we can't give out samples from . . . "

Chris paused, listening to the caller with obvious strain showing on his face.

"Look, I really don't care what group you represent . . . No, Doctor Francis is not here . . . No, I don't know where he can be reached . . . "

After a moment more he hung up, holding on to the handle as if to keep himself from flying around the room in rage. In response to his obvious discomfort, Rita let out a long sigh, throwing down the manuscript on which she had been concentrating.

"How long is this going to go on? Who was it this time?"

Chris was trying to keep his voice under control.

"A group of atheists who think the existence of the clone means that they can prove Jesus was only human, not divine. They want the DNA so that they can sponsor research."

Bill Pierce stood up and began stuffing papers and journals into his backpack. "I can't take any more of this!" His normally intense features had taken on a tortured configuration.

"I'm going to the medical library to hide out for a while. I've got prelims coming up next month and I need time. All of this is just getting in the way."

"Bill . . . calm down . . . please."

"Don't tell me to calm down!"

For a moment he stood before them, coiled in anger, his black hair in disarray, his thin frame contorted by tension. With a sudden violence, he grabbed his pack and bolted for the door. The others watched in silence as Bill ran from the lab. He had been accepted to the graduate program less than two years previously. During that time, he had performed marginally well in classes and had not impressed the faculty. His nerves were on edge. He knew that his future in the department hinged on his success in the preliminary examination, a rite of passage that all second year students must endure.

Rita was a more senior student and already past that critical stage in her career. She could look on Bill's outburst with the benefit of this broadened perspective. Nevertheless, the atmosphere that had prevailed in the lab during the weeks since the press conference had shaken her normally focused behavior.

"Bill's right. It's impossible to get anything done in the middle of this. What is he going to do?"

Gesturing toward the office wing of the building, Rita indicated that the "he" in this case referred to Josh. She leaned back, half-sitting on her desk. Her brown hair was pulled tightly back and held in place with an elastic band, accentuating the angular lines of her face. She dressed plainly in a studied attempt to de-emphasize her natural beauty; her appearance indicated that she intended to be taken seriously.

Rita had been actively sought after by the department and had turned down opportunities at Caltech and U.C. Berkeley to come to Arizona. Her scientific sense was sharp and her manner aggressive when it came to her discipline. She commanded the respect of her peers and of the faculty. Chris Warren was no exception to this rule.

"I don't know, Rita. He seems so lost, almost frightened in some ways."

"Listen. Yesterday, I tried to talk to him about my work. There's another group that seems to be on exactly the same track as me."

She picked up the manuscript she had been reading earlier and held it out for emphasis.

"It took him a while to realize what I was saying. He hadn't even read this paper. He gave me some vague answer about changing the emphasis enough to make it publishable. He didn't understand that I'm going to be scooped even before I start writing my dissertation."

Chris knew her well enough from their three years in the lab together to sense that she was struggling with a decision.

"What will you do?"

"I'm not sure yet. I hate to say it, but I may have to consider changing research directors."

"Give it some time, Rita. That won't help him right now."

"That's true, but I may have no choice."

* * * * * * * * * * * * * * *

The hall outside Josh's office was empty as Leslie walked up to his door. The whining chatter of printers could be heard coming from adjacent rooms. That and the muted sound of a radio playing as background noise were the only evidence of activity on the fifth floor.

She was worried about him. She had spent most of the morning supervising the mounting of a new exhibit at the Center. It was hard to keep her mind on her work. On the spur of the moment she had taken some time and walked south to his building, hoping to catch him for a few minutes.

The door to his office was slightly open. She could see him sitting at his desk, elbows propping up his head, his face buried in his hands.

"Hi, love . . . what are you . . . "

She stopped as he swung around in his chair. His face was drained of color, waves of shock and fear washing through his eyes.

"What is it? What's happened?"

She went quickly to him and cradled him against her. On top of the mass of paperwork and journals on his desk were two piles of opened mail. He had been receiving letters since the day after the press conference and she had seen many of them. In general, there were two types. One group accused him and all the others at the University of blasphemy and sacrilege for daring to experiment with the shroud. This constituted the largest number, since Rev. Edwin Slaughter had preached to his television flock against science in general, and Josh in particular. He had encouraged a letter writing campaign that had borne fruit.

The other letters came from individuals or groups who wanted Josh to send them a sample of the DNA clone. Some requests were from scientists who wanted the molecule for research purposes. Most, however, were religious appeals, asking for the DNA to use in various worship services. These letters bothered him more than the denouncements. He tried to cling to the rational and scientific position that there was no proof regarding the actual source of the DNA.

Josh had been severely distracted by all of this, but, until now, he had not been terrorized. Leslie noticed that one letter lay separate from all the rest. She picked it up, still holding him protectively against her with one arm.

> March 18, 1999
> Dr. Francis:
>
> The Shroud is real. It is the authentic winding sheet of Christ. The DNA you have isolated is, therefore, the DNA of Jesus. Your experiment should never have been done. Now, it is too late.
>
> You must return the Shroud and this DNA to the rightful caretakers. We are the Custodians of the Cloth. You must arrange that it be returned to us. Otherwise, you will suffer the consequences.
>
> Arimathea

"What is this Josh? Who is this from?"

"I don't know. It came today. A lot of the letters are crazy or even sad. I've been able to ignore them. But this one, Leslie . . . this one frightens me."

"What is 'Arimathea?' "

"All I can think of is the part in the Bible about Joseph and the sepulcher."

"Of course. The man who gave his tomb for the burial of Christ. But, I don't understand. You've received threatening letters from the Reverend's followers, saying worse things than this. Why has this one upset you so much?"

Josh pulled away and looked up at her, his voice trembling.

"At Laurent's seminar yesterday, during the questions and answers, a man used these same words . . . 'caretakers' and 'custodians.' This letter sounds the same."

"Who was he? Did he identify himself?"

Josh had seen Nikos but had also seen the man with the sandy hair in the audience. He was confused. Which one had asked the question? Who was the threat?

"He didn't give a name; he only asked the question. I don't remember which one he was. I can't really describe him. But I'm afraid it's someone who's here in town."

"Why?"

He handed her the envelope.
"Look at the postmark and date."
Leslie read:
"Tucson, Arizona. Mar. 18, 1999."

Interlude Four

Gallipoli
1366 A.D.

He could not move. The sword that had pierced him had passed through his body from front to back and had severed his spine. Although paralyzed, he could feel his blood draining onto the stone floor of the chapel. The pain was searing, more intense than any he had experienced during his long life. Through the agony that screamed inside of him he could hear the sound of the men leaving, the clanking of their scabbards and bucklers and the crunching sound their boots made as they stepped on the ruins of the door.

He was dying. He knew that. But he also knew he had done everything possible and had still failed. What else could be expected from a man of his age pitted against three soldiers who could have been his grandchildren?

When the attack began earlier that day, every man in the city who could wield a weapon was pressed into its defense. Moslem, Christian, or Jew; it did not matter. The invaders must be turned back. Aristos was not included. At sixty-three and with a crippled right leg he had little fighting worth left to offer.

There was one service he could perform, not for the city but for the Society of which he was a member. As soon as he could, he hobbled off in the direction of the small chapel, trying to avoid those streets where the fighting seemed most intense.

Above the entrance to the building was a simple carving of the three crossed nails and the name that made it outwardly appear to be a chapel dedicated to St. Joseph of Arimathea. The door had already been torn down. Inside he found three of the invading soldiers, helmeted and with swords drawn, rummaging in the ruins of the interior. One of them had already found the cedar chest containing the shroud.

"No, no! Don't take that!"

The men turned with practiced skill, ready for an attack. They spoke in a language that he could not comprehend.

"*Qui est-il? Est-il Chrétien où Islamique?*"

"*Je ne sais pas.*"

Aristos waved his arms, trying to signal to the men his intention. He only succeeded in alarming them further.

"This is a chapel. Please, do not desecrate it. There is nothing here that you can use. There is nothing here of value."

The men looked at each other, as puzzled by the foreign words as by the old man's intentions. The one who appeared to be the leader picked up the cedar chest and began walking toward the door. He pointed at Aristos with his sword and spoke to one of the soldiers.

"*Jean, tué lui.*"

"*Mais, il est vieux.*"

"*Je m'en fiche! Allez y!*"

Again, the words were meaningless to him. Aristos saw only that the precious chest and its contents were being removed. He rushed forward, screaming in protest. The young soldier had been turned in response to the order. The sudden movement made him react protectively. He spun around and held out his sword as a guard. Aristos ran himself onto the blade, forcing his body all the way to the hilt.

The eyes of the soldier widened as they saw the red stream begin to flow from the mouth, open in anguish, of the man impaled at the end of his arm. He pushed against the struggling form with his free hand.

"*Merde!*"

The leader was unconcerned with what had taken place, his mind fixed on returning to the main force. Maybe some of the items they had found would be of interest to the Count. Perhaps even the contents of the chest he cradled under his arm. He was anxious to move on.

"*Il est mort. Allons! Vite!*"

Aristos, freed from the steel that had supported him along its length, sagged to the floor. The young soldier stood over him for a moment, drops of blood falling from his blade. A look of sadness passed over his face.

"Je suis . . . je dois . . . "

He could not find the words he needed and, saying nothing further, followed the others into the street.

Aristos heard the sounds of their departure fade. Indeed, his own leave-taking was near. The shroud had left the care of the Society. In a way, he was glad to be gone as well. It was cold now, at least for him. As the light dimmed he could hear, at last, the water as it lapped gently against the shore of the island he knew as a child. It called him home.

CHAPTER FOURTEEN

SAN RAFAEL, CALIFORNIA
MARCH 22, 1999

"Costa. A Mr. Hawkins is calling from Tucson. He didn't say what it's about."

By his own design, Cheryl screened all of his calls, but there were times when he wished he had installed a private line. He depressed the "talk" switch on the intercom.

"It's all right. I'll take it."

He watched the lights on his phone console flash as Cheryl transferred the caller to him. He pressed the button and lifted the receiver.

"Hello?"

"Mr. Tarquin?"

"Yes."

"This is George Hawkins."

"Yes. Please tell me what's happening. What is your status?"

"Yes sir. The shroud is still being held in a safe inside the dating laboratory facility. All of the scientists and even the priest maintain that there is no proven connection between the cloth and any historical person. The public outcry is continuing, however. Several news reports have focused on the biblical account of Christ's death and burial, and legends of what happened to the burial cloth. Two days ago, the priest from France . . . Father Carriere . . . spoke on the campus and was questioned extensively about the origins of this shroud."

Hawkins said nothing about Nikos' appearance at the seminar nor about his statement at the end. He and his partner were unsure of the relationship between father and son and had decided to wait until their client asked for this type of information.

"Mr. Tarquin, we have, of course, mounted a number of operations for you in the past. Unlike the others, however, we're not sure about our objectives at this time. Perhaps you could be a bit more specific and tell us what your interests are in this case. Maybe you could . . . ”

The voice trailed off. Costa was certain that the investigator had sensed his own mistake. Nevertheless, he decided to deliver the necessary rebuke. He paused several seconds to let the weight of the silence have its effect.

“Mr. Hawkins, have we not negotiated your fee? Is it not sufficiently large for this operation?”

“Yes, sir.”

“Then you will never again question my reasons or motivation. These matters are not your concern. I have given you detailed instructions. If you cannot execute them, I will contract with another firm. Is that clear?”

“Yes, sir! I'm sorry. It won't happen again.”

“Good. Anything further?”

“Yes, sir. We believe that, if you wish, we can successfully expropriate both the shroud and the DNA samples and deliver them to you. We have studied the physical situation and we see no problem in accomplishing this.”

“Thank you. But you will do nothing, repeat, nothing, without my explicit instructions. For now I need to know the whereabouts of the shroud, the DNA, and all of those involved. And how is my son?”

“He . . . ah . . . seems to be fine. He's apparently trying to learn all he can about the shroud. As far as we know, he has not made contact with any of the University people.”

“Okay. You will keep me posted and . . . ”

He was interrupted by Cheryl's voice through the speaker at his side.

“Costa. I have Nikos for you on line two.”

“Just a minute, Hawkins.”

A quick push of buttons on his console placed the investigator on hold and connected him with his son.

“Hello, Nikos. Wait a moment while I finish this other call.”

He manipulated the telephone lines again, juggling two of the pieces in the strategy he was directing.

"Hawkins, report back in three days. You have my home number."

He disconnected abruptly, not waiting for an acknowledgment.

"Nikos, how are you? What have you got for me?"

"I'm doing well, Papa . . . uh . . . I haven't found out . . . that is, I don't know if . . . what I'm trying to say is . . . "

"Nikos. Just tell me what you know."

He could hear his son's deep intake of breath as he prepared himself.

"The shroud, of course, is real. The scientists and the priest don't know that yet or they're not admitting it. The press, on the other hand, is reporting the story as though it's authentic. They've made the public believe. I'm trying to get to talk with one of the scientists as soon as I can. Perhaps I can still persuade them to let us make an offer on the shroud."

Costa moved the phone away from his mouth so that Nikos would not hear the sigh of exasperation that escaped his lips. He knew that his son couldn't see his head shaking as he tried to formulate some response.

"Good work, Nikos. You're doing fine."

"Papa, I think I should stay here. One of us should be here in case anything happens."

"Yes, of course. You're right. You keep in touch . . . keep me informed. I'm counting on you, Nikos."

"Yes, Papa. I understand."

Costa depressed the switch to end the conversation and sat back in his chair. He had set in motion an enterprise designed with one purpose: the return of the shroud to the Society.

Of course, Nikos was in Tucson solely as a diversion. Costa had no confidence in his son, no matter how motivated he might seem. He chose to keep him busy at the University until he could bring into play the final stroke of his operation.

His principle tactic was to use the legitimate and powerful weapon of Rome, in the person of Msgr. Corsini. Costa believed that, since the shroud was discovered at a Benedictine abbey, it would be a relatively simple matter to have it turned over to the Vatican Museum. From there, it would ultimately be returned in triumph to the Society. He would see to it that a proper chapel was built to house it. Perhaps they would no longer need to be a secret organization, but instead, one with an elite and respected membership.

The DNA that had been produced was another matter. Since this substance had been derived from the shroud, it too belonged in the care of the men and women of Arimathea. He did not know if it was the DNA of Christ that had been isolated. He had no way to judge since he had no training in biology. But he would take no chances.

His backup plan was ready, in the event that Msgr. Corsini failed. Hawkins and his associate were primed. In the past, he had employed them to break into places more secure than a university research laboratory. He had no doubt they could, on his order, steal both the shroud and the DNA. The lesson of history forced him to hold this alternative as an absolute last resort.

In 1578, after more than two centuries in the possession of various royalty, a different shroud had been brought to Turin, Italy. The Society had known of this cloth all along, since they had, in fact, created it as a decoy. Its appearance first in Lirey and subsequently in Chambery and Turin had been duly recorded by the leadership. Through popular belief, however, this one came to be thought of as the winding sheet of Christ.

Within the Society, there existed a small group who yearned for the glory that having even this false shroud would bring. In their view, ownership of the winding sheet the faithful believed in would do as well. Privately, four of these men conspired to steal the relic from the cathedral in Chambery were it was kept before moving to Turin. Early in 1532 they made their attempt. They were interrupted during their crime by a young priest who, unable to sleep, had quietly entered the great church in the predawn hours. In their haste to escape, the thieves knocked over a candle, setting fire to the altar cloth and damaging the shroud.

The men were caught and tried. Their crime had very nearly exposed the Society. Only their silence and the efforts of certain high Vatican officials had prevented the investigation from going beyond the attempted robbery. The memory of the failed theft had long reaching effects. From that time onward, membership in the Society was severely limited and, in addition, less emphasis was put on recovery of the sacred relic. Thus, Costa found himself the head of a largely ceremonial organization.

In his mind, Costa pictured the scene at the next meeting of the Society's leadership. The room they used was on the upper floor of a nameless building in Gallipoli. Over the years it had been converted into a ceremonial chamber. The walls were decorated with tapestries that rivaled those found in any of the major museums of Europe. The room contained paintings and statues, many of great value, depicting episodes in the life of Christ. An altar had been built and consecrated such that the room was a functioning chapel in which Mass could be offered. The center of the space was filled by a massive wooden table, ornately carved and complemented by matching, deeply cushioned chairs for each member. Light was provided almost exclusively by candles burning in sconces along the walls.

There they congregated, twelve men and women from the upper echelons of their professions; officials of the church, politicians, and those who, like Costa, had high status in private business. There were other members worldwide, but only the elite were invited to this annual event. The garments were twentieth century, the robes of the past having given way to ornate sashes of crimson. They wore their medallions openly during this time.

Costa, as president, was master of the ceremony. He imagined that, as was the custom, he would stand before them and lead the chant.

"The Cloth is the Symbol of our Christ."

The others would respond.

"And of His Resurrection."

"The Cloth is the Symbol of His sacrifice."

"And of our salvation."

The members would always recount the deeds of those who went before them, reciting a litany of heroes.

"Benjamin BarSimon, who bore the Cloth to safety."

"The nameless crucified one, who gave the ultimate gift."

"Miriam the martyr, who kept her vow and preserved our charge."

"Aristos of Spetsai, who died in valiant defense of the Cloth."

At this point, there would normally be words, added to the ritual after the loss of the shroud, pleading for its return. Instead, Costa envisioned that he would place before them the gold reliquary box, containing their recaptured prize. He had already written the new text.

"The Cloth of Christ is returned to our care."

They would respond.

"And to the care of our descendants."

These visions fueled his passion for the strategy he had begun. Costa had decided to take the shroud and the DNA derived from it by force only as the last possible choice. He had also decided that, if this choice must be made, he would see to it that this time it would succeed.

* * * * * * * * * * * * * * *

TUCSON, ARIZONA

Nikos slowly lowered the telephone receiver onto its cradle on the table beside the bed. His fifteenth-floor hotel room near the campus faced north, giving him a spectacular view of the Catalina Mountains that underscored the Tucson skyline. In contrast, the room itself was plain, spare, and generally uninviting. With the drapes closed and the scenic panorama hidden, the tiny chamber became the image of a monk's cell. After nearly two weeks, Nikos noticed neither the expansiveness of the landscape nor the small-ness of his quarters.

The conversation with his father had produced a tension within him that threatened to splinter his back. He tried to force himself to relax, breathing slowly and deliberately, in and out, clenching and unclenching his fists. He knew much more than he had let on to Costa, and now he had a strategy of his own design.

During the first few days following his arrival and the press conference, he was a lost soul, walking the campus and driving his rented car along city streets to no purpose. He got to know the University, its buildings and its resources. He found the Main Library and became a familiar figure among the stacks and carrels. Using catalogues and departmental descriptions, he learned as much as he could about the faculty members involved in the dating project: their training, their specialties, and, most importantly, what he perceived to be their potential weaknesses.

Nikos spent hours tracing the history of the abbey at Hautecombe. He read volumes concerning the Savoy royalty and Amadeus IV, the Green Count, who had stolen the sacred shroud from the chapel in Gallipoli. That ancient city was also the object of his study.

The plan he had formulated had taken shape slowly during this time. The day of the confrontation between the mall preacher and the scientists had clicked everything into focus.

He had convinced himself that he could intimidate the scientists into selling the shroud to him. After all, they did not believe it had any religious significance. He built a scenario in which they would let him take the relic simply to get rid of the threats and public outcry. The look of fear on the face of Dr. Francis when the preacher had directly accused him made this man the prime target for the assault.

He needed an address, preferably a post office box. There was a postal substation near his hotel, but this was unacceptable, since it might be too easy to trace the person who had rented the box. He traveled to the northwest part of the city. Using a fictitious name and an address taken from a street in that area of town, he leased P.O. Box 325677, at zip code 85740.

Nikos chose to begin with a warning letter. He had brought with him, as he usually did when traveling on business, a lap-top computer and small printer, and using these had produced his first message that echoed the questions he had asked during the priest's lecture. He thought signing the letters "Arimathea" a stroke of genius. The biblical reference would lend the air of mysticism he sought and could not, he believed, lead anyone to the Society itself.

He would send letters to the others, Dr. Sutton, Fr. Carriere, and Dr. McGovern. But it was the series of letters to Dr. Francis that he felt would be the key. He had already mailed two; one should have been received. Dr. Francis could expect one each day, increasingly threatening and hopefully instilling greater fear. The young scientist would have no choice but to negotiate the return of the shroud. And then, Nikos would return to his father a victor, bearing before him the prize that Costa desired.

CHAPTER FIFTEEN

WASHINGTON, D.C.
MARCH 22, 1999

The view from the window was classic: to the left, the U.S. Capitol building; below, the tree-lined circular drive leading up to this seat of American political power; and, in the distance, the slender obelisk of the Washington Monument, poised against the late afternoon sky. The senior senator from California had earned this suite in the Senate Office Building by years of careful and sometimes ruthless maneuvers.

The Reverend Edwin Slaughter enjoyed the spectacle from this window while awaiting the arrival of Sen. Sam Johnson. The two friends met often, either in California or here in the District. Slaughter was such a familiar figure that the senator's staff, ignoring normal protocol, let him come and go in the office at will.

He had been a busy man. During the past two weeks he had waged a vigorous campaign against the desecration inherent in the work on the shroud and, more importantly, in the isolation of DNA that was from Christ Himself. Each of the past two Sundays, using his television pulpit as a battle station, he had lashed out at the "godless university scientists and the Church in Rome, who should know better." Exhorting his listeners to mount a crusade, he pressed them to write letters of complaint. He gave out the addresses of all those at Arizona who were involved in the project or who were in the University administration. His efforts were beginning to show results.

Normally, as a part of these eastern trips, Sam Johnson prevailed on him to give, on one day, the morning invocation for the Senate session. That morning, atop the ornate dais at the front of the historic chamber, Slaughter prayed for deliverance from the "secular humanists who had so cleverly captured the minds and hearts of so many." If there were any senators present who disagreed with him, they had no way of objecting.

Slaughter stood with his hands in his pockets and his shoulders hunched over in fatigue. It had been a long day, filled with meetings at the East Coast offices of the Christian Revivalist Movement. He watched as the street lamps lining the Mall began to wink on in response to the deepening twilight. Another hour or so and he would be stretched out on the bed in his hotel room, letting some of this tiredness drift away.

"After all these years I still think that's one hell of a sight."

Sam Johnson tossed his briefcase onto the couch near the door, loosened his tie, and crossed the room to stand beside his friend. The two men could not have been more different.

Edwin Slaughter was big: overweight with advancing age and, therefore, large in both size and stature. His broad face told the family history of Eastern European immigration, with stops in the Midwest. The tendrils of hair that clung like a diadem around his scalp held no traces of the dark brown of his youth. He was enough over six feet tall so that he towered above most people he met.

Trim and compact, Sen. Johnson was often described as one of the Capitol's most athletic politicians. Almost a head shorter than his friend, he did not dominate a crowd physically as much as psychologically. He had managed to keep most of his hair into his later years, although the color had changed from its original Scandinavian blond to pure white. His rugged good looks and Western swagger were all he had needed to gain attention when he had first come to Washington. His political skills had carried him the rest of the way.

The two had been inseparable throughout their childhood. In high school they had both made the starting lineup in football. The papers of that time were full of stories in which Slaughter, at right guard, opened gaping holes in the opposing defense so that Johnson, at halfback, could scoot through on his way to a state record in yardage and scoring. The pattern had continued through their military service together and, when Sam Johnson declared himself in politics, Edwin Slaughter was there to lead the charge.

"So, Eddie, what do we need to do next?"

Sam Johnson spoke as he walked away from the window and began opening cupboards at the wet bar that occupied the center of one wall. Some in Washington said that the only reason Johnson did not seek the Presidency was that he would have to be satisfied with less luxurious office space than he currently occupied. The room was dominated by the large oak desk, situated in its middle. To one side was an entertainment console, complete with three television monitors and an area for food and drink service. Another wall contained shelves lined with books and tokens of his political career. Above, displayed against the wood paneling, were framed photographs chronicling Johnson's life to that point. Many included Edwin Slaughter: the two as high school athletes; both men posing at a military depot in Saigon; the senator and the reverend on either side of the President in the Oval Office.

Conference tables were arranged in two areas so that separate small working meetings could be held. A door to the left led to a private apartment.

Johnson poured out a good measure of Jack Daniel's for himself and a glass of diet soda for his friend. Rev. Slaughter had no moral objection to alcohol. It was, however, a personal demon against which he waged a constant struggle. His friend was a silent and constant ally in this battle. The senator handed him the glass and took a seat in the great chair behind the desk, swiveling around to face the window.

"Can we stop them, Sam? Can we keep them from doing any more work with the shroud or that DNA?"

"I don't think we can do much about the shroud. After all, the Catholic Church and the government of France will likely see to it that they have a say in what happens next. But the work on the DNA . . . that's another story. I've been thinking about this. I've served on enough scientific subcommittees to have a good understanding of what these kinds of clones are about. From what I know, you could produce huge vats containing the cells that have the DNA. What would you do with it? Would you sell it, for instance?"

"Good God, of course not! You can't sell the DNA of Christ!"

"I'm just asking, Eddie, not suggesting, okay?"

Slaughter stalked along the floor, hands behind his back, face lost in thought.

"But we could see to it that everyone had some . . . any Christian who wanted to could have a little bottle with some of the DNA of Christ. If the shroud and the DNA wind up controlled by the Church of Rome, the relics would be kept in some holy of holies and trotted out once a year for the privileged to view. The common man would then never have a part of this link to his Savior for himself."

Slaughter stopped his pacing and turned toward the senator.

"Is there a way we can get this DNA?"

Johnson reached across to the communications console on his desk and pressed a button.

"It just so happens I've had my top legislative assistant working on this for the past week. Margaret, ask John Billings to join us, please."

The young woman who had entered in response to the signal nodded and left.

"He's been with me for about a year. He comes from Fresno and did law school at Stanford. His family owns a lot of acres of cotton in the central Valley."

"I know the name. They're Episcopalians, I believe."

"That won't matter, Eddie."

John Billings was at that time making his way quickly from his office down the hall. In his hand was a brown legal file case, with folders neatly organized and tabbed. He had been waiting for this call.

Like the senator and Rev. Slaughter, Billings had grown up in a San Joaquin Valley farming community. Beyond that, little else could bind them together. The young lawyer did not share their extreme conservatism, nor did he share their religious convictions. What he did share with Sen. Johnson was an enormous appetite for power. Shortly after his arrival in the District, he had contracted a serious case of "Potomac fever" and did everything he could to effect the only known cure: a permanent position in Washington.

He stepped into the office after a single knock, not waiting for an answer. He stood ready in the center of the room.

"Yes, Senator. You needed to see me?"

Billings was much shorter than either man. He looked more the affable accountant than the aggressive lawyer. The three-piece suit and quiet tie matched perfectly the narrow face topped with straight black hair. However, behind the horn-rimmed glasses were eyes that were coldly observant, as if marking a target or measuring a victim.

"Yes, John. I think you know Reverend Slaughter. Perhaps you could tell us what you've found out about this University of Arizona situation."

While the senator was still speaking, Billings shook hands with Slaughter, placed his case on the edge of the desk and drew up a chair. The Reverend took a seat in one of the plush chairs nearby.

"I've investigated each of the faculty members involved in the research project to date the Shroud of Hautecombe, as it has come to be called. I have here information about their activities. Which one would you like to hear about first?"

"Start wherever you wish, John."

Billings took the file case and, holding it on his lap, extracted a smaller folder from within. This he opened, referred to for a moment, and began to speak.

"I have very little information on the priest, Father Laurent Carriere, who brought the shroud from France. He is not a part of the University. The director of the dating laboratory is Doctor Richard Sutton. He is not a U.S. citizen. On the other hand, he is a well-known chemist with an excellent international reputation. He has research support from a wide variety of sources, including industry in this country and abroad. Doctor Dennis McGovern played a small role in the project. He is an assistant professor and seems to be somewhat of a free-spirit. His politics seem rather liberal. He has a reasonable amount of research funding. However, he has kept a low profile throughout this episode and has had little to do with the work in question. Finally, there is Doctor Joshua Francis, also an assistant professor. He is the one who conducted the cloning experiment and, in my opinion, is the most vulnerable."

Sen. Johnson sat forward in his chair, sensing that they had reached the critical point of the report.

"And why is that, John?"

The lawyer made a small adjustment to his glasses and removed another folder from the case.

"Doctor Francis has a single research grant from the National Institutes of Health . . . I believe . . . yes, from the National Cancer Institute. He has published only one research paper in the four and one-half years since he has been at the University. This means he is in danger of not receiving tenure."

Slaughter could no longer remain silent.

"Is he the one working on the DNA? Is he the one with the clone?"

"Yes, Reverend. I have a contact within the University administration. I have been informed that Doctor Francis has been asked to delay any further work until the public reaction dies down. But, as of now, he has it."

Johnson rose from his chair, signaling that he was ready to give Billings a direct order.

"John, I agree with Reverend Slaughter that this research is blasphemous and sacrilegious. We want this work not just delayed but stopped completely. I want you to work on this as a top priority."

With an air of calm efficiency, Billings closed his folders and returned them to the case.

"Yes, sir. I understand. There is one small problem. Doctor Francis is a minority, African-American . . . he lists himself as 'Creole' . . . we'll have to proceed with caution to avoid any possible legal action later."

"Can you take care of this yourself?"

"Yes, Senator. I really don't see any problem. I've already explored a set of options."

"Good. I don't need to know the particulars yet. Keep me informed on a daily basis."

Billings stood up to leave.

"It's good to see you again, Reverend. I hope everything is going well back home."

"Well enough, thank you. I hope you can give us some encouraging news soon."

As the door closed behind the departing lawyer, the two men returned to their seats.

"He's very intense, Sam."

"I know, Eddie. But he's good. He'll get the job done."

"I don't want anyone hurt in this. I get the impression he could be pretty cold and pitiless when he's after something."

Johnson laughed and slapped his desk.

"Come on. We're all like that in one way or another. He's young. It shows a bit more on him than it does on us."

CHAPTER SIXTEEN

HAUTECOMBE ABBEY, FRANCE
MARCH 23, 1999

Fortunately the lake steamers had not begun their daily trips from Aix to the abbey. As it was, a small army of journalists and tourists managed to navigate their way around the lake by land, to arrive each morning at the front gate of the monastery. Gustav Holden waited in the northern gardens, steeling himself for the day's invasion. He could already see the advance contingent of cars descending on him after traversing the Col du Chat high above the western shore.

His prized sanctuary was becoming more and more like a carnival grounds. The announcement of the true age of Laurent's shroud, which he refused to even think of as "the Shroud of Hautecombe," initially resulted in a deluge of telephone calls to the monastery offices. The level of interest overwhelmed the abilities of his single assistant, Fr. Cand, and meant that an additional priest had to be assigned to this work, upsetting the delicate balance of effort he had established.

The phone calls were followed by visits, the first being a reporter for the magazine, *Paris Match*. That article appeared the weekend after the press conference in Tucson, and featured photographs, descriptions, and detailed directions to the abbey. Since then, representatives of the media had assailed Hautecombe in a fury. That day alone, he was expecting crews from Télévision Suisse Romande, the French language network from Geneva, and CNN.

The first cars of the day were pulling into the parking lot outside the gate leading to the monastery church. As doors opened and closed, depositing visitors out onto the gravel entry way, the voice of Maurice LeFebvre could be heard.

"Now, if everyone will please remain quiet and orderly. Remember, this is a monastery, a place of worship. The church is not open yet; the first tour will begin in fifteen minutes. Certain areas of the abbey are not open to the public. If there are any news agency representatives, please follow me to the office."

He repeated parts of the message in halting English. Maurice had assumed the role of gatekeeper along with his other duties. He was fiercely protective of the grounds and of the priests. In addition, by controlling the movements and behavior of the visitors, especially the press, he could distract any attention from himself.

The last thing Maurice LeFebvre wanted was for his picture and name to be seen outside the confines of the monastery. After all, the real Maurice LeFebvre had died many years earlier in a fiery explosion during an aborted robbery in Montpellier.

The old caretaker had seen much during his life. One very painful lesson was that leaders were not to be trusted. The tragedy of the French experience in Indo-China could be blamed not on the troops, but rather on the leaders, both military and political. Like many of his comrades, he had returned home embittered and cynical.

He had gravitated into the world of crime in Southern France, both as a means of survival and of protest. Initially, he was convinced that the leaders of the underworld shared his views. Almost too late, he realized his mistake.

The bank in Montpellier was supposed to have been a simple job. Three men, including Maurice, had been chosen to enter the building, explode the safe, and leave with stacks of francs. Hours before the break-in, he had accidently overheard a conversation in a local bar in which it was revealed that the robbery was designed to fail. The police needed a public relations coup. The head of the crime syndicate had agreed to set one up, in exchange for relaxed enforcement. The men chosen for the job were considered expendable. Even worse for him, Maurice had been recognized as he left. They could not let him survive the night.

The balance of the evening was spent in hiding. He tried to reach his comrades before they started, but could not find them without exposing himself. Using back alleys and streets that remained dark, he made his way slowly to the bank. This route delayed him and the others started on their own. The bomb they had been given to detonate the safe was more powerful than they knew.

He had arrived just as the blast ripped apart the wall of the building, filling the early morning air with smoke and debris. Scattered amidst the wreckage he had found all that was left of his companions.

He had made his decision instantly. His knowledge of the deal, struck between the crime organization and the police, made him a danger to those in power on both sides. As the alarms of the city began to sound, he exchanged his identity papers with those of the dead and unrecognizable Maurice LeFebvre. He made his escape, leaving his former life buried in the rubble of the bank vault. The man he had been was presumed dead, and his former name all but forgotten, even by the caretaker of Hautecombe. The new man he had become would have nothing more to do with authority.

Maurice would meet the day's contingent of visitors, give his brief speech, and usher any members of the press quickly into the administration wing. For the rest of the day, especially if there were any filming being done, Maurice would essentially disappear.

Fr. Holden considered this behavior a bit odd, but never questioned the old man directly. He was only too happy to have someone, anyone, fill the role of warder.

Holden listened to the discussion at the front gate for a moment longer, then turned and walked through the garden. He entered the abbey and made his way to his office, resigned to another day of disturbance.

No sooner than he had settled into his chair, he heard the sounds of several voices in the outer office. His door opened to admit Fr. Cand along with Maurice. Behind them he could see a man and a woman, Americans from the style of their clothes, journalists from their demeanor. Maurice spoke in a conspiratorial voice.

"These two want to see you, Father. I don't think they speak French."

Holden rose to greet his visitors, his expression far from welcoming. He spoke in English, a language he very seldom used.

"Please, come in. You are from the American news organization?"

The young woman spoke first. Holden did not expect this.

"Yes, Father. I'm Ellen O'Neil, producer, from the CNN office in Paris. This is Mark Foster, my assistant."

She extended her hand, smiling at the priest's confusion.

"We drove down from Geneva last night and stayed in Aix-les-Bains."

She had trouble with the word "Aix," trying to pronounce it without sounding the final "X."

"The rest of our crew, along with the equipment, will be here in about an hour. We came early so we could get the ground rules settled with you."

Her speech was quite rapid and Holden was having difficulty keeping up with her.

" 'Ground rules?' I do not understand."

"I'm sorry, Father. I mean, how would you like us to behave? Where can we film? What areas are closed? Will you be available for an interview?"

"Ah, yes. I see. Phillipe Cand, my assistant, will help you. He speaks English somewhat better than I. There will be some time we can meet later this morning."

He looked past her to the young priest waiting at the door and spoke, this time in French.

"Father, please see to it that this news team understands the restrictions we have. I don't want to be disturbed until at least 10 o'clock. I leave the rest to you."

"Yes, Father"—then, in English—"Please follow me."

The group left the office, with Maurice closing the door and leaving as quickly as possible, distancing himself from the reporters.

In the outer office there was an awkward silence, broken by the CNN producer.

"He doesn't seem too pleased that we're here, Father."

The priest smiled and shook his head.

"I am afraid our abbot is rather disturbed by all the attention. After all, this is a monastery. My name is Phillipe Cand. I think you will find everything you need to see will be available to you."

"Thank you, Father."

"Please, you may call me Phillipe. If you will come with me, I can show you where to start."

Holden heard the muffled voices move off down the corridor. His head dropped into his hands as he groaned under his breath.

"This is only the beginning."

* * * * * * * * * * * * * * * *

Late afternoon found Holden again in his office. The day had gone better than expected. The interview with the American news team had been strained because of the subject and the language. The Swiss crew had also arrived, and that interview had actually been more difficult. With no barrier of words behind which to hide, Holden found himself exposed to intense questioning, particularly about the authenticity of the shroud. He found it necessary to continually escape, using the "we have no firm evidence" defense, a statement that left the listener open to draw the obvious and more sensational conclusion.

There had been one major crisis laid before him. For several days, the abbey had been the reluctant host to a team of investigators from the Vatican Museum. The two men were not priests and yet had been given quarters in the cloistered section of the monastery. The disruption of daily routine had been immediate. Some of the younger priests were fascinated by the entire episode, and the presence of the two researchers merely added to their enjoyment. The attraction was so great that they were often drawn away from their normal duties. For the older men, including Holden, the breach of the peace and order of their way of life was irritating.

After the noon hour, Holden had been called to the library. Father leClerq, one of the senior members of the order, was stationed outside the door, his face livid with rage.

"Gustav. Thank God you're here. Those men must be told to leave. This cannot go on."

"Calm down, Jean-Pierre. What happened?"

The elderly priest was the picture of the tonsured monastic, the smooth dome of his head rising above the meager fringe of gray hair. He drew a deep breath and folded his hands in front of him.

"I was beginning my customary afternoon meditation, seated as always by the window overlooking the lake. I had barely opened Aquinas when those . . . " he struggled to find a permissible descriptive word, could not, and continued " . . . people from Rome came bustling over. They said they needed my table. They asked if I would move. My God, their French is barely intelligible."

The abbot knew that his old friend could be excitable, but he too was outraged at these continued violations of their way of life. He entered the library, trying very hard to cast himself in a neutral the role.

Holden had mediated the dispute, although siding with his priest, and asking the two researchers to be more considerate and restrict their work to unoccupied areas of the library. Since the men spoke little French, communication was difficult. And since they were from the Vatican, they were not inclined to be apologetic. The abbot left with only a temporary and uneasy truce in effect.

At 4:30 that afternoon he had to place an international call to Laurent. He had been receiving pressure from all sides, asking him to force the historian to return, bringing the shroud back to Haute-combe. The pressure had come from his own Benedictine order, from the Vatican, and even from the French government. Consequently, he telephoned Laurent at least every three days.

Phillipe would handle the logistics of the call. In Tucson, where it was eight hours earlier, the staff at the University Catholic Center were beginning their day. He heard a series of clicks, a period of static-tinged waiting, and then the telltale single ring of the American phone system that told him the connection was completed.

"Good morning. Newman Center. May I help you?"

"Good morning. This is Father Cand at the Abbey of Haute-combe, calling for Father Carriere."

"One moment, please. I'll get him."

Phillipe heard the sound of the receiver being set down and someone bumping a chair as he rose from a desk. After several seconds, the familiar voice of Laurent was on the line.

"Yes, hello."

"Laurent, good to hear you. How are you doing?"

"Good morning, Phillipe . . . or should I say 'good afternoon.' I'm doing well. And how are you? What's happening there?"

"Very hectic. You're missing all of the activity. Father Holden wants to speak with you. Hold the line."

Phillipe left his desk and stepped to the door of the abbot's office.

"I have Laurent on the line, Father."

"Thank you, Phillipe."

Holden held his hand on the telephone and waited, eyes closed, as he composed himself for this conversation.

"Hello, Father Carriere. I hope everything is well with you."

"Thank you. Yes, I'm fine. Very busy, as you can imagine."

"And when do you think you will be returning? How soon will your work there be finished?"

The same question each time. Holden could already hear the gist of the answer, even before Laurent began.

"Well, there's still a good deal more to be done here. I expect that it should take a few more weeks."

"That's unfortunate, Father. A number of things have been going on at the abbey. The Vatican researchers seem to have found something in our library. I was certain you would want to be present to work with them."

There was silence at the other end for a moment.

"What Vatican researchers?"

"Oh, didn't I tell you? The Vatican has sent two young men . . . medieval specialists, I believe . . . to look through the archives of the monastery. They've been at work about three or four days now."

"May I ask who sent them?"

"Monsignor Corsini. He's the head of the Vatican Museum, isn't he?"

"Yes, yes. In what area of the archives are they working?"

It was clear that the idea of other investigators sorting through these records was disturbing to Laurent. Holden had counted on it.

"Oh, all parts. The request from the Vatican was that they have access to everything. When you return, I'm sure they would be happy to bring you up to date on their findings."

Holden could almost touch the tension that existed at the other end.

"I'll try to finish as soon as possible, Father."

"Good, good. And you'll be bringing the shroud with you?"

"Of course. Why do you ask?"

"I'm concerned for the safety of our relic. We all look forward to your return. God bless you."

The dial tone sounded after the connection had been broken. Only then did Holden replace the receiver on its cradle.

Phillipe came into the office, this time holding a number of papers. These he spread out on the desk before the abbot.

"Could you look at these, Father?"

"What are they?"

"I have been making some projections. Normally, in March we have only a small number of tourists. During the last two weeks that has changed. Based on this, I expect that during the summer season, the number will be dramatically increased over years past. The steamer company in Aix is considering adding extra trips due to the inquiries they have received already. If I'm correct, during the next few months the abbey would have a substantial increase in revenue from fees and donations. If that happens, we may not need to request support from the Order this year."

"Thank you, Phillipe. I'll look these over."

As his assistant left, Holden got up and walked to his lakeside window. One of his least pleasant duties each year was balancing the books and finding that, in order to keep Hautecombe in the black, he would have to seek extra funds from his superiors. Each year this happened he feared the Order would intervene, changing in some way the sanctuary he had so carefully tended.

If Phillipe was correct, they might be safe this year. He sighed, remembering the French saying, *"À quelque chose malheur est bon."* There was something equivalent in English, having to do with good coming from an ill wind.

CHAPTER SEVENTEEN

THE VATICAN
MARCH 24, 1999

"Yes, Father Holden, I understand . . . I'm certain it was quite upsetting . . . no, I believe they were wrong . . . nothing I've told them suggested that they could . . . yes, I'll make sure it doesn't happen again."

Msgr. Corsini spoke fluent French, as well as three other languages. He could use words to charm or to cajole. The irate priest had been playing directly into his net during the last few days.

"Father Holden. On another matter. Do you have any idea, as of yet, when Father Carriere will return? I trust you have spoken to him of the urgency of this matter."

Corsini waited while the answer was delivered.

"And does he know that our research team is at Hautecombe now? . . . Excellent. I'm sure that news should hasten his plans along. And what of the shroud? Does he have it with him? . . . Well then, does he have access to it?"

The news that the cloth was no longer in the hands of the priest disturbed him. He would have to alter the situation to his advantage. Perhaps a letter, on Vatican stationary, to the president of the University would be in order. Corsini knew of the strong connections between Arizona and Rome, especially of their collaborations in astronomy. He was certain such a letter would have the desired effect.

He finished his conversation with Holden, giving assurances that the disturbances caused by the Vatican investigation would be minimized. He thanked the abbot for his call and wished him a pleasant afternoon.

He was dressed that day in what he called his "Holy City uniform": formal black cassock, purple sash around his waist and, waiting on his desk, his biretta, the square, black cap with projecting vanes that so identified the Roman Catholic clergy. His mane of gray hair encircling a face of classic proportions made him appear as though he had escaped from a Renaissance painting on display in the gallery.

Msgr. Corsini needed to think, and he did this best in the open air. He left his corner office, exiting into a small, private hallway. At the end, a door led out into the Vatican Gardens, passing next to the Pinacoteca Court where tourists could stop for refreshments. He walked south along the Avenue of the Gardens, the dome of St. Peter's looming up before him. Next to the avenue on his left stretched the length of the Belvedere Palace, housing a large portion of the museum's collection.

Looking inward through the windows on the west side, he could see the heads of visitors as they processed through halls lined with tapestries and murals, and past alcoves filled with statuary, on their way to the apartments of the ancient popes and his own beloved Sistine Chapel. The press of tourists increased as Holy Week approached.

Strolling with his hands clasped behind his back, his head held high, he fell naturally into the part demanded of him by the surroundings. Any of the throng looking out into this private section of the Vatican could almost believe he was indeed an actor, hired to give the proper dressing to the backdrop of palms and pines.

He turned to his right, following the smaller paths that led deeper into the garden and away from public view. As he continued, he met a few other clerics: two Carmelite priests in brown robes and flowing white copes; a Franciscan missionary, still looking dazed from what must have been a recent arrival; and a trio of Dominican nuns in traditional habit. As usual, few words were spoken. A slight nod of the head, perhaps a "Good afternoon, Father" uttered with some deference to his ecclesiastical rank. In all, the encounters resembled the courtly behavior associated with royalty of past centuries.

Corsini followed smaller and smaller walkways, making for a region of the gardens behind the papal villa and offices of the Pontifical Academy of Sciences. Here, he found a small and hidden alcove created by hedges enclosing a fountain, presided over by two ancient Roman statues that were not included in the museum's regular displays. Stone benches completed the setting.

He sat and let his mind review his situation. The historian, Laurent Carriere, was the most urgent problem. During the year he had spent at the museum, the young Jesuit had developed a reputation as an aggressive and ambitious scholar who was loathe to share the spotlight. The abbot had done well to give Carriere the information that other investigators were in competition with him. There was still another piece to be moved, and Corsini had begun this the day before with his call to the office of the Papal Nuncio in Washington, D.C. He was confident Laurent and the shroud would soon be on their way back to Europe.

The cloth would return to Hautecombe accompanied by the fanfare of world attention. Holden had already agreed to transfer the relic to the Vatican Museum as soon as possible, wishing a speedy return to his solitude. The museum director had promised that the shroud would receive "expert documentation" and "careful and complete examination" in the hands of his research staff. If necessary, he could transfer Carriere to the museum, a prospect that seemed to please the abbot immensely.

Once the shroud was at the Vatican, the Society would have to be patient. It might take some time for the notoriety to die down. Of course, there would be no proof that the relic was in any way connected to Christ. Corsini would personally supervise this aspect of the research. It would simply be a piece of cloth that was nearly 2000 years old, important for historians, but of no religious significance. Eventually, the relic would find its way into the vast storage areas of the museum where access to it would be limited. After all, the Dead Sea Scrolls, relics of supreme importance, had been kept from scholars for years by those in control in Israel. It would be a simple matter.

In a few years he would be able to quietly transfer the shroud to the Society. At their next meeting, the leadership would have to discuss the various possibilities the return of the cloth presented. They could choose to remain secret, keeping their charge safe and passing on its care as before the tragedy of Gallipoli. On the other hand, there was the opportunity for a bold stroke. They could reveal themselves, document their history and the history of the winding sheet of Christ, and enshrine it in glory for all the world to see.

Costa Tarquin was a proponent of the latter course of action. He had already spoken of donating huge sums of money, practically his entire worth, to build a new chapel, not in Gallipoli, but in some safe haven. Perhaps in Rome, maybe in one of the Catholic cantons of Switzerland, possibly even in the United States.

Corsini was unconvinced. Display of their precious charge might mean the threat of another loss or, even worse, its destruction. There were enough terrorists in the world who might see this as the perfect target. Even Michaelangelo's *Pieta*, a universally revered work, had been the victim of a fanatical attack in St. Peter's itself. No place could be considered truly safe. He firmly believed obscurity was the best protection for the relic.

He heard footsteps approaching, stopping for a moment, and then continuing to the alcove. He looked up as his assistant, André Bernay, stood where the enclosing hedges were parted by the walkway, barely able to conceal his triumph. Somehow, no matter where the director chose to hide, the man always seemed to find him.

"Monsignor, sorry to disturb you."

"How did you . . . never mind. What is it?"

"Something very interesting has come up. As you know, we have been slowly building a computerized database with information related to our collection. The job is far from complete, although a large number of entries have been made. Over the last few days, I have been searching through that information. I used as search criteria two sets of key words: 'The Shroud of Jesus Christ' and 'Arimathea.' "

Corsini displayed no emotion, keeping his features unchanged, merely interested.

"Yes, go on. What did you find?"

"There were several times where the two words coincided. Obviously, most of them would be references to the New Testament descriptions of the death, burial, and resurrection of Our Lord. But three or four seem to be very different. I have not yet had a chance to look at the original text, but I think this could have something to do with the document I found earlier. In a few days I should be able to have more information."

The director nodded and motioned with his hand, indicating he understood.

"Excellent, André. I think that's good use of the new resource, although I'm not sure there's anything to this. How many people do you have working on this with you?"

"Only myself, Father. I didn't want to pull anyone else away from their work."

"Good, good. I think we should have someone follow up on this. However, I have something else for you. How would you like a field assignment?"

The scholar's eyes brightened. It was one thing to catalogue the finds of others; it was quite another to dig for information at the source.

"Where, when?"

"Our team at Hautecombe is running into, shall we say, some minor conflicts with the clergy. I need you on site to supervise the research and to keep the situation calm."

Bernay laughed, rolling his eyes.

"Don't tell me . . . it's Marco. He charges into a room with all the subtlety of a bull elephant. I can almost picture his relationship with the good monks of the abbey."

"I'm glad you understand. Is it possible for you to leave in the morning?"

"Yes, Father. But what about this?"

He held out the folder containing the results of his preliminary computer search. Corsini took it from him and laid it on the bench.

"I'll assign someone to pursue this for you while you're gone. It's not a problem."

"Thank you. It will be good to have my hands 'dirty' again. I'll have to go and close up some things on my desk right away."

Bernay left, clearly elated and totally distracted from his other projects. Corsini watched him leave the alcove and listened to his receding footsteps, all the while resting his hand on the brown folder at his side.

CHAPTER EIGHTEEN

TUCSON, ARIZONA
MARCH 30, 1999

The letters were increasing in frequency and intensity. The latest message demanded the return of the shroud or else, in the words of the author, " . . . your life will be terminated." All of the notes ended with the cryptic "Arimathea" printed at the bottom.

Josh had informed the University police about the threats. In response, he was told many people at the University received that kind of mail, especially when their names had been featured prominently in news articles. Their advice was to forget it; they offered no assistance.

There was other mail, many pieces from the followers of Rev. Slaughter and his Christian Revivalist Movement. These had become trivial. The focus of his fear was the receipt of the next threat. Josh also suspected he was being followed.

He was seeing the sandy-haired man everywhere he went. Josh was convinced this was no student. Even though he dressed the part, he never seemed to be heading to or from class, never had a book open, nor was he ever seen with other students, except for one equally suspect man. He was always in the periphery of Josh's vision, whether at the Student Union in the center of campus or at the medical school several blocks to the north.

As Josh approached the Life Sciences South Building he swiveled his head from side to side, almost in the manner of the prey searching for the predator he knew would strike. He opened the glass doors to the first-floor lobby and crossed quickly to the elevators. He kept his back against the two metal panels while he waited for one or the other car to descend. The bell sounded and he stepped inside. No one was following, for the moment.

The doors slid open to the lobby of the fifth floor, revealing a scene of confusion. Most of the departmental office staff were there,

181

along with students and technicians from the adjoining laboratory area. Everyone seemed to be gathered at the head of the corridor on which his office was located. Josh walked slowly to the rear of the crowd.

"Oh, Doctor Francis. Thank goodness you're here. Maybe you can do something about this."

Josh pushed his way to the front of the crowd, where he saw two men and a woman next to his office door. They were all kneeling, hands folded and heads bowed as if deep in prayer. He cautiously moved toward them, waiting for any sudden motion.

"Who are you? What do you want? What are you doing?"

One of the men, positioned a bit ahead of the others, spoke.

"Doctor Francis. We have come to receive the Blood of Christ."

"What did you say?"

"You have the Blood of Christ. Through what you have done in your laboratory you have brought us this precious gift. It is a sign of the coming of the millennium, as promised in Revelation 20. We are here to receive it from you."

The man tilted his head back and put his tongue out, eyes closed, and hands pressed together across his breast. The others followed his lead.

Josh began to tremble, his voice barely under control.

"Get out of here! Get up. Leave . . . now! Somebody call the campus police. I have nothing for you."

He grabbed the man by his arms and jerked him upright, shoving him into the crowd. Suddenly, he pulled him back, holding him so that their faces were inches apart. Josh's words came out in a whisper.

"Are you Arimathea?"

"What? What are you talking about?"

"I said, 'Are you Arimathea?' Is that your name?"

The eyes that glared out at the man were filled with a strange mix of anger and terror. This was not what he expected. He wrenched himself away from the fierce grip and staggered backward.

"No! . . . let go . . . we're leaving."

The three ran past Josh to the stairway exit at the end of the hall. Josh, with the crowd of onlookers at his back, watched the last of them disappear through the door.

He recovered his briefcase from where he had dropped it and, with no words to his colleagues, closed himself in his office.

He continued to shake uncontrollably for several minutes. On his desk was the series of frightening letters he had received. In the top left drawer was the rack containing the preserved bacteria in their glass ampules. It was not his habit to store such samples outside of his lab, but he had done so only because of their importance. The clone was his future, but for now it made him and his laboratory targets.

After he had calmed himself, he found a small plastic case lined with cushioning foam used to ship vials of biological materials. He transferred the four sealed containers into this case, snapped it shut, and dropped it into his briefcase. He would destroy any other existing samples of the clone in his laboratory, making sure the only possible source would be these ampules. Mac had already done this with the extracts from the shroud and he would follow suit. When this madness was over, perhaps his work could continue. Until that time, he would keep the ampules with him and would tell no one.

* * * * * * * * * * * * * * * *

Laurent waited in the lounge of the Newman Center for the arrival of his visitor. The "visitor," in this instance, was Monsignor Patrick Bennett, the assistant to the Papal Nuncio, the diplomatic representative of the pope in Washington, D.C. A telephone call yesterday had announced that Laurent should make himself available between 10 a.m. and noon the next day. Msgr. Bennett would be stopping in Tucson for a few hours on his way to meetings in Los Angeles. When Laurent asked what the nature of this meeting would be, he was simply told that the interests of the Vatican in matters related to the shroud would be discussed.

At 11:30 a.m., a taxi stopped in front of the Center. Laurent watched from within as the passenger paid the fare and got out. He was short, thin, and balding. He wore the black suit and collar of the clergy with no evidence of his rank. Laurent knew nothing about this man, other than his name. Had he asked the right people in Washington, he might have found out that Msgr. Bennett was from an old Bostonian family, that his appointment to the papal office in D.C. was considered a step toward a bishop's miter, and that he was well known in diplomatic circles as a tough negotiator. One thing he would not have found out was that, beneath his black shirt, he wore the gold medallion of the Society.

Laurent met him at the door.

"Good morning, Monsignor."

"Hello, Father Carriere. It's good to meet you. Is there somewhere we can speak privately?"

Laurent gestured to the hallway leading away from the lobby.

"Yes. There is a conference room over here."

The room, used for occasional small meetings, was simple, with a table and folding chairs in the center. The walls were wood paneled and adorned sparsely, highlighted by a plain crucifix. Laurent waited for Msgr. Bennett to enter and then closed the door to ensure that they would be undisturbed.

"Please, sit down, Monsignor."

"Thank you. This is my first time in Tucson. I'm sorry I can't stay longer. It seems to be a fascinating city."

Laurent waited for what the Americans called "small talk" to end. He was anxious to get to the heart of whatever matter brought this man to him.

"Your shroud seems to have caused a good deal of commotion. By the way, I hope you don't mind that we speak in English."

"No, that is fine."

"Tell me, Father. What do you think about the origin of this relic?"

The question seemed straightforward. Laurent answered without hesitation.

"I believe we can verify nothing more than its age at this time. There is no evidence linking this piece of cloth to any individual, especially to Jesus."

"Exactly so. That's the Vatican's position. That's why we must be very careful about what happens next. Arrangements have been made with your abbot, Father Holden, that, as soon as you return to Hautecombe, the shroud will be brought directly to Rome."

"Excuse me. Holden has agreed to this?"

"Of course. It's the only way we can prevent wild speculation. In Rome, facilities exist for a complete examination of the history of this cloth, facilities not present at Hautecombe or even here in Tucson."

Laurent suspected they were trying to take the shroud away from him.

"But I am the one who found the cloth. I have done the initial research into the origin. I do not understand why this is being done."

"Oh, did I forget to mention? You are being offered a post at the Vatican Museum. Father Holden has reluctantly agreed that you might better serve the Church there."

Laurent did not think Holden's agreement had been at all reluctant.

"Will this be a temporary position?"

"No. Quite the opposite. You would be a member of the permanent research staff, specializing in medieval studies. That is, if you choose to accept."

Bennett's smile was disarming. Laurent had expected a battle. Instead, he was winning a victory with what appeared to be no contest.

"What of the shroud? Who will continue the research regarding its origin?"

"Naturally, you will be involved in this. After all, as you've said, you've done the initial work. All we ask is that you finish up here within the next few days and return to Hautecombe with the shroud. You will be in Rome as soon after that as possible."

Laurent had been caught completely off guard. He was at a loss for a response. Bennett rose, indicating an end to the meeting, and strode to the door.

"I'm certain you'll find this most attractive. You deserve the position and the accolades because of your discovery. Now, if you could show me to the office, I'd like to get a cab back to the airport. I have a 2 o'clock flight to Los Angeles."

As Msgr. Bennett left the building, he grinned in recognition of his own abilities. The mission had been ridiculously easy. The young Jesuit would be trapped by his own ambition.

Minutes later, the dazed and confused historian watched as the taxi carrying Bennett pulled away from the curb. He remained in the lobby long after the cab had left, peering through the window of the Center, as if he could discern in the wake of the man's departure the meaning of this encounter.

* * * * * * * * * * * * * * * *

Richard Sutton waited outside the president's office in the Administration Building. His appointment was scheduled for 1 p.m. President Varner was known for her punctuality and he expected no delay.

The LAC director had not been spared the public outcry that had been occurring over the shroud. He had been the recipient of letters, mostly negative, and telephone calls, mostly bitter and accusing. The laboratory staff was developing a siege mentality. Their work was suffering; something had to change.

"President Varner is ready for you, Doctor Sutton."

He was ushered in and found Elizabeth Varner on her feet behind her desk, ready to greet him.

"Hello, Richard. I suspect there's some problem or you wouldn't have been so insistent on this meeting. Please, sit down."

Sutton remained standing, as did Dr. Varner. He spoke without any further ceremony.

"I'll come right to the point, then. This shroud business has upset things terribly. I do believe it must be sent back to France. We can no longer function properly in this atmosphere. I'm afraid I can't be responsible if anything should happen."

Dr. Varner retrieved a folder from a tray on top of the desk. This she opened and displayed for Sutton.

"Richard, take a look at these." As she spoke, she lifted each sheet of paper and tossed it to one side. "Here is a letter from the abbot of Hautecombe, ensuring us the shroud rightfully belongs there. Here is another from the director of the Vatican Museum, claiming ultimate responsibility for the relic. Here, a letter from the French Ministry for Culture, again citing ownership. Another, from Senator Sam Johnson, chiding us for performing these kinds of experiments and warning that possibly the shroud and certainly the DNA clone should be kept at the University until further investigation. There's even a letter from a Count Melano in Aosta, Italy. He claims to be descended from the Savoy royalty and, therefore, the sole heir to the shroud."

Sutton was bending forward to examine each piece as she spoke. He looked up as she finished, already knowing the answer to his question.

"What does this mean for us?"

"It means, Richard, that neither the shroud nor the clone is leaving this campus until the legal staff has a chance to sort out our liability. All we need on top of everything else is an expensive lawsuit to recover something we shouldn't have let go. No, the shroud stays here for the time being."

"I don't think my staff can stand much more of this attention."

Dr. Varner heard his words, but the haunted look on his face told her he was speaking more for himself than for anyone else.

* * * * * * * * * * * * * * *

Late afternoon found Laurent seated on an iron bench in the inner courtyard of the residence portion of the Newman Center. One-story red brick apartments bordered the patio. Potted plants and hedges lent an air of peacefulness to the setting. He felt anything but peace.

His head was bowed and his arms were resting on his knees. He did not see the Dominican priest standing across from him.

"What is it, Laurent? You look defeated."

Father Simon Bell had been a university chaplain since the day of his ordination. As he approached his fortieth birthday, the age difference between him and the students seemed even greater. In spite of this, he had not lost his sensitivity for their problems, nor had they lost their trust in him. He had a reputation as an excellent counselor. It was in this spirit that he approached Laurent, who looked up from his dark musings to respond.

"Oh, Simon . . . hello. I am all right, really. There is nothing to worry about."

Simon took a seat next to him. Fr. Bell was marathon-thin, with a sun-weathered face that had resulted from years and miles of running. With age he was slowing, but not stopping.

"I didn't get a chance to meet your visitor today. He looked important."

Gently, Simon drew him out until, without realizing it, Laurent had told of the calls from Holden, the visit from Msgr. Bennett and the pressure to return with the shroud. He mentioned the position in Rome and his years of waiting for such an opportunity.

"Then it sounds like you should be happy. You've got what you wanted."

Laurent looked at his hands before answering.

"I am not sure, Simon. This offer to work in Rome. Something is wrong. In English you say 'I see a rat' . . . is that correct?"

Simon laughed. "You mean, 'I smell a rat.' "

"Yes. Somehow the offer does not seem sincere."

"Why did you come here, Laurent?"

"I do not understand."

"What was your purpose? What did you hope to accomplish here?"

"Of course, I came with the shroud to have it examined and the age determined."

"Certainly, that's true. But what were your real reasons? What do you think this shroud means? Before you reply, I know all of the 'facts,' as you call them. Don't answer now as a medieval specialist, but rather as a priest and a man. What are your feelings about it?"

"I do not know. I have never thought about this point."

"Perhaps this relic is with us as a challenge. Maybe our faith is being tested. Possibly you need to examine your motives. Did you come here for the historical and religious reasons associated with the shroud? Or, did you come here for yourself? There's a set of questions to ponder."

Simon rose from the bench and walked slowly across the court-yard, entering the door leading back into the main building. Laurent was left sitting as before, except that his gaze was fixed on the empty space left by the departing priest.

* * * * * * * * * * * * * *

Leslie lay awake, one arm draped over Josh, watching the digital face of the bedside clock as it registered 2 a.m. He was asleep now. Minutes earlier he had cried out, fighting underneath the bed covers. She had soothed him, quieting him with her voice. He had never come fully alert and slipped quickly back into another, hopefully calmer, dream.

She knew about the letters and the threats. Today those "people" were at his door. She was frightened, more because of the terror he could no longer hide than anything else.

Before dinner he had collapsed across the bed in exhaustion. As she prepared the table for their meal, she had to move his open briefcase. She saw the plastic box and inside the four ampules, the same ones, she believed, that she had seen in his office. He never mentioned that he had brought them home.

They ate dinner sitting on the couch with the TV tuned to Channel Four. The evening news was on in the background, but they paid little attention until they heard the words "Shroud of Hautecombe" as the lead-in to the next story. Tom Brokaw was turning the narration over to a reporter in the field.

On the screen was the face of Rev. Edwin Slaughter in a clip taken from one of his recent television ministry shows. The stage setting for his sermon, with its immense pulpit and the choir on tiers behind, made Rev. Slaughter seem even larger than his true physical size. He thundered in the time-honored style of many evangelical preachers. His topic was Dr. Joshua Francis.

"It must be clear to all of you that this Doctor Francis, this godless scientist, is indeed in league with the Antichrist so terrifyingly described in the book of Revelation. To have experimented with the precious Shroud of the Saviour was truly a sacrilegious act." The camera showed the congregation nodding in approval and Slaughter continued. "But some good can come from even this. Write to Doctor Francis and to his University. Persuade them to change their minds and their hearts. You can ask them to stop the blasphemy before it is too late."

The reporter described the letter writing campaign the CRM was pushing, with a shot of the mail being delivered at the University Administration Building. A brief cut from the news conference at which the shroud dating was announced ended with a freeze-frame of Josh's face, caught in mid-sentence.

At the end of the report, Leslie set her plate and his aside and lowered the volume. "Did you know that was being shown?"

"No. I had no idea. These letters have been appearing steadily from the followers of Slaughter, but I didn't know about this report." He looked at her, anguish on his face. "Do you think what I've done is a sacrilege?"

"Oh, Sonny, of course not. You couldn't have guessed beforehand that this would happen. Don't do this to yourself."

"Les . . . I don't know how to put this . . . I think there's more to the shroud than the data and the historical facts. All of my training says to ignore the hysteria and continue the investigation. Still, a part of me wants to walk away from the confusion and believe again, like I did as a child."

She pulled him to her and held him close. She could feel the shudders in his body as he fought to understand and to reconcile the conflict between his old self and this emerging person.

They went to bed and made love in the gentle way she had come to know during the last few weeks. She held on to him as the minutes crept slowly across the face of the clock, and awaited the coming of sleep, or an end to the night.

CHAPTER NINETEEN

TUCSON, ARIZONA
MARCH 31, 1999

The glowing red lines of the numbers on the digital clock re-formed themselves to read 2:00 a.m. Nikos sat up on the bed, took a deep breath, and after a long moment, let it out as though unleashing the vanguard of his energy. It was time to go.

His letters had been a failure. Not one response had appeared at the post office box. There seemed to be no obvious change in the pattern of behavior of Dr. Francis. In addition, it seemed that, any day, the priest would finish his work and decide to leave, taking the shroud with him. What he needed was some additional leverage.

His new plan was born of desperation. During the course of his daily activity, he had followed the movements of the faculty involved in the project and knew which buildings held their labs and offices. By posing as a reporter over the telephone, he had learned that the shroud was being held in an impregnable safe in the LAC facility. The DNA clone, however, he was certain was still in the possession of the young scientist who had made it.

If he had the clone, perhaps he could arrange a trade. The scenario he had created convinced him this was a possibility. For two days he had worked out the minute details of his attempt. At last he was ready. He was also armed.

Several years before he had bought and licensed a gun, a .38 caliber pistol. The pretext had been his frequent trips from San Rafael into San Francisco to attend to the sales and shipping needs of DSI. The wave of crime in the inner cities, so much a part of the fabric of the nineties, had swept through the culture, leaving in its wash a citizenry bearing arms in a way never envisioned by the founding fathers.

Nikos imagined that the gun provided him with a large measure of protection. Now he took it with him on every business trip, secreting it in his checked luggage to avoid detection as he boarded a plane. The pistol, in its small holster, along with a box of ammunition, was still in the leather suitcase at the foot of the bed. He removed it and set it down on the dresser as he prepared himself.

A series of packages from stores in a local mall lay on the bed. Quickly unwrapping the clothes he had purchased, he began to dress. Posturing in front of the mirror, he judged the overall effect. He did not see himself for what he appeared: a caricature of a thief, his costume copied from movies rather than practice. Instead he saw a powerful figure clad in black pants, shirt, and jacket. His hands were covered with black leather driving gloves to complete the effect. The pistol, in its holster, was at his waist.

He left his room, descended to the lobby of the hotel and walked quickly out into the parking lot, hoping no one at the desk had seen him. The drive to the Life Sciences South Building was short, with no traffic on the street. The parking lot next to the building was empty. He turned off the engine and headlights and waited.

This same drive had been practiced on the two previous nights and, each time, he had clocked the passage of the University police patrol car. As expected, the cruiser appeared at the corner of Park Avenue and Lowell Street at 2:15 a.m. Nikos slid down behind his steering wheel so his car would appear unoccupied. The officers took no notice of the parking lot as they crossed in front of him. They were engaged in an animated conversation and their car rolled slowly past the building and continued east.

Nikos opened the door and stood next to his car. The south facade of the building was bathed in the eerie yellow of the sodium vapor street lamps. All of the windows on this side were dark. He began a meticulous walk around his target, convinced, at least from the outside, that the building was deserted.

Metal staircases zigzagged their way down both the western and eastern ends of the building, connecting the various floors with ground level. Architecturally, the stairs added an external flair to the structure that could only be achieved in the warm, dry climate of the Southwest. But the University planners intervened, insisting that at the landings there be some protection from illegal entry. In answer, the designers sketched in, on the east end, a circular wall of concrete, ten feet high, preventing access to the stairs except from inside the building. However, vanity insisted that the wall match the overall motif. It had two inset bands running along its length at roughly four and six feet above the ground.

Nikos approached the guard wall and, using the indentations as handholds, quickly pulled himself to the top. From there he could reach the railing of the staircase and jump. The noise of his feet hitting the metal platform of the landing resounded through the empty plaza. He crouched low, waiting for some sign of movement in return.

He made his way upward to each level, checking for a door inadvertently left open and watching at each turn for anyone in the street below. On the third level he found one that was closed but not locked, relying on the security of the guard wall. After a quick survey of the street area below, he entered the laboratory wing of the building.

The listing in the University directory had told him that Francis' office was on the fifth floor. The service elevator at the east end of the building took him up two more flights.

The hallways were dimly lit by one or two overheads left on for the convenience of the night watch. All doors to the laboratories were closed. He realized he did not know which rooms belonged to Francis. In this part of the building there were only numbers. Taking a chance, he pulled down the handle on the entrance to Room 514 and looked in.

Nikos was completely unfamiliar with biological research. The whine of centrifuge drives, the constant clicking on and off of relays, and the glow of panel lights on the instruments made the room seem as though it were being attended by some ghostly army of technicians. Even if this were the Francis lab, where would he begin to search for the clone? He closed the door and stepped back into the hallway.

The office he wanted was number 574. He passed through the double doors separating the laboratories from the administration area. The lobby contained an open stairwell descending one level. Rooms were arranged in clusters around this central space. Directional signs on the walls indicated that 574 was to the left.

Outside the door a nameplate identified the office: "Dr. Joshua Francis, Department of Molecular Biology." This time he found a lock in his way. The translucent glass panel that filled the center of the door revealed nothing of the interior.

He had come too far to be blocked by this. Taking the gun from his pocket and reversing it to use as a hammer, he struck the glass near the doorknob. Once, twice, a third time. The only result was the echo of his activity throughout the building. In desperation, taking a full swing, he brought the metal butt of the gun hard against the pane. A large, jagged opening appeared as glass shards flew inward. He reached in and opened the door from the other side.

The spill from the lamps in the plaza north of the building provided enough light for his mission. The office was a jumble of books, magazines, and papers stacked on the desk, the adjoining bookcase, and even the floor. The computer console and keyboard were just visible amid the apparent disarray.

How would he find the clone? What it would look like? In a glass jar, swimming in formaldehyde, reminiscent of old science fiction movies? Locked away somewhere, barely identifiable to the uninitiated?

First, the obvious: the desk drawers. Nothing. More papers and the expected office supplies. He rummaged around on the desk, scattering journals and memos as his search became more frantic. His attention focused on the bookshelves. Perhaps hidden behind this volume—no, this one—or this one. The books opened crazily as he sent each crashing to the floor. His frenzy was interrupted by the sudden glare of headlights reflected from the street below.

His manic activity changed abruptly, replaced by an immobility triggered by fear. Below, he could see a police car had stopped at the curb west of the building. An officer got out, flashlight in hand, and walked across the grass toward the main entrance.

Someone in the plaza below, perhaps a student out late and returning to the dorm, may have seen his shadowy figure and reported suspicious activity. Or, it could be a routine visit by part of the night crew. In any case, he knew he had only seconds to escape.

The violent activity of moments before gave way to an icy restraint as he analyzed his situation. The policeman would come into the building at the office end, using the main elevators. His best chance was to escape in the opposite direction.

He left the room and ran back down the hall, into the laboratory area and to the end of the building where the door led to the exterior staircase. As his hand rested on the push bar, he realized how easily he could be seen and heard descending the metal steps. The service elevator he had used before was at this end of the hall. He pushed the call button and heard the welcome sound of the ascending car. An eternity later, the metal door slid open and he was on his way to the first floor.

At the bottom he found himself in a small loading area with three exit doors. His sense of direction and of the layout of the building told him one of these would let him out into the space between Life Sciences South and the building to its east. He opened it cautiously, fully expecting to see a waiting cop with gun drawn. No one was there, as yet. His car was in the parking lot to the south, only about twenty-five yards away. There was no way to guess how close the nearest patrol was. He would have to risk the street and the lights.

Trying to walk normally was next to impossible, as his legs, under the impetus of his pounding heart, moved faster than he intended. In a matter of seconds he found himself at the side of his car and into the front seat. He ducked down as the lights of a second patrol car swung around the corner. After this next wave of officers had entered the building and were out of direct sight, he started the engine. Without headlights, he drove across the lot and onto the nearest city street.

Driving back to the hotel, Nikos hammered out his frustration on the steering wheel. In spite of everything, he had not been caught, but had come away with nothing to show. Even though Francis would no doubt feel even more threatened than before, Nikos was still powerless to force them to turn over the shroud.

Interlude Five

L'Abbaye d'Hautecombe
Lac du Bourget, France
December 15, 1602

Father Luc Reynard hurried down the steep embankment to the shore of the lake. His footing constantly slipped out from under him as he made his way through low bushes. He was already covered with brambles and bleeding from several cuts. Below, voices were shouting, urging the last stragglers on. He saw very little. The thick layer of scudding clouds that pressed down upon the alpine valley obliterated what little moonlight there might have been at two in the morning.

He stopped to jerk the hem of his cassock away from a clutching branch. The panic that had infected the entire abbey since the news of Duke Emmanuel's rout at Geneva had reached its height earlier that evening and had not abated. Everyone, including the abbot himself, was certain that, at any minute, the forces of the Calvinists would emerge from the woods bordering the elevated clearing, the "high comb," on which they lived. At that point, all of their lives were forfeit.

Beyond their lives was the need to prevent the sacrilege that these iconoclasts would wreak upon their chapel. The day had been spent packing up, hiding, or even reverently destroying every statue, picture, vessel, or other religious object.

Luc was the most senior of the monks who served as sacristans in the chapel. As such, it had been his responsibility to care for the golden reliquary enshrined on the altar. This, above all, must not fall into the hands of the enemy.

A new wall was being built such that the vestibule could accommodate a larger ceremonial entrance. The work had been completed, except for a small section next to the monument of Amadeus VI, the Green Count. Luc had done much of the work himself, enjoying again the use of the trade he had learned as a young boy, following his father from one mason's job to the next.

He had been the last one in the chapel that evening, staying long after the others had taken the smaller statues and crucifixes away to safety. Without witnesses, he had removed the reliquary box, wrapped it in several layers of cloth, and lowered it into the narrow space in between the stone walls of the church and vestibule, through an opening that had been left near the top. Working faster than he could remember, his hands moving on their own, he had lain the stones in fresh mortar to seal the hole.

No one had any idea how long it would be until the abbey was once again in their hands. His only thought had been that the reliquary and its contents should be hidden for as long as necessary. Until their return, its location would be known only by those monks to whom he eventually chose to reveal his secret.

He had stepped back and removed his mason's apron. His hands were encrusted white from his labor. It was time to go.

As he approached the edge of the lake, the light from a lone lantern flickered over the four small boats. Tethered to the shore, the skiffs that held a single mast and a crude lateen sail seemed more than fragile.

"Hurry, please, Father. There's not much time."

He clambered over the side, finding a seat along the gunnel in the center of the craft. With the press of time and fear, the boats were dangerously overloaded, the water coming close to swamping the vessels even as they floated near the shore.

The winds that had swirled across the surface of the lake earlier, pushing the clouds into the valley, now blew steadily as the chill storm gathered its strength for a descent from the peaks above.

"Shove off! Quickly, before it's too late!"

The four boats were forced away from the shore and out into the open water. Several of the younger men applied the oars to steady their drift while the sail was adjusted. The wind was in their favor, coming out of the northwest and pushing them toward Chambery and safety.

They were more than 200 yards off shore when the first blast of the gale struck. As if slapped by an unseen hand the small boats heeled over in recoil. Those sitting on the gunnels who had no handholds were thrown into the December waters of the lake. Luc was among them.

At an earlier time in his life he would have laughed at the mishap and either climbed back aboard or turned and swam for shore. At an earlier time he would have had the strength. Instead, the wool cassock, weighted down by the water, dragged at his arms and legs. His thrashing movements only served to entangle him further. The shouts of those still in the boats were counterpoint to the cries of those sinking beneath the dark surface of Lac du Bourget.

The first mouthful of water caused a surge of adrenaline that propelled him back to the surface. It was a temporary reprieve. A prayer to the Virgin raced through his mind as he slipped a last time beneath the roiling waves.

CHAPTER TWENTY

TUCSON, ARIZONA
MARCH 31 - APRIL 1, 1999

The office door was crisscrossed by a large "X" formed of yellow plastic ribbon with the words "Police Line: Do Not Cross" emblazoned at intervals along its length. Josh tried to focus on it, his eyes burning from lack of sleep.

The call had come at 3:30 a.m., startling both him and Leslie. He had groped for the phone next to the bed, his voice slurred with sleep as he answered.

"Yes, hello . . . "

"Doctor Francis? Sorry to disturb you. This is Officer Vega of the University police. I'm afraid that someone has broken into your office. Your laboratory has not been entered, as far as we can determine. We'd like you to come down and tell us what might be missing."

The news had brought him instantly awake. Minutes later they were on their way, flying along vacant streets, as though getting there sooner would somehow lessen the damage.

Several patrol cars, both University and city, had been parked near the main entrance with lights flashing. Josh and Leslie were stopped at the door until he showed his identification.

The fifth-floor lobby had been a flurry of activity, reminiscent of the previous morning. This time the crowd consisted of uniformed men scouring the floor, looking for anything that might be evidence. Josh had picked his way through, Leslie in hand, both of them trying hard not to interfere with the work.

At the door to his office they had been met by a University police officer.

"Doctor Francis, I'm Officer Joe Vega. Thank you for coming in right away."

Josh had taken the extended hand but had not registered the words that were being said. Instead, he had looked at what was left of his office. The broken glass on the floor told the story of the forced entry. Everywhere he looked he saw books and papers strewn about. Journals had been trampled in an attempt to get at other things on the bookshelves. Drawers hung open, their contents protruding out at odd angles. Officer Vega was still speaking.

"I know it's probably hard to tell, but we need to know if anything is missing."

"They didn't get what they came for."

"Sir? How's that?"

Josh turned his attention to the policeman.

"I said, 'They didn't get what they came for.' "

"How do you know that?"

"Because I have it with me . . . at home."

"What? Who do you think did this? What do you have that someone might want?"

Josh walked over to the desk and retrieved the stack of letters. He held out the entire set to the officer.

"I have been receiving these messages, about one each day, for the past eleven days. Each one gets progressively more demanding, more threatening."

Joe Vega had been methodically trained in investigative procedures. He did not touch the papers himself. Instead, he took a manila envelope from among the debris, emptied its contents, and had Josh place the evidence inside. He continued his questioning.

"What did they want here? The shroud is in a safe over there." He gestured out the window at the massive Gould-Simpson Building on the other side of the plaza.

"I think they were after the DNA clone I produced. I'm sure we'll find nothing else is missing."

They had looked and he was right.

He had returned home with Leslie but neither of them could sleep and he was back in his building at 9 a.m. His office was officially a crime scene. The ampules containing the clone were still in his briefcase, and were now with him wherever he went.

"Doctor Francis." He turned as his name was called to find the main office receptionist waving a pink message slip.

"I was about to tape this to the wall next to your . . . well, outside your office. You received an urgent call from"—she referred to the paper—"Doctor Helen Wright at NIH. You must get in touch with her this morning."

NIH was the universal shorthand for the National Institutes of Health, that collection of congressionally-mandated units charged with curing the physical ills of the country. More often than not their budgets, and therefore their various missions, became the subject of heated political battles rather than reasoned scientific inquiry. The research to which Josh's laboratory was dedicated was funded by a grant from the National Cancer Institute, one of the largest of the organizations.

"Thank you. May I use a phone in the office? I'm afraid I can't . . . "

She cut him off before he could mention the tragedy.

"Certainly. No problem. You can use Jean's desk for a little privacy. She's away for the morning."

Once alone in the borrowed office, Josh took a deep breath to search for some remnant of his composure. He dialed the Bethesda number and waited.

"Grants Management, may I help you?"

"This is Doctor Francis, calling for Doctor Wright."

"I'll see if she's in."

While he waited, seated at the desk, he held the phone to his ear with one hand as the other massaged his forehead, trying to relieve the tension.

"Hello, Doctor Francis. Thank you for calling back."

"Your message sounded urgent."

"It is. As you know, the Institute must keep track of all our grants and contracts. Of course, we've heard of your latest experiments using DNA isolated from this relic called the Shroud of Hautecombe. We are assembling a small panel and we'd like you to appear in person to discuss this work."

Josh was not sure how he should interpret this news. Were they interested in his results because of the scientific excitement, or was there some other reason for this meeting?

"When would you like me to come?"

"As soon as possible. Would tomorrow fit your schedule? I know it's short notice, but the members of our panel can all meet on Friday morning."

"I suppose I could fly out in the morning and be available on Friday. Who will be on the panel?"

"Oh, just NIH staff members. You'll know some of them. Let's say 9 a.m. Friday morning, Conference Room 15 in Building 31C. I've taken the liberty of reserving a room for you at the Holiday Inn-Bethesda, on Wisconsin Avenue. We'll see you then."

"Fine, I'll bring . . . " Before he could finish she had broken the connection.

* * * * * * * * * * * * * * *

"But it would be the most secure place to keep them."

Josh argued with a reluctant Richard Sutton that the samples of the DNA clone would be best stored with the shroud in the LAC safe. The director was totally opposed, especially after what had happened the night before.

"I don't like any of this. We've never been under this kind of pressure and scrutiny before. It's impossible. I wish the relic had stayed in that wall in France. And what about the burglary of your office? These religious fanatics could do serious damage here. Remember what happened several years ago when those animal rights maniacs destroyed an entire building."

"Please. I have nowhere else to go with the ampules. I'm afraid to keep them in my lab or office or even my home."

Sutton sensed that his young colleague had come to the same realization as he. They were dealing with something that went beyond the walls of the University.

"Come with me."

He led Josh out of his office and down the hall to a small room off the main examination suite they had used that first day. The cubicle housed a desk with a computer keyboard and terminal, and a massive safe bolted to the floor in one corner. No handles or combination knobs were visible on its front door. Instead, a series of cables ran from its back to the computer.

"This safe can only be opened by someone with access to the appropriate codes. I want you to know them, since your samples will be inside. The code words are known only by myself and my administrative assistant. Also, you should have keys to the building and this room in case you should ever need them. Harry will see to it."

Sutton typed the word "SAFE" after the screen prompt. The program activated and requested a name. He entered "LACSAFE" and was queried for an authorized name.

"Use my name here." He typed, "SUTTON." The program next asked for the password. Sutton's fingers skipped over the keyboard but the screen showed "XXXXXXXX."

"You must use the password 'CHRIST'S.' " As he was speaking, he wrote the letters on a piece of paper next to the computer. "Enter the word exactly like this."

Josh looked at him with open amazement. The director realized the confusion.

"Oh, it's not what you think. The password is simply my college at Cambridge. It's a bit of irony I haven't found time to alter."

He pressed the "enter" key and, after a moment, the thick steel doors slid open in two directions from a barely perceptible seam, revealing a shelved interior. Alone in the center was the gold reliquary box containing the shroud. Josh put the small plastic case of ampules alongside it, juxtaposing the ancient and the modern. Sutton was again at the computer console.

"To close the door, you simply quit the program." By way of example, he typed "QUIT" and the doors glided shut, clicking into register and leaving a smooth, featureless surface.

The director rose and faced the young man.

"Doctor Francis. I am sympathetic, you know. I don't really want to be involved in this any longer, any more than you do. I wish there were some way that these things could disappear. But that's not possible. As long as the president of the University says so, we will keep them safe in here."

* * * * * * * * * * * * * * *

APRIL 1, 1999

What little early morning traffic existed in Tucson was rapidly thinning as Leslie returned from the airport. Josh had walked through the balance of the previous day in a trance, arranging for his flight and collecting the papers he would need for his meeting. He had spent some time in the afternoon talking with Laurent, sharing their concerns with the closeness that their friendship had produced. During the night, she had awakened twice to find him out of bed and at the window. Neither of them had slept very much.

There were not many houses on the cul-de-sac where Josh lived, so she noticed the strange car at once. As she parked in the gravel driveway, she saw the man at the front door.

He was dressed completely in black with his hands hidden in the pockets of his jacket. When she got closer to him, she could see that his clothes were rumpled, as though he had slept in them. His hair was uncombed and he was in need of a shave. Leslie would have thought him an unfortunate derelict except for two things: the expensive look of his clothes and the manic expression on his face. Caution made her stop some distance away from him.

"Can I help you?"

"I'm looking for Doctor Francis."

"I'm afraid he's not in right now."

"When do you expect him back?"

"Look . . . what is it you want?"

"Is he at the University? In his office?"

Leslie was not intimidated in most situations and was immediately on guard. Her instincts told her she must get rid of this man as quickly as possible. She went on the offensive.

"Perhaps I can get you some help. I'll phone the police and ask them to send a social services representative over. I'm sure they will take care of whatever is wrong here."

The mention of the police had a noticeable effect. The man jerked his hands free and waved them in front of his body, warding off the idea.

"No, no! That's okay. I'll be on my way. I'll try to see Doctor Francis another time."

He began to edge his way toward the street and his car. As he passed in front of her, she caught a metallic flash from inside his jacket. Suspended from a chain around his neck was a gold medallion. In the brief instant of that passage she saw the design and her photographic senses registered the raised image of three crossed nails.

CHAPTER TWENTY-ONE

BETHESDA, MARYLAND
APRIL 2, 1999

Wisconsin Avenue passed through Bethesda on its way from the Maryland suburbs into the spoked array of arterials feeding the District. The name changed from "Rockville Pike" to "Wisconsin" as it crossed the Beltway. At this point, the busy street separated two large government reservations: the U.S. Naval Hospital on the east and the main grounds of the National Institutes of Health on the west. Josh walked slowly north on Wisconsin Avenue early on the morning after his arrival. He had spent another sleepless night, this time at the Holiday Inn two blocks south of NIH. He had about 45 minutes before his meeting with the NIH investigative team and, in order to clear his mind, had decided on a long walk across the "campus," as NIH referred to its facilities. His preoccupation with the coming events caused him to miss the man who left the hotel behind him and followed along about a half-block distant.

He veered off Wisconsin Avenue and followed a footpath up the hill toward the massive National Library of Medicine. He walked along the series of streets weaving through the campus, following the signs to Building 31C that housed much of the central administration of the Institutes. The grounds themselves were impressive, with large expanses of lawn and trees decorated with the first leaves of spring. The park-like scene was interrupted occasionally by buildings of obvious governmental architecture. The brick sameness of the structures was broken only by the columns and the facade of Building 1, the original Public Health Service home. Building 31C was on the extreme northern edge of the campus, surrounded by large parking lots. The man following him waited at the edge of one of these lots, withdrawn back into the trees.

The briefcase Josh held contained his notes, his experimental results, and everything else dealing with the shroud project, except the samples of the recombinant DNA clone.

The meeting was to be held in a conference room on the tenth floor. Josh took the elevator, got off in the lobby area, and found the receptionist.

"Good morning. I'm Doctor Francis. I have a meeting . . . "

"Yes, Doctor. Down the hall . . . Room 15." The young woman gestured to her left.

Her directions brought him to the door, where he arrived two minutes before the appointed time. He took a deep breath and reached for the handle.

The small conference room was paneled in a light-colored wood and had two large windows with heavy red drapes, pulled aside to admit daylight. A table was already prepared with note pads, pencils, glasses, and small carafes of water. There were four chairs to one side and a single chair opposite. A group of five people were at one window and, as Josh entered, they fell silent and turned to face him.

"Good morning, Doctor Francis." One of the men detached himself from the group and approached Josh with his hand extended. "I'm Eric Nevins from the Division of Research Grants. We haven't had a chance to meet." Nevins was a short, rather intense man wearing heavy, black-framed bifocals.

"Good morning."

"Let me introduce you around. You already know Doctor Helen Wright, your grant administrator from the National Cancer Institute."

"Yes, I do. Good morning, Helen. Nice to see you."

"Hello, Josh." The difference in age between the NIH administrator and the young professor showed in her conservative attire: a navy blue dress, little jewelry, and no makeup. Her round face was outlined by unstyled, gray hair. She did not make eye contact.

"And this is Doctor William Jarvis from the research staff at NCI." Josh certainly knew Dr. Jarvis by reputation, although they had never met.

"Good to meet you, Doctor Francis." The handshake was perfunctory and the tall, ascetic-looking senior scientist moved away.

"This is Mister Stephen Kane from our legal department."

"Legal? I don't understand." Josh shook hands with the young lawyer but looked around at the others.

Kane smiled, "Oh, I'm here in case there are any questions . . . you know . . . protocol questions . . . that sort of thing."

"Finally, let me introduce you to Mister John Billings, legislative assistant to Senator Johnson." Billings shook hands with Josh but said nothing.

Josh was caught off guard. "Excuse me? I'm not sure what your interest is here."

Dr. Nevins interrupted, "Mister Billings is only an observer. Well, shall we get started?"

The group took seats around the table, with Billings choosing a chair near the window. Josh remained on his feet, now quite unsure of himself. "Please, Doctor Francis, do sit here." Nevins gestured to the chair opposite the other four. The inquisition had begun.

"As you know, we'd like to discuss with you the recent line of investigation you've initiated concerning the DNA clone obtained from what is being called the Shroud of Hautecombe. Would you describe for us how you became involved in this project, and exactly what the nature of your experiments has been?"

Josh opened his briefcase and removed his papers and folders of data. He began to spread these out in front of him, rehearsing once more his presentation as he arranged his material. He would show them how his accidental discovery would lead to an entirely new line of investigation for him. "I'd like to begin with the circumstances that brought the shroud to my attention. Next, I'd like to show you the results of the cloning experiments I performed. I also have for you copies of a preliminary outline of a publication describing these results." He was warming to his task.

Nevins coughed and sorted through the documents before him. "Excuse me, Doctor Francis. Before you begin, there's something else we'd like to discuss." He glanced quickly over at Billings and continued. "Let's see, your research is currently funded by a grant from the NCI, number RO1-CA4503782, correct?"

"Yes."

"Well, we asked you to meet with us to discuss the nature of your experiments. Since the results have produced a great deal of public attention, we're interested in what might be the NIH's role in this. By the way, the title of your grant proposal is 'Motility Factors from Normal and Transformed Human Cells,' is that correct?"

"Yes, it is."

"Good. Please tell us how your work on this topic led to your experiments with the DNA from the shroud."

"Well, the experiments are unrelated. The shroud project came up separately."

Eric Nevins pressed his point. "And did you have separate funding for this new project?"

"No."

"Did you pay for the project using funds from your NIH grant?"

"Well . . . yes . . . I guess so. Everything in my lab is paid for by this grant. But it was only a small amount of supplies and a small investment of personal time."

Nevins sat back, removed his glasses, and spread his hands across the papers in front of him. "You see, that presents us with a real dilemma. The experiments you performed were, in point of fact, unauthorized."

"Unauthorized? What do you mean? I've done nothing that every other scientist doesn't do routinely. I've simply pursued an interesting lead."

For the first time Dr. Wright spoke, softly but directly, to Josh. "Doctor Francis, these experiments were not a part of your original grant proposal. Also, you did not inform us of this new direction in any progress report. By the terms of your grant with NIH, these experiments were unauthorized. I'm sorry."

In silence, the group across the table watched Josh, waiting for his response. Billings, the legislative assistant, sat upright in his chair, his expression unreadable. Josh gathered his strength and addressed Nevins.

"What does this mean?"

In a deliberate motion, Nevins leaned forward in his chair. "I'm afraid, Doctor Francis, that this means we will have to terminate your NIH grant for misuse of funds."

"What? You can't do this! Doctor Jarvis . . . certainly you don't agree with this?"

William Jarvis had achieved a great deal of fame, but he had been on the NIH staff for most of his career. He had learned the hard way that there were times when you did not interfere with the administration. "I'm sorry, Doctor Francis. There's nothing I can do."

The back of his chair caught him as Josh's body sagged. This couldn't be happening. His entire career was coming to a close in this room. His breathing became more and more labored.

From the side of the room, John Billings spoke, his voice laced with an icy stillness. "Doctor Nevins. Would you say a word about the recombinant DNA clone?"

Nevins looked uncomfortable, but proceeded. "Doctor Francis, the recombinant DNA clone you have constructed must be surrendered to the NIH."

Before Josh could respond, Stephen Kane, the NIH lawyer, cut him off. "We have studied the legal issues here. We believe that ownership of the physical results of experiments funded by NIH resides with NIH and, therefore, with the government."

Taking the lead again, Nevins tried to close the discussion. "Doctor Francis, unfortunately we are informing your University today of this action. We require that you submit your recombinant DNA clone to us as soon as you return to Tucson. We are truly sorry we've had to take this action."

Josh gripped the arms of his chair as the room closed in on him. He could contain himself no longer. "You bastards had this set up before I got here."

"Doctor Francis, please. This kind of behavior isn't going to help you in any way."

"Help with what? What more can you do to me?"

Josh jumped to his feet, grabbed his briefcase, and stood before them, his anger flowing unchecked. A numbing fear built in his stomach. He was out of control, stumbling as he crossed the room to the door.

"You don't know what you're doing. It's wrong. You just don't know . . . "

His audience sat in silence. Helen Wright looked at Josh, her eyes reddened, wordlessly pleading with him for a calm he could not possibly find. William Jarvis looked away, his attention on anything or anyone but Josh. The others simply watched him and waited.

He turned and groped for the handle of the door. As it opened, he could only think of getting out of the room, the building, and the city. The doors of the elevator closed before him and he barely saw the lobby and the eyes of the young receptionist who had watched him stagger down the hall.

As the door to the conference room swung closed in Josh's wake, the other participants in the meeting sat focused on either the table in front of them or the empty space where the young scientist had been. Billings rose from his place by the window and approached the table. "Of course you will see to it that the recombinant DNA clone is turned over as soon as possible?"

Nevins snapped his head around. "Shut up! Just shut up. We did your dirty work. We cut his chest open and ripped out his heart. Leave us alone to clean up the rest of this mess."

Billings adjusted his coat as he went to the door. He paused before leaving and smiled, "I'm sure Senator Johnson will be quite pleased with the outcome of this meeting."

* * * * * * * * * * * * * * *

Josh got out on the first floor and walked toward the exit of Building 31C. He stood for a moment, trying to gain some composure. The rage was subsiding, but the fear was growing. Everything was shattered. He held on to the handle of the main doors for a moment to steady himself. It was then he noticed the figure at the far side of the parking lot. The man was standing half-hidden behind the trees. He wore a checked sports coat and looked unremarkable except that he was staring directly at the building doors. But the feature that riveted him into Josh's eyes was the familiar sandy color of his hair. The fear in his stomach took on a new flavor. This threat was not to his career but to his life.

Josh did not know the NIH grounds extremely well, but had looked at a map before his walk from the hotel. He knew Building

31C had exits on all sides. It would be possible for him to leave at its western end and to work his way back to the Holiday Inn from the opposite side of the campus. Turning away from the door, he was suddenly face-to-face with John Billings. The lawyer had followed him and stood waiting in the center of the entry lobby. With great effort, Josh controlled the scream rising in his throat.

"Doctor Francis. I'm glad I caught you."

As Billings came closer, Josh stiffened, trapped between two enemies. The lawyer sensed this and stopped short, keeping his distance.

"It must have been distressing for you up there." Billings gestured at the ceiling. "You really had no way out. When the Senator and the Reverend both want something, they pull out all stops to get it."

"Reverend? I don't know what you mean."

"Come on. Surely you're aware that that little 'conference' was engineered for a purpose? Johnson and Slaughter want your clone. But I have an idea how we can be one step ahead of them."

The word "we" set off alarms in Josh's mind that suppressed everything else for the moment. A coldness crept over him.

"What are you talking about?"

"Your clone, of course. Look, there's a potential market out there that's bigger than you can imagine. Here's my idea. I'll set up a company with you, here in the District. You give me exclusive rights to represent this DNA you've isolated. We'll see to it that church groups, private citizens, or whoever wants to use the clone can only get it through us. There's no reason why you shouldn't profit from your discovery. Your colleagues are doing it every day. I'll handle any legal challenges from NIH or the Senator or anyone else . . . "

For Josh, Billings' words began to fade and be replaced instead by that telltale rattling that was an instant warning to his Southwestern-trained senses. He began to sidestep slowly, circling the man who stood coiled in front of him. Unblinking eyes followed him, accompanied by a flickering tongue and the incessant buzz of words. As he edged along, he was cautious, constantly computing the distance between them, wary of the danger of a strike.

" . . . you can call me on Monday. Better use my home telephone rather than my office."

Josh was now backing away, into the long corridor heading to the other end of the building.

"Yes . . . yes . . . of course. I'll call. Give me some time to think this through."

At first he walked, but then nearly ran to the other doors.

In his room at the hotel, Josh stuffed his small bag with the few items he had used and left. He checked out at the front desk, signing his bill off to the NIH and grimacing at the irony. As he looked to one side, he saw the sandy-haired man walking into the lobby. Panic began to take over as, in mute terror, Josh mouthed the word "Arimathea." Without thinking, he left the side door of the hotel and jumped into a waiting cab.

"Go! Go!"

"Hey, man, I'm waiting on a fare."

"Just go!" Josh pushed a handful of bills at the driver. The cab pulled off onto Wisconsin Avenue heading toward the District. His pursuer watched him leave from the street and, with a practiced wave, hailed another taxi. The cab with his target was already several blocks ahead.

Josh struggled to regain some rational thought in the midst of his hysteria. The cab was passing through Bethesda and into Chevy Chase, the last suburb before the District. They approached the business center where Josh saw signs for the D.C. Metro. He ordered the driver to stop and sprinted the few steps from the curb to the entrance of the Friendship Heights Metro Station.

The descent to the station took him through a concrete tube, gliding down a slowly moving escalator. The roughly formed walls of the tube leading into the station were lit indirectly, lending a surreal cast to the Metro entrance. The entry tube contained three escalators. The one Josh was on went down, the one on the far left came back up, and the center escalator, used at rush hour in either direction, was stopped to form a staircase. Unlike the entries into the London Tube or the Paris Metro, the walls were devoid of advertising. The result was a futuristic starkness that only served to intensify the cold fear that enveloped him.

He tried to appear as casual as possible. Some commuters, who had the freedom to display their haste, walked down the moving staircase, speeding their journey by even a small margin. Standing to the right to allow their passage, he managed for a while to keep his eyes unfocused. Inevitably his attention was drawn to a man on the rising escalator who seemed to be paying special attention to him. The man's eyes locked with his for an instant, causing Josh's breath to catch in his throat. The other man looked away and continued his climb to the streets of Chevy Chase above.

The bottom of the long escalator emptied into a vestibule containing, on the left, a large Metro system map and a listing of fares to points within the District and, on the right, a bank of automatic travel card dispensers. He desperately wished to attract no attention and so walked straight to the fare machines. A young woman approached and he tensed. She fumbled with her purse as she spoke.

"Excuse me. Do you have change for a ten?"

"What?"

"Do you have change for a ten . . . you know . . . like ten ones?"

He opened his wallet and found a five and five ones. "Will this do?"

"Thanks."

The girl proceeded to get her travel card. Josh stepped up to a vacant machine, found another five dollar bill, fed it in, and punched the button to deliver the card. He crossed to the turnstiles, inserted the magnetic card, and walked down the stairs to the train platform.

Josh had a choice of two directions from the center aisle of this station. The Red Line went from Shady Grove near Rockville and curved down through the District in a large "U," returning to Maryland in Silver Springs. Friendship Heights was on the Shady Grove arm. He chose the Silver Springs direction so that he could connect with the Blue or Orange Lines at Metro Center and make his escape through the District and, hopefully, to National Airport.

Since it was not rush hour, he could not lose himself in a crowd. The platform was nearly empty at mid-morning. The commuters were mostly women who appeared to be at various stages of pre-Easter shopping. One or two men in suits could be government types out on official business or away from their offices for other excuses. One young woman, blond, shapely, and overdressed for the hour of the day, stood nervously at the edge of the platform. He knew he would take the train toward Silver Springs, but waited at the Shady Grove side, hoping to throw off any pursuit. No one seemed to be paying any attention to him, which only increased his wariness.

The inbound train was arriving, announced by the flashing lights along the edge of the platform. As it squealed to a stop he drifted in its direction. The doors hissed open and a garbled voice announced, "Red Line to Silver Springs." He stepped into the car and, as he turned to face the door, expected to see the his pursuer. No one other than his fellow commuters appeared. The doors closed with electronic precision and the train lurched once and began accelerating. As the platform slid by, he watched for any sign of recognition among the people remaining on the station platform. The train picked up speed, the faces began to blur, and at last, the station view was replaced by the concrete walls of the underground tunnel. He had made his escape.

The train approached the Metro Center Station. According to the map on the wall next to the door, this was where he should change to the Blue Line in order to get to National Airport. Josh left the car along with the fastest commuters, following the signs and symbols. He rode the escalators bringing him to the correct level and waited on the platform for the next train.

The Blue Line ascended from its underground tunnel before it crossed the Potomac River on its way into Virginia, passing north of the Watergate Hotel. Josh let the scenery slip by without notice, preferring to concentrate on quelling the residues of his fear. The train halted at the elevated platform outside National Airport. Josh stepped out of the Metro car, walked downstairs to street level and a waiting shuttle bus to the terminal.

The interior of National Airport was in its normal chaotic state, since both departing and arriving passengers entered and left through the same doors. He wound his way through the crowds to the boarding area for his American Airlines flight to Dallas and his connecting flight to Tucson. He found a corner from which he could see the entire lobby. As soon as the flight was announced, he was in line and on his way to his seat.

He had been watched. The man he had lost by his jump to the Metro stood near a bank of pay phones not far from the American Airlines lobby. When Hawkins realized Josh was no longer in the cab he was following, he went directly to the airport. He knew the itinerary as well as his subject. As Josh boarded his flight, the man picked up a receiver and dialed a number in Tucson. "He's on his way back to you."

CHAPTER TWENTY-TWO

TUCSON, ARIZONA
APRIL 3, 1999

The St. Thomas More Chapel was in darkness as the congregation awaited the beginning of the Easter Vigil service. Josh could make out the vague forms of those around him only because of the dim illumination from the street lights that filtered in through the stained glass windows. He felt rather than saw Leslie next to him, her hand touching his on the edge of the pew.

Four days ago Laurent had asked him to come to this service. At first, Josh had taken it as a polite invitation. Later, he realized Laurent was quite serious. After the events of the last three days, he himself felt a need to be there, if only for the moments of peacefulness it might provide.

Josh had been raised in a Catholic family, had attended parochial schools, and had been faithful to his religion. Walter's death had changed all of that.

Josh could not accept his brother's death. The rest of the family, steeped in Catholic and Creole traditions, had grieved intensely and then had given in to the inevitable loss, trusting their faith. Josh, instead, had blamed God.

And so, he had drifted away from his religion and accepted, in its place, the objectivity of science as his sole philosophical base. He attended church infrequently at best, usually at Christmas or whenever he visited his parents in Albuquerque.

Leslie too had early religious training. But where Josh had rejected his spirituality, she had welcomed hers. Josh strove to make the world fit his notion of order, founded entirely on scientifically testable facts. Leslie accepted the world as she saw it through the eye of her camera. A scene was captured in her mind in much the same way that she recorded it in silver grains. At times there was little she could do to change it. Surprisingly, she was a keener and more objective observer than Josh, especially of those things not covered by theory or instrumentation.

The evening's ceremony had started outside with the lighting of the New Fire. The group of priests, together with the lay ministers of the Newman Center, began to enter from the rear of the church. In the lead was Laurent, holding in front of him the Paschal candle with its freshly ignited flame casting a circle of light in the darkened chapel. A voice intoned the chant:

"Light of Christ."

The choir and the congregation answered in the same mode:

"Thanks be to God."

Two lay ministers transferred the Paschal light to small tapers of their own and then on to candles being held by all in attendance. As the single flame was multiplied and passed around, the darkness gave way to a chapel illuminated by the combined glow of hundreds of small fires.

The group of celebrants proceeded forward to the altar, stopping twice more to repeat the chant. As a boy, Josh had always been touched by this sharing of the fire. He found the same emotions sweeping into his consciousness again.

The Easter Vigil service was one of the longest of the Church year, with many scriptural readings from both the Old and New Testaments. Josh tried to follow along, using one of the missals available in each pew. He could not concentrate on the text and found himself taking in the entire scene before him.

The chapel was simple in design and yet elegant. Dark wooden beams supported the ceiling, with matching posts descending on either side to the floor. High windows at the back and on both side walls contained stained glass representations, some of saints, others of the desert. Small circular chandeliers hung down at several points and these, along with spotlights directed toward the altar, had been turned on, the small candles having been extinguished after the opening of the service.

The altar itself was in the middle of a raised floor at the front of the church. Within this area, seats were available so that worshipers could encircle the broad ceremonial table. Like many Catholic churches, following the reforms of Vatican II, the tabernacle was no longer at the center of the main altar, but was kept in a small side chapel. The choir and musicians were near a piano to the left of the platform.

On the wall behind the altar was a majestic natural sculpture. The wooden skeleton of a saguaro cactus had been rescued from the desert. The sun-bleached ribs of the fifteen-foot tall remains formed the stark shape of a cross. The remnants of the two arms extended outward, symbolizing both death and benediction. The arms were draped with a length of pure white cloth in deference to the feast of the day.

The large Paschal candle dominated the altar itself, with the clergy and lay ministers gathered around. Simon Bell was the principal celebrant of the Mass, with Laurent and another resident priest as his assistants. As Josh's attention returned to the service, Laurent was reading one of the Old Testament prophecies related to the coming of the Messiah.

The scripture readings were followed by the sermon and the reception of new members into the Church. Josh was vaguely aware of the proceedings, his mind wandering elsewhere. The service approached that section of the Mass wherein the events of the Last Supper were remembered and re-enacted. He heard the words spoken by priests for thousands of years in the rite that Catholics believed transubstantiated the bread and wine into the body and blood of Christ. Father Bell held first the circular host of unleavened bread and then the crystal chalice with wine and water.

"This is My Body . . . This is the cup of My Blood . . . "

Josh suddenly remembered words in Latin that he had heard as a young child, not knowing the meaning at the time:

"Hic est enim calix Sanguinis Mei . . . "

His attention was focused on the altar and, at the same time, on his fellow worshipers. All stood as one for the singing of the Lord's Prayer. The custom at all Masses at the Newman Center was that everyone in attendance hold hands during the Our Father. As Josh entered into this link, he felt another unaccustomed surge of emotion.

At the Communion, the pews emptied one by one as the congregation went forward to receive the bread and wine. Josh rose and walked up the aisle together with the others. He approached the altar and was facing Laurent, who held up a small wafer of unleavened bread for him. He saw friendship radiate from the priest's eyes as he personalized the Communion ceremony for him.

"Josh, the Body of Christ."

Josh accepted it wordlessly and placed it in his mouth. He stepped to one side where a lay eucharistic minister held a small chalice out to him.

"The Blood of Christ."

This time he said "Amen" and took the cup and allowed the wine to touch his lips, tasting only a small amount.

He found his way back to the pew where Leslie waited. As he sat next to her, he felt a wetness along the sides of his face. It was then he realized he had been crying.

* * * * * * * * * * * * * * *

"Laurent, you must come with us. We have to talk."

They were outside the chapel as the last of the crowd departed. It was after midnight in the early hours of Easter Sunday. Laurent was still dressed in the vestments he had worn during the Mass.

"I do not understand, Josh. What is so urgent?"

"It's about the shroud."

Laurent turned toward the church door.

"Just give me a moment to change."

While they waited, Josh and Leslie agreed that her house was the closer. When the priest returned they walked across the street, got into Josh's car, and drove off.

After coffee had been prepared they gathered in the living room. Leslie was preoccupied with the image on the medallion she had seen three days earlier. Off to one side, she sifted through files of contact sheets and photographs she had accumulated over the years. Josh was sitting on the edge of the couch. He spoke with a new found confidence.

"I can't explain the feelings I had tonight. I haven't had emotions like that for years, not since I was a child. But there they were again. And then it struck me. Those people tonight were there not because they sought proof, but because they believe."

Laurent leaned back in his chair and folded his arms.

"Of course they believe. What does that have to do with the shroud?"

"Those people tonight were there to celebrate events that happened almost two thousand years ago. They were not asking for evidence, only for a simple retelling of the story. Now, we have a relic that has been dated to about 30 A.D. We have a clone that was constructed using DNA found on this relic. We have no objective evidence that this cloth has any relationship to Christ. On the other hand, we have the conviction of a large segment of the public that this is, indeed, the Shroud of Jesus. Think what harm someone could do if they used the cloth or the DNA in the wrong way.

Consider what damage might be done to the idea of faith; one sect warring against another for possession of what might become objects of worship."

"Suppose that what you say is true. What can we do about it?"

"We can prevent anyone from getting either the shroud or the DNA clone. We can destroy them both."

Laurent leapt from his chair.

"*Non, non! Mon Dieu! C'est fou.* Are you mad?"

"Calm down, please, Laurent."

The young priest sat back in his chair, bringing himself under control.

"The shroud is an important artifact. Its age alone makes it unique. In addition, there is the possibility that it could be connected to Christ. The Vatican has records going back for centuries. No one has even begun to look there. What if the link were proven? You would destroy the only existing relic that could be positively associated with Jesus? That would be senseless."

Josh waited until he had finished and then pointed at Laurent.

"Are you saying that as a historian and scholar, or as a man of God?"

"That is not the issue, Josh. You are talking about destroying something that is irreplaceable. What harm will come from preserving something so rare? If it should be found that the shroud is authentic, that it is the winding sheet of Christ, so much the better for the world. In this case, I will return the sacred relic to France and it will be in the hands of the Church. What will be the problem?"

Josh shook his head.

"Laurent, your view is not objective. Think for a minute of another faith, not your own. I recall a little of my Comparative Religion class from high school. Suppose the Shiite Muslims found a document, certified as authentic, which claimed that Muhammed had named his son-in-law, Ali, as his rightful successor. What would happen to the tenets of the Sunni followers of Islam? Would they then give up their belief in the leadership of the caliphs? Or would sectarian battles break out? Rewrite this scenario as the Catholic Church suddenly having possession of the True Shroud of Christ. Certainly a great cathedral would be built for its veneration. But what would happen between Catholic and Protestant, between the

Eastern churches and Rome? What would become of years of ecumenical progress? Your view that the Church would only use the shroud for good is idealistic, at best."

Laurent was at a loss to dispute the possibility, however remote it might be. But he persisted.

"Surely the shroud is in no imminent danger. Why not wait until we have more information?"

"Because there are forces at work trying to seize both the shroud and the clone. The University has received letters from several sources claiming ownership of the relic. On Friday, I learned that Reverend Edwin Slaughter, the televangelist, with the help of a powerful senator in Washington, is trying to gain possession of the DNA. I have been ordered . . . ordered, Laurent . . . to turn over my samples to the government. I don't know how much . . . "

Leslie had been silent for much of the exchange. She came upon a photograph in her files that made her face pale. She spoke, her voice quiet but with an intensity that caused Josh to stop in mid-sentence.

"Josh. It's worse than you thought."

"What? Why do you say that?"

"The man I met after you left on Thursday . . . the one waiting at your house? He was wearing a medallion around his neck. I saw an image on it . . . " she reached for some paper and sketched the symbol she had seen " . . . something like this . . . three crossed nails. I've had an uncanny feeling since then that I'd seen it somewhere before. I've finally found it. Here's a picture I took several years ago in Turkey, in the town of Gallipoli. There's a museum of archaeology in which partially reconstructed ruins are displayed. I photographed some of them as an assignment piece. Here . . . look at this."

She handed him the black and white print. The display consisted of a portion of a restored doorway from what must have been a temple or church. There were various symbols carved on the stone fragments of the posts. The large slab which had served as the lintel, had a central relief, worn down with time, but recognizable as the same crossed nails. Below the symbol, Greek letters could be made out, forming the word "Arimathea."

Josh was very still; his eyes fixed on the image. In one deliberate motion, he dropped the photograph to the floor. He had no doubt about what must happen next.

"We have no choice. Whatever we decide to do with the shroud and the DNA, we have to get them away from here."

Laurent made one last appeal.

"That is impossible. They are both under lock."

"I know that. I can get them out."

CHAPTER TWENTY-THREE

TUCSON, ARIZONA
APRIL 4, 1999

Josh parked on the street north of the Gould-Simpson Building. He asked Laurent and Leslie to wait, despite their fear of being discovered.

"I'm authorized to be in this building after hours. If someone comes along, just tell the truth . . . you're waiting for me."

His key admitted him to the building's lobby, lit only by a single bank of overhead fluorescent tubes and the illuminated clock, reading 3:00 a.m. The elevator rose swiftly through the unoccupied floors to the level of the LAC offices. As the doors opened, Josh tried to take on the appearance of the tired professor, forced to work late on some experiment or other. He had brought along a vinyl shoulder bag he normally used for sports equipment. No one was present.

He walked past the main administration suite to the door of the small room holding the safe. His second key opened this lock without incident. The room was dark, save for indicators glowing on various computer terminals. He would have to risk full lighting. The room was on the interior of the building, so nothing should show on the outside.

Following Sutton's instructions, he turned on the computer that allowed him to open the safe and stepped through the sequence until he was asked for the password. After typing the series of letters, he received the response "INVALID PASSWORD: ACCESS DENIED."

What next? He had typed in the letters C-H-R-I-S-T—no, wait— that was not the name of the Cambridge college—C-H-R-I-S-T-'-S— that was it. Once more, being sure to include all the necessary characters, he entered the password. After a moment he was rewarded with the whirring of gears and the scraping sound of the metal doors parting. The room light gleamed from the gold of the reliquary box, reflecting onto the plastic case containing the ampules.

The vinyl bag was large enough to contain both items. At the computer terminal he typed "QUIT." The doors to the safe glided shut, showing no external trace of his activity. He turned off the lights and was locking the door when he heard footsteps approaching.

"Doctor Francis?"

"Oh! Hello . . . Officer Vega, right? You startled me."

"Sorry, sir. I'm . . . ah . . . on my rounds and . . . may I ask what you're doing here?"

"I left some paperwork here after my last computer session. I needed to get it to finish up at home." He patted the shoulder bag. "Actually, we were coming from church and an early breakfast . . . my friends are down in the car."

"I see. Well, don't let me keep you. Happy Easter."

"Happy Easter to you, too."

Josh moved off in the direction of the elevator, trying very hard to walk as normally as possible. He stood, praying for the car to arrive, studying the bulletin board next to the doors. At the sound of the bell, he looked back to see Vega still watching. Smiling and waving, he stepped in and pushed the button for the main floor.

Vega waited until the doors had closed, then took out a small pad, noted the time, and made a series of entries.

Once in the lobby, Josh walked quickly out of the building and climbed into the driver's seat of the car, handing the vinyl bag to Leslie.

"We're leaving . . . now."

He turned the car around and headed first west to Park Avenue and then south, away from the campus. As they passed the corner, they were observed by two men seated in a darkened sedan. Hawkins had watched through binoculars as Josh entered and then left the building.

"I'll bet he's got it in that bag he was carrying. Damn! It look's like he's done our safecracking for us. Okay, follow, but not too close. This time of night he could pick us up easy. I'll track him with the glasses. Let's see where he's taking it."

* * * * * * * * * * * * * * *

They drove east on Interstate 10, away from the lights of Tucson and into the early morning dark. Josh was running and, like any animal being pursued by a predator, he made for familiar ground: home. At first, this was not a conscious decision. He wanted to put as much distance as possible between them and the University.

Leslie and Laurent had said nothing during their mad dash through the city streets to the freeway. As they crossed through the southern foothills of the Rincon Mountains, marking the eastern edge of the Tucson valley, Leslie asked the necessary question.

"Where are we going, Josh?"

"I'm not sure yet, baby. I guess I'm heading for New Mexico."

"Albuquerque?"

"No. I can't bring this problem to my family's doorstep. Probably Santa Fe."

She began to understand. Josh was fleeing not for cover, but for sanctuary.

* * * * * * * * * * * * * * *

Josh Francis had grown up in Albuquerque but had come of age in Santa Fe. For most of his young life he had spent summers in that northern New Mexico city. Especially during the opera season, the town was filled to capacity with tourists and opportunities. From his early teens he had worked each year at La Fonda, one of the hotels, waiting tables or doing other odd jobs.

He had made a lifelong friend during those years. Carlos Fuentes was a Santa Fe native he had met the first summer. They worked together in the noted hotel owned by Carlos' uncle. Their free time was spent with Carlos introducing Josh to the wonders of the Sangre de Cristo Mountains that hovered over the city. Walking beneath Truchas Peak was as close as Josh ever came to feeling spiritually at ease. Santa Fe would always be that kind of place for him.

Carlos had shown him more than the glories of the wilderness. His friend, although only one year older, was in many ways Josh's mentor. He was one of those people who, almost at birth, seem to be gifted with a deep understanding of life. He had been and remained the only person, other than Leslie, who knew the essential Josh.

The time after Walter's death had been hard for Josh, even though Carlos was also at the University of New Mexico. They had spent the following summer together and the warmth of the Fuentes home had been enough comfort that Josh almost forgot his anguish. Carlos had spent long hours walking with his friend in silence, letting him release his pain. During those three months they had forged even stronger bonds between them.

It had been on one of their hikes in the Pecos Wilderness that summer that Josh confessed to Carlos his bitter distrust of God. They were walking through a grove of aspens whose leaves trembled with the slightest summer's breath.

Carlos raised his hand to the shimmering canopy.

"You know, Sonny, the amazing thing is that, no matter what we decide, all of this still manages to continue to be. All of it has a purpose. You, too, have a purpose, which will be made clear in time. And the wonder is, Sonny, that, in spite of what you say, God still trusts you."

* * * * * * * * * * * * * * * *

They were through Lordsburg by sunrise and continued on to Deming. Josh had driven this road enough times that most of his moves were automatic. The interstate highway system goes from Tucson to Las Cruces, connecting there with I-25 leading north to Denver. Instead, he took the Hatch cutoff, a state two-lane highway stretching diagonally from Deming across rolling hills to the small Rio Grande farming community many miles north of Las Cruces. Josh bought gasoline and followed this route, driving northeast and away from the interstate. Far behind, but not lost, Hawkins and his partner continued their surveillance.

They followed the river northward along I-25, heading toward the major population center of the state. All three were exhausted. Even though they had shared the driving, no one had slept. They talked little, avoiding in particular the topic of the shroud.

Laurent watched the miles of arid landscape drift by and tried to piece together the broken path that had lead him from Hautecombe to this flight with his precious find. The offer of a position at the Vatican had been the prize he had sought. Why was he now repelled by the idea? Simon Bell had asked him to examine his motives. The confusion of events made that difficult. On the other hand, it was easy to see the changes that had been wrought in Josh. The two men had grown close during the short time Laurent had been in Tucson. He had witnessed the rapid progression from purely objective scientist to the man who the evening before had pleaded the case for belief over fact. Again and again Laurent's eyes came back to the vinyl bag in which rested the shroud and the DNA.

Leslie had taken this drive with Josh twice during their time together. Because of the way her mind processed images, each billboard and small town was familiar enough from those trips that she barely registered its passing. Her eyes, when she could keep them open, drifted to Josh.

She had seen him crying in church the night before, the sight of the tears shaking her at first. It was the look that had come over his face that made her realize the tears were of release rather than remorse. Even now he appeared relaxed and, for the first time in days, focused. In a strange way this affected her own mood, elevating her spirits in the midst of their frenzied escape.

At about 10 a.m. they stopped a second time, for both gas and food, in Socorro. Josh carried the bag into the restaurant. He could not bear to leave it, even in the locked car. They ate a hurried and late breakfast. The men in the sedan watched from across the street.

Their flight continued. At noon, they were in the center of Albuquerque, where I-40 runs east and west. His family lived to the northeast, in the foothills of the Sandia Mountains. In spite of the heart-wrenching tug the sight of the Candeleria Road exit caused, he knew he could not stop here. He did not slow down, but continued north, following the river valley toward the state capital.

By early afternoon, the jewel of Santa Fe glistened in its setting against the Sangre de Cristo range. Josh knew exactly where he was going. He drove to the old section of town and La Fonda Hotel.

Carlos still lived in the city, and had become the manager of the hotel where he and Josh had once been summer help.

They parked a few streets to the east of the hotel; the building occupied the entire block at the southwest corner of the famed plaza and spaces were at a premium. Josh took only the shoulder bag. They walked together into the lobby, where Josh asked to see Carlos.

The hotel was old and one of the most popular. The open beams and heavy wood style that had become synonymous with the name of the city was evident throughout. Adobe walls and pastel colors accented the furnishings. Josh was, as usual, at home. Leslie had been here before with him and loved it almost as much as he did. For Laurent, in spite of their headlong flight, the sight was enchanting enough to cause him to gape openly. A loud voice brought them all around.

"Sonny! Why didn't you tell me you were coming?"

Carlos was taller than Josh and much larger. He was not at all overweight, only muscular. He enveloped his friend in a hug that all but crushed him.

"And Leslie, too! This is wonderful."

She was included in the three-way welcome. Carlos had curly black hair and wore a full beard, giving the general impression of a great and gentle bear. His exuberance cooled as he looked at them more closely.

"Something is wrong. Tell me later. Right now, what do you need?"

"We could use two rooms, if you have them. We've driven all night."

Carlos stepped over to the registration desk and, after a few words with the clerk, returned with keys.

"Why two rooms?"

"Oh. I forgot to introduce my friend. This is Father Laurent Carriere from France."

"Welcome, Father. Perhaps after you have all had a chance to rest, we can talk a bit. You have these rooms and you are not registered here. Will that help?"

Josh gripped his old friend by the arm and held him for a moment.

"Thank you, Carlos."

"It's nothing. You know where these rooms are . . . third floor, in the rear. I've got to get back to my office. We're about to start serving Easter dinner and there's trouble in the kitchen. Call me when you're ready to talk."

Outside, Hawkins and the other investigator had found Josh's car and were beginning a systematic search of all the hotels near the plaza.

* * * * * * * * * * * * * * *

"And what do you intend to do now?"

They had finished a dinner sent up to the rooms and were seated on chairs and on the bed. Carlos knew of the cloning, both from the newspaper reports and from Josh's phone calls weeks before. He listened now to the most recent additions to the story, including their flight from Tucson with the shroud and the DNA. Josh tried to answer his friend's question.

"We don't know. I'm in favor of destroying everything to keep it out of the wrong hands. Laurent is opposed to that, for both historical and religious reasons."

Laurent nodded his agreement. Carlos looked at each man, then at the vinyl sports bag.

"May I see it?"

Josh took out first the gold reliquary and then the plastic case. He opened each, revealing the satin pouch holding the cloth in one and, in the other, the four glass ampules containing the preserved bacterial cells. Laurent had not seen the vials before this. To him they looked like miniature wine bottles, an impression that would be burned into his memory. Carlos bent over the table, touching first one and then the other. He turned to Josh.

"It would be a very heavy burden to bear if you were to destroy these things. You don't know what they really are. You must be cautious. What leads you to your suggestion?"

"It's not what they are that's important. It's what they signify. If they are misused, they could harm the faithful. I mean, Christ asked people to follow Him without proof. Look what He said to Thomas. If these things . . . the shroud and the DNA . . . are offered as 'ultimate proof,' how will that change the response of people to Christ's call? I can't be responsible for that."

Carlos looked at Josh, searching his face, weighing his answer. "Well, my friend, you have changed. Remember our discussions? Perhaps now you can see what I meant by *Hamlet*, Act One, Scene Five."

Carlos prepared to leave.

"Anything I can do to help you, just tell me. Sonny, may I speak to you alone?"

They stepped into the hallway and walked a short distance away from the rooms. Carlos spoke in a low voice.

"Two men have been asking for you. They described all three of you, saying you are friends they were supposed to meet. Unfortunately, someone at the desk told them you're here. They have stationed themselves at the front and the side exits."

"Is one of them a medium built man with sandy hair?"

"Yes."

At that word, Josh's heart began to pound and his stomach went hollow.

* * * * * * * * * * * * * * *

Hawkins had placed a call to San Rafael as soon as they identified the hotel. He was certain their employer would not be happy.

"Mister Tarquin? Hawkins. I'm afraid Francis and the priest have left Tucson with the shroud. We've followed them to Santa Fe, and we're watching their hotel."

Costa sat at the desk in his home office, his Easter guests forgotten for the moment.

"This is getting out of hand. I'm coming down there tomorrow." He tapped a few buttons on the computer console to his left, opening a separate link to airline reservations. "There's a morning flight to Albuquerque . . . United Airlines . . . arrives at 11:50 a.m. . . . one of you pick me up at the airport. Keep track of what they do. I want to know who they meet in the hotel, understand?"

He hung up before Hawkins could respond. Costa thought for a moment and then dialed a Tucson number.

"Hello, Nikos?"

The voice at the other end sounded distant and strained."

"Yes, Papa?"

"It's time to come home. You're finished there."

"But what about the shroud?"

"It's not in Tucson any longer."

"How do you know that?"

"Because I've had two men tailing the biologist and the priest. They left Tucson last night with the shroud and have gone to Santa Fe. I'll take care of it from here. You come home. I don't want to argue about this."

Again, he hung up. He was starting to loose his temper.

* * * * * * * * * * * * * *

Nikos watched the telephone for a long time, as though he expected the instrument itself to ridicule him. His face burned with a combination of rage and humiliation. It was like every time before, all the way back to high school. His father had set him up. Again he was being asked to get out of the way, like a good boy. Not this time. Nikos was not about to roll over and perform as commanded.

He grabbed his suitcase, jacket, car keys, and gun, and ran from the room. He would be in Santa Fe the next morning.

CHAPTER TWENTY-FOUR

SANTA FE, NEW MEXICO
APRIL 5, 1999

The lights of a small town are especially eerie at 4 a.m. They shine for no one except those who can't find the solace of sleep. Josh was at the window of the room that looked out onto the empty street. Leslie had long since given in to her exhaustion and lay fully clothed across the bed, covered by a light blanket. Laurent had gone to his own room hours ago. They had resolved nothing.

That wasn't quite true. Josh had made his own decision. He had brought the clone into existence. It was his responsibility to deal with it. The shroud must be left for Laurent. Notes to each of them, saying he would be gone for several hours, lay on the dresser. They were to meet him in front of the Cathedral of St. Francis, the major church in Santa Fe, at 2 p.m.

He took the plastic case with the ampules from the table where they had been on display earlier and returned them to the vinyl bag.

For a moment he watched Leslie as she slept. Her hands were curled beneath her chin in childlike innocence. He could see, if only in his mind, the depths of her eyes. He reached out and gently, without waking her, shifted one lock of hair that had fallen onto her face. He opened the door and slipped silently into the hall, closing her behind him.

The main exits were being watched. But he and Carlos knew every possible way to leave this hotel, particularly if they didn't wish to be observed. At the end of the third-floor hallway, on the side of the hotel away from the plaza, was a metal fire escape that could be used to get to the street. Better still, it allowed access to one of the various levels of the roof of the pueblo-styled building. From there, he could work his way to the east end of the hotel on Cathedral Place before descending. He could get to his car unobserved.

Everything was as he remembered it. Climbing up the external stairs, he reached a point where one section of the hotel roof joined another. Using various metal staircases and crouching low, he made his way along the length of the building. Using another fire escape, he lowered himself down onto the sidewalk along a deserted Cathedral Place. In minutes he was at his car, pausing to listen for any signs of pursuit. Quietly he opened the door, got in, and drove away, leaving the center of town and heading south toward the interstate.

He stopped at a shopping center to use the telephone. His plan required that he place a call to *The Santa Fe New Mexican.* Reaching a reporter who covered the night desk, he revealed his name and that he had taken the Shroud of Hautecombe from the University of Arizona. For proof, he invited him to call Dr. Richard Sutton to confirm this news. There would be a press conference on the steps of the cathedral at two that afternoon. He made another call to the news department of the local television station. This time he left the message on their answering machine.

Interstate 25 swings in a wide loop south of Santa Fe on its way around the southern end of the Sangre de Cristo mountains that extend down from Colorado. Josh followed this route until he reached the Cowles exit. There he drove north following a two lane highway that wound along the Pecos River toward its source. At the small village of Terrero he turned left onto a dirt road, leading to Holy Ghost Creek.

As he reached the campground at the end of the road, the first light of morning was beginning to show in the eastern sky. Patches of snow were evident in some of the more sheltered locations of the canyon. He parked and, from the storage area of the Bronco, retrieved hiking boots, a warm jacket, gloves, and a small backpack he kept supplied for day hikes. Into this he placed the plastic case of ampules. He changed into the heavier clothing, laced up the boots, and locked the car.

Shouldering the pack, he started up the trail that began where the road ended. The path traced the creek, fording it several times as it ascended between the canyon walls. Although the winter had been exceptionally mild, there was still a good deal of snow. He walked through the pine and spruce forest feeling the exertion of

240

the hike as the sky became brighter. The trail rose sharply at one point, requiring numerous switchbacks, sometimes through knee-deep drifts, as it struggled up toward a ridge above the creek.

Here he veered left onto another trail, and continued along the top for two miles. A branch forked left again, leading to Spirit Lake, a favorite of his. The glacial mountain lake sat nearly at the top of the entire range, ringed by pines and spruce, overshadowed on one side by the granite slopes of Santa Fe Baldy. Snow covered its banks and the surface was frozen, save for the center, where bright blue water rippled in the morning breeze. Beneath his jacket, he was warm from the exertion of the climb but could still feel the subfreezing chill of the air.

He cleared the snow from the surface of a boulder and sat down at the edge of the lake. During the climb he had tried to make up his mind. To destroy the clone seemed to him the best course. But, if it was real, if it did contain the DNA of Christ, what then? Carlos was right; it would be a terrible decision with which to live. If he could not bring himself to destroy it, perhaps the best thing would be to put it beyond anyone's reach.

From his backpack he retrieved a small sack made of dull green polyethylene netting and some nylon fishing line. He took the plastic case out and opened it once more. The four ampules lay against their cushion, each one with its powdery brown contents that might mean so much.

There it was. In the end, he couldn't bear to part with the ampules; at least not with every one of them. Had he really made them, or was the hand of God somehow at work here? He did not know the answer to that question, but he did know that his faith had returned because of the experiment he had been called upon to perform.

He took one vial out and placed it in the breast pocket of his shirt. He closed the case and, using the fishing line, tied it tightly and dropped it into the sack along with a good sized rock, sealing them in with the drawstring. The ampules were made of thick glass, designed to withstand the vacuum and ultracold of laboratory storage. They would be safe where he intended to send them.

The ice at the edge of the lake was thick enough to support his weight. Holding the sack in one hand, he took a few cautious steps toward the center. Loud cracking noises echoed in the stillness. What little experience he had with cold country told him that if he fell through the ice he was as good as dead. He lowered himself onto the surface, spreading his weight out as much as possible. In this position, he began to crawl slowly outward, pausing to test the ice in front of him.

He made it to within 25 feet of the water when he found he could go no further without the risk of breaking through. The surface of the ice was smooth, having been exposed to sun and wind for several days. He lay atop the crystaline plain, his arms and legs straining to either side. With a deliberate but powerful motion of his right arm, he swung the sack containing the samples as hard as possible along the surface, sliding it to the center of the lake. The bag stopped before it reached the water, poised on the thin edge of the ice shelf. Then, as he watched, the weight of the sack and its contents broke through. The samples disappeared into the lake.

The return to the shoreline took all of his concentration. Almost every motion produced the loud popping that he knew meant another fracture in the ice. He fought to contain the panic that urged him, against all logic, to stand up and run. By the time he reached the section he knew could support his weight, he was sweating and panting as though he had indeed sprinted the distance several times over.

At last he began to recover; his breathing returned to normal. He sat for a while, watching the water in the center of the lake, as if he expected the sack rise up above the surface. He touched the single vial in his pocket, knowing that he would keep it secret.

Finally, he took up his backpack and began the descent to his car and to the city.

* * * * * * * * * * * * * * * *

News of Josh's impending press conference had spread beyond the two telephone calls he had made. Both the newspaper and the TV reporters had checked and confirmed the theft at the University of Arizona. Sutton was quoted as saying that both of the items in question were missing. A University policeman had encountered Professor Francis outside the room containing the safe early Sunday morning. There was little doubt he had taken the shroud and the DNA samples.

By 1:45 p.m. the major news networks had set up their cameras in front of the sandstone facade of the cathedral. Members of the print media, both local and wire service, had gathered. State and local police were on hand as well.

Leslie and Laurent arrived at about that time. They had spent most of the day in the hotel with Carlos, although they had made an early morning expedition to a bookstore near the plaza. Carlos did not attend the press conference.

An astute reporter recognized Laurent from earlier stories as the priest who had found the shroud. He was besieged by a host of others, all seeking comments about what might have happened.

"I am sorry. I have no idea. I am waiting to hear from Doctor Francis."

Five minutes later, Costa Tarquin reached the plaza, accompanied by the two private investigators. When Hawkins had discovered that one of the three people had slipped through his surveillance, he was livid. Neither he nor his associate had ever taken their eyes from the two exits of the hotel. They had followed the priest and the girl early that morning, but found it was only a shopping trip. During the day, they heard police transmissions regarding the 2 p.m. appearance at the cathedral. Hawkins personally drove to Albuquerque to meet his employer, instructing his associate that under no circumstances must he lose the other two.

Costa and the two men took up positions in front of the steps, waiting along with the others.

To one side of the cathedral was a grove of trees. Keeping well back in this space, away from the crowd forming in the square, was Nikos Tarquin. He had driven all night and had spent all day trying to find some clue to the location of the scientist and the priest. A radio report told him of the expected press conference.

Nikos could see quite well from his vantage point. He recognized the priest and the girl from Francis' house. A little further back he saw his father and what must have been his two private detectives. The smile that spread across his face was not one of humor, but rather a grimace of pain.

By two o'clock everyone was looking around, not knowing from which direction he might come. No one paid much attention to the cathedral itself. The top of the steps was dominated by a series of huge brass doors, reminiscent of some of the great churches of Europe after which it was modeled. One of these doors opened slightly, and Josh walked out and stood at the top of the stairs. Only then did most of the crowd notice him, appearing before them as if out of nowhere. There was a chaotic clamoring of questions as the reporters pressed forward to meet him.

Josh had spent most of the time since his return inside the great church. The vaulted solitude had allowed him time to seek the composure he needed for what he must do next. He was ready to face the press and the others. He took a deep breath and held up his hands for their quiet and their attention.

"My name is Doctor Joshua Francis. I am a professor of molecular biology at the University of Arizona. As you may know, I have been involved with a project to date the Shroud of Hautecombe. I am the one who constructed the recombinant clone using DNA extracted from that shroud.

"Yesterday, in the early morning hours, I took the shroud and the only remaining samples of the clone from a safe at the University. I did this for the following reasons."

Josh looked around at the people gathered before him. There were Leslie and Laurent. Beyond them, he saw the sandy-haired man and his companion, along with another person he did not recognize. He faltered a bit but did not weaken. Swallowing hard, he continued.

"Although the shroud dates from about 30 A.D., we have no evidence that it has anything to do with Christ. And yet, many people have laid claim to the shroud and the DNA because of the general belief that it is real. I believe that only harm can come from this. I am afraid that this relic and the DNA I have isolated will be used in the wrong way."

Costa listened to Josh with growing trepidation, sensing what was to come. His face paled and he sagged back onto Hawkins, as though he had been hit when he heard Josh's next words from far away.

"Therefore, early this morning, I took the shroud and the remaining samples of the DNA clone into the mountains." He pointed toward the gray peaks of the Sangre de Cristo range. "There, with great reverence, I burned the shroud and the samples, scattering the ashes when I finished. I have destroyed them to keep them from being misused."

Nikos, too, had heard Josh's announcement. While the scientist was speaking, Nikos had inched out from his site of concealment and, by the end of the statement, was at one side of the crowd, near the front.

Leslie, looking around to witness the effect of Josh's words, saw Nikos and recognized him as the man with the medallion. She gripped Laurent's arm and pointed, but was too late.

As Josh spoke the words, "I have destroyed them," a chord inside Nikos that had been winding tighter and tighter over the years finally snapped, releasing what little restraint was left. He cried out a loud and barely intelligible "No!" that resounded throughout the plaza. He reached inside his jacket and withdrew the gun from its holster.

When Josh finished his announcement he was poised with his arms at his sides, his gaze flowing over the crowd. He heard the cry from somewhere and turned his head. A man he did not recognize was pointing at him. Too late, he realized that the hand held something metallic glinting in the afternoon sunshine. He saw a flash of fire and a cloud of white smoke.

The bullet smashed into Josh, piercing the vial he held in his left breast pocket. The steel projectile continued on its way, driving shards of glass and the last of the DNA into Josh's body. The bullet ripped into his heart and exited through his back, falling to the steps, its lethal energy spent.

Josh staggered, driven from his feet by the impact. He crumpled to the steps and fell on his back. His eyes closed on the sight of the blue sky above his head.

For one instant everyone and everything formed a macabre tableau. And then, as if on cue, everyone acted at once. Police nearest to the gunman disarmed him and pushed him to the ground. Leslie, in spite of the jolt to her very soul, ran to Josh. Laurent had recovered first and had gotten there ahead of her.

There was nothing that could be done. Laurent laid his hand on Josh's forehead, praying for his fallen friend. Leslie was at his side, her face buried in her hands. Blood was spreading along the steps, pouring out of the body from the gaping holes in front and back. Within this widening pool, Laurent noticed a tiny fragment of glass. He recognized it as the top of one of the vials. He picked it up and slipped it into his pocket, saying nothing.

EPILOGUE

AUGUST, 1999

GALLIPOLI, TURKEY

Costa Tarquin stood on the embankment overlooking the Dardanelles, the strong wind blowing across the water from the Turkish heartland directly into him. The lines in his face had deepened during the past four months as the aftermath of that day in Santa Fe drained more and more of his spirit from him. The shroud was forever beyond his reach. This had become the least of his concerns.

His son would come to trial within weeks for the murder of Joshua Francis. Costa had assembled the best possible team of defense lawyers he could find. In their opinion, the most he could hope for was some kind of insanity defense. In all likelihood, Nikos would remain in jail for many years. Whatever the outcome, Costa would live with the knowledge that he had driven his son to commit an unforgivable crime.

As a corollary to this personal disaster, it was clear that the Society would be exposed during the judicial process. Nikos had not been secretive about his motives. He had talked freely with investigators and with his own lawyers about Arimathea, its history, and his family's involvement in its leadership. The world would at last have the evidence that the scientists and historians had lacked: the shroud that they had lost was the one used to bury Christ.

Predictably, the Society had asked for his resignation as president. Msgr. Corsini had been selected as his replacement. Rumors circulated that at the next general meeting, here in Gallipoli, Corsini intended to introduce a plan that would convert them from secret to public. He would propose that they become a part of the service arm of the Church, similar to the Knights of Columbus. Costa was resigned to this. Without the guardianship of the shroud as even a potential goal, there was little else to do.

Centuries of tradition would come to an end because of him. The weight of this had not fully descended on him. As it did, he would sink further into the black pit he had excavated for himself.

* * * * * * * * * * * * * * * *

SPIRIT LAKE
SANGRE DE CRISTO MOUNTAINS, NEW MEXICO

The waters were still now, with only an occasional late afternoon breeze to disturb the surface. Earlier, as she had crouched under her shelter, waiting for the summer thunderstorm to beat itself out against the faces of the peaks, the lake had been in turmoil. Leslie had watched as the pelting rain and hail churned the surface with a million small eruptions. She had taken a series of photographs during the height of the storm, part of her continuing collection of the many moods of the lake.

Josh had been buried at home in Albuquerque. There was nothing left for her in Tucson. She had resigned her position and moved to Santa Fe. In spite of the tragedy of that day, she could not stay away. The city held her like a magnet from which she could not escape.

During the last few months she had relived every moment of those final days. Many things had became clear afterward. Carlos told her details of Josh's life she had never known. His cryptic Shakespeare reference, for instance, recalled a time during their college days when they argued back and forth about religion and faith. "There are more things in heaven and earth, Horatio, than are dreamt of in your philosophy." But, in the end, Carlos had played Horatio to Josh's Hamlet.

Carlos had helped her get settled, introduced her to several gallery owners, and generally made her feel welcome. She had returned to her art, turning her lens on images she found in the richly varied countryside. Many of these photographs were already being well received by the local exhibitors. The Spirit Lake photos, however, were not for exhibit or sale.

The short note Josh had left for her on the day of his death was another reason that brought her to the mountains. She no longer needed to read it, having memorized the words in the days and nights afterward:

> Dear Les,
>
> Carlos was right. To destroy either of these things will be a serious matter. The shroud I must leave for Laurent. He found it and it's up to him to decide what to do next. I'll take the clone and make a decision for myself. I need to walk somewhere that will allow me to think clearly. I'll be back this afternoon. Meet me in front of the cathedral. I've called a press conference for 2 p.m. By then, I will have chosen.
>
> I will love you always,
> Sonny

Her deepest instincts told her that Spirit Lake was the place he had chosen for his "walk." She knew his feelings for these mountains and this lake in particular. She had no idea what he had done. The fate of the clone was likewise a mystery to her. But somehow she knew that he had been here that day. After each of her hikes she was back in her darkroom, searching in the images she had captured, trying to discern a clue, trying to look back in time.

The sunlight was glancing off the surface of the lake, making the water look as if it were on fire from below. She picked up her camera for one more series of pictures.

* * * * * * * * * * * * * * *

L'ABBAYE D'HAUTECOMBE
LAC DU BOURGET, FRANCE

The last steamer of the day was on its way back to Aix-les-Bains, leaving a broad wake across the surface of the lake. Its passage signaled the end of another round of summer tourist activity at Hautecombe. It also meant Laurent could return from his self-imposed daily exile into the fields below the abbey.

The priests and brothers respected the fact that he did not wish to speak of his time in the United States. Visitors were not so kind. Everyone wanted to see the church where the shroud had been found and to talk to the priest who had brought it to America. Laurent would have been on constant display. An earlier version of this same man would have relished the attention. It was not so any longer.

Josh's short note had left charge of the shroud to Laurent. The priest and historian knew that he could not destroy the cloth. But he could not argue against his friend's fears. He determined to return the shroud to France in secret, postponing any decision as long as possible. He and Leslie had gone out that morning and purchased a number of books, mostly related to Southwestern plants. With the help of Carlos, they had packaged the reliquary in plain paper and included it in a box stuffed with the gardening references along with volumes on Santa Fe history, photo essays on the region, and local cookbooks. The box was sealed and addressed to Monsieur Maurice LeFebvre, the caretaker of the abbey. Included was a note from Laurent asking that the old man hold on to the package, leaving it untouched, until his return. He knew Maurice and he could trust that this would be done.

Laurent might be identified, simply because of the notoriety he had received. Therefore, Carlos agreed to ship the package, using the distraction of the press conference to preserve their secrecy. And so the shroud traveled home, via Federal Express, with no attendant fanfare or ceremony.

After the tragedy of Josh's death, Laurent had begun to withdraw into himself. By the time he returned to Hautecombe, he had become more reclusive than even the abbot, Father Holden.

He had decided that since the world believed the shroud was destroyed, he would see that it remained hidden from the public's consciousness. He enlisted the help of Maurice. Together, using materials they found in the abbey's workshop, they fashioned a completely sealed plastic case, into which they inserted the reliquary. Maurice, working in the gardens outside the cloister, excavated a deep pit, ostensibly for modifications to the watering system. Late one night, some two weeks after his return, Laurent and the caretaker lowered the shroud into its resting place. Maurice had filled in the hole and eventually, when summer drew nearer, planted a bed of roses in the plot.

As the steamer reached the midpoint of the lake, Laurent appeared at the edge of the garden wall. He walked slowly, his head bowed in thought. He fingered a small silver locket that hung from a chain around his neck. In it could be found a fragment of glass, still stained with blood. He passed the rose garden in which Maurice was busy with a hoe.

"Good afternoon, Father. All is well?"

"Hello, Maurice. Yes, yes . . . all is well."

The priest continued on toward the vacant abbey church, leaving the caretaker alone in the garden. Maurice would keep the secret simply because he did not trust anyone in power. He understood the burden of trust the young priest had given him. He also understood a good deal about the importance of the shroud, and even more about those who sought to exploit it.

Maurice bent again to his labors. As he worked, something shiny fell from his open shirt and hung suspended from his neck. He quickly placed it back against his skin, closing the top buttons in spite of the warmth of the day. Had Laurent or anyone else been looking, they might have seen a golden medallion that had been given long ago to a man who everyone believed was dead, but who now bore the surname "LeFebvre." Had they been able to examine it in detail they would have seen on its face the image of three crossed nails, and underneath, the word "ARIMATHEA."

THE END

Author's Note

All of the locations I have mentioned in this novel do exist. The Abbey of Hautecombe sits on the western shore of Lac du Bourget in the Savoy Alps and can be visited either by car or by lake steamer. The buildings mentioned on the University of Arizona campus are, in general, as I have described them. High in the Sangre de Cristo Mountains (the name means "Blood of Christ") above Santa Fe you can find Holy Ghost Creek, running out of Spirit Lake.

Order Form

Please send _____ copies of *Sangre de Cristo* at $13.95 each to:

Name:_____

Address:_____

City:_____State:_____

Zip Code:_____

_____copies at $13.95 each = $_____

Sales Tax. 7% Az Residents: $_____

Shipping Charge: $_____

Total Enclosed: $_____

Shipping: Book rate, $2.00 for the first book and 75 cents for each additional book. Please allow three to four weeks for surface mail. Air mail, $3.50 per book.

Please send order form and make check or money order payable to:

Spirit Rider Press
2920 E. Mabel Street
Tucson, Arizona 85716-3848